In a Cat's Eye

Edited
by
Kelly A. Harmon and
Vonnie Winslow Crist

Pole to Pole Publishing
Pole to Pole Publishing
Baltimore

In a Cat's Eye

ISBN-10: 1-941559-12-3
ISBN-13: 978-1-941559-12-3

A Pinch of Chaos ©2016 by Christine Lucas
Three Wizards and a Cat ©2016 by A. L. Sirois
Tenth Life ©2016 by Doug C. Souza
The Canticle of Grimalkin ©2016 by R. S. Pyne
Cats of Nerio-3 ©2016 by Steven R. Southard
A Familiar Story ©2016 by Elektra Hammond
A Sudden Breeze Through an Open Door ©2016 by Jeremy Gottwig
Mark of the Goddess ©2016 by A. L. Kaplan
Kings of the Concrete Jungle ©2016 by K.I. Borrowman
Catspaw ©2016 by Gail Z. Martin
Masquerade Night ©2016 by Alex Shvartsman
Another Man's Cure ©2016 by Joanna Michal Hoyt
Nemesis ©2016 by Jody Lynn Nye
The Neighbor's Cat ©2016 by Gregory L. Norris
Grimmun ©2016 by Oliver Smith

Egyptian translations from Sir E.A. Wallis Budge's *Egyptian Book of the Dead*, and *Legends of the Gods*, both in the public domain.

"The Brazilian Cat," reprinted by arrangement with the Conan Doyle Estate.

Library of Congress Control Number: 2016954053

In a Cat's Eye

In a cat's eye, all things belong to cats.

~ English Proverb

Table of Contents

A Pinch of Chaos

Christine Lucas

Starving yourself isn't going to save him, Khemes wished he could tell Ankhu. He wanted to grab him and shake his grief away, but no one—not even his trusted servant of many years—dared such insolence toward the High Priest of Anubis. Instead, Khemes offered him once more a simple supper of dried fish, bread and beer.

"Please, neb-per. Please, my lord. You need to eat." When had his face grown so pale, his shoulders so slumped?

"I am not hungry, Khemes." The voice that could—and had—commanded the dead had grown low and weary. "Give it to Ne—" his voice faltered—"to some unfortunate beggar." Give it to Nedjem, he'd almost said. But the poor cat, slayer of frogs and sparrows, would never eat anything again. Not even a twitch of his whiskers, not even an inquisitive sniff at the scent of fish. He lay on Ankhu's bed, his breathing labored, littered by the occasional attempt to purr when Ankhu stroked his fur. After a long, pampered life—longer than those of his predecessors—the time to embark on Ra's Solar Barge and travel to the Afterlife had come.

"As you wish, neb-per." You will see him again, he wanted to shout, but his tongue was harnessed by an old promise.

Khemes bowed and took the meal back to the kitchen, where two of Nedjem's soon-to-be-widows took care of it. There were fresh loaves of bread, baskets of figs and dates, but even the jugs of Mareotic wine had lost their appeal. Dragging his bad leg—damn that old, stubborn wound—Khemes made his way back to his master's chambers. He treaded slowly, carefully, to avoid tripping over Nedjem who loved napping where it was most inconvenient. He wiped his eyes before entering the room; it would take a while for his body to accept the absence his mind already knew.

The breeze carried the choir of the frogs and crickets all the way from the Nile, along with a whiff of honeysuckle. Outside, Nedjem's usual hunting grounds were bursting with life. Inside, neither man nor cat seemed to notice him, as he entered the room. He poured water into a mug from the alabaster urn by the window and offered it to Ankhu, who just shook his head. Khemes sighed and sat on a cushion under the window, rubbing his aching leg. It would be a long night.

Troublesome dreams denied him any kind of rest that night; Apep, the Serpent of Chaos, gloated over his fallen enemy with the soft paws and sharp claws, defeated not in combat, but from age and disease. Khemes started from his sleep with a gasp at first light. Damned be his tired mind and old bones, he'd dozed off and left his master alone in his hour of grief. Ankhu sat hunched at the foot of his bed, clutching Nedjem's body on his chest.

Khemes cupped Ankhu's shoulder. "I'm sorry, *neb-per*. You did everything you could. Let him go now." Empty words, he knew it. But he had to say something. He had to *do* something. And he would. In time.

"No. I cannot. Not yet."

Three times Khemes tried to gently remove the cat's body from Ankhu's arms, and three times he failed. This was not good. He'd never seen his master so distraught before. Perhaps he should call someone? Perhaps—

"Fresh water."

"As you wish, *neb-per*."

He sprang to his feet at Ankhu's request, and the sudden movement rekindled the burning ache in his thigh. It didn't matter. He couldn't read or write his own name—despite Ankhu's valiant efforts over the years. But this much he knew: healing always began with water. Cool water from the sacred Nile, to wash away whatever ailed body and soul. He rushed to the kitchen for a fresh jug and when he returned, he found Ankhu donning his priestly garb: the long, white robes, the collar of multicolored beads and the leopard skin over his shoulders. Once the High Priest had quenched his thirst and washed his hands, Khemes helped him apply the kohl around his bloodshot eyes. With the dead cat a tiny parcel wrapped in white linen in his arms, Ankhu left for the *per-nefer*, the Pure House, for the embalming. Khemes followed him, holding a parasol over his master's head to protect his sensitive skin from the scorching sun.

When Ankhu placed Nedjem onto the stone slab to prepare him for eternity, Khemes leaned by the wall, drenched in sweat and lightheaded. It was too much: the smell of embalming fluids, the incense that failed to cover the stench of putrefaction, the feeling that Duat's guardian demons stared at him from every shadow, from every corner and crevice—he wanted out, out, under the sun, away from all this death. But he gulped down the bile and rubbed his gut to calm his heaving stomach. The High Priest needed no distractions while he performed the ritual. He needed someone to watch over him quietly. Loss of sleep and fasting had taken their toll.

How could Ankhu's hands be steady, holding the scalpel? How could the linen bandages unfold so effortlessly? How could his eyes be dry? This was his trusted companion—from kittenhood until his death last night— he was cutting open. The terror of sparrows and fishmongers, the cat whose paws had trod the paths of the dead beside his master, and the beloved of novice priestesses. His master's guard against intruders, Nedjem had often alerted him of the presence of ghosts and foul entities, even burglars—Cretan thugs who had no idea whose house they'd broken into. The idiots were probably still running.

He, too, would miss the rascal. Nedjem took great joy in pestering Khemes, who'd lost track of the times he had cleaned up broken pottery and shredded linen, replaced figurines and cutlery and dried

11

fish stolen from the pantry. Then, he'd trot purring at him and rub his head against Khemes' bad leg, and all would be forgotten. And now, he had to take care of his grieving master who'd fasted and stayed awake and recited prayers that brought no comfort. Ankhu's final service to Nedjem would come to an end, once he'd placed the small mummy into his family's tomb by his mother's sarcophagus. Then, Khemes' own task would begin.

A boring task. At dusk each day he waited by the city gates for the mute priestess to come into town and show him the way. A lonely task—he sat with a jug of beer at the feet of a great granite Sphinx, where he had first met her many years ago. A silent task, for only two others knew of it: a mute priestess and a dead cat. He needed magical skills to start a conversation with either of them. Bast knew he was as mute and deaf when it came to magic.

Three months and countless jugs of ale later, Ta-miut, the priestess, hadn't come. Ale lost its appeal, his household duties suffered, the other servants complained. His master barely noticed, sometimes in deep prayer, sometimes reciting incantations that summoned the dead. He lost weight. His long silences and wandering thoughts while in Court and Temple drew attention. Rumors spread of all sorts of maladies ailing the High Priest: insanity, senility, even magical ailments from consorting with the dead, the undead and whatever lay between. One night, Khemes found him sitting with his back rigid on his bed, stroking Nedjem's cushion beside him. He hadn't let anyone wash it or throw it away.

"Why hasn't he come to me?"

Khemes almost dropped the tray of food he'd brought. He'd seen his master tired, sad, even desperate, but never defeated.

"The spirits of long-dead pharaohs and sorcerers have come at my command, but not him. Why? Did I fail him?" *Has he forgotten me*? Ankhu didn't speak those last words, but Khemes heard them lingering in the cat-less room around them.

Because he's not dead, you idiot, Khemes wanted to shout, but held his tongue just in time. It was not his truth to tell.

"When did Nedjem—or any cat—come when commanded, *neb-per*? Do not despair. He'll come in his own time, as in life."

"Perhaps you're right." Ankhu fixed his gaze on his lap. "Perhaps…"

Enough was enough. Khemes dropped everything at the kitchen, grabbed his walking stick and a water skin and made his way to the city gates. Grief he could deal with. It was normal. Feeling like a failure was not—not for his master. The failure was his and his alone, for waiting so long to take matters into his own hands. He'd track down Ta-miut and get this over with. What if his absence was noted? When he'd return, he'd bring Nedjem with him and all would be back to normal. Ma'at—Harmony and Balance—would be restored once more in his master's home.

Even if that required of him to force the hands of the gods.

Ta-miut resided in a remote shrine of Bast half a day's walk south of Thebes. Nothing more than an old, broken-down statue, a worn tent and countless cats in a clearing by the Nile. No one knew where she'd come from; she'd walked into Thebes one day from the desert, her tongue cut off and her bare feet bleeding. Her talents for healing earned her a place in the Temple, but she preferred her solitude amidst fur and paw. She'd aided noblemen with their wounds, servants with newborns, even an old, crippled servant weeping for his master's dead cat almost two decades ago.

Khemes knelt amidst the reeds to throw water on his burning head. It had hit him hard—he never expected to care for anyone else so much, least of all a cat. The memory of that grief would follow him to his deathbed and beyond. So would the memory of Ta-miut's clear blue eyes—eyes of a princess from a faraway land—on her wrinkled face that day at sundown. As Ra's Solar Barge began its nightly journey, she held her index finger to her lips. *A secret. Between the two of them.* She took out a pouch of ground herbs from the folds of her dress and blew them to the breeze, then pointed at that direction. *Go.*

His thick—and tipsy—head hadn't understood at first. A shove at that direction by her bony hands helped a little. Her kick got him going in search for Bast's blessing. Or Bast's prank—that much was still unclear.

Where was she now?

With his gut in a knot, Khemes started walking alongside the Nile again, picking figs from the nearby trees as he went. Their sweetness brought a welcome relief from the bad taste in his mouth: sand and heat and worry. Ta-miut was old. Old people got sick. Old people died. Nedjem would be lost, if something had... A horsefly landed on his cheek and he slapped it away, a little bit too hard. Such thoughts attracted bad luck. Good thoughts only. Ta-miut was well, only distracted with the birth of many litters. Or by aiding some spoiled princeling with his wounds from hunting or sparring. She'd be under her tent by the shrine, just over that cluster of palm trees, with her arms full of kittens. And she'd be well and happy.

Only she wasn't.

She couldn't be, when two of her cats ran past him under the acacia trees, growling, ears twitched back and eyes wild. The sound of metal on stone followed. Men yelling. Cats hissing. More cats fleeing. Khemes fell flat on his belly. Robbers? Deserters? Whatever those men were, he was no match to them. He couldn't be. He should go back and alert the guard. Yes. That's what he should do. If he could crawl around with as little noise as possible, they wouldn't notice him. He'd be safe—

An arm's length away, a sand-colored cat cowered by the trunk of a palm tree under a thick fern. A young cat, barely a year old, the poor thing sat trembling. It looked at him with eyes huge and unblinking, judging him. Not just this cat—all cats, Nedjem amongst them, were judging him through those eyes. Perhaps even Bast herself. Should he leave now, one day his cowardly heart would be weighed and found heavy. His face fell in the dirt. *Damn.* He should have learned by now that forcing the gods' hands came at a cost.

He discarded the water skin and clutched his walking stick tighter—good, sturdy wood. It might crack a few bones. He started to crawl forward, toward the clearing, over fallen palm tree leaves, shrubs and rotting fruit. More cats were hidden all around him and watched his crawl in silence. Someone yelled in a tongue unknown but vaguely familiar. Khemes hunched behind a thick palm tree and dared a peek around the trunk. Ta-miut curled up by the remnants of her tent, sniveling. Two bandits. Hairy, dirty bastards. Foreigners, most likely. One paced around cursing, one sat on the ground, leaning against the feet of Bast's statue with a badly wounded leg. Very badly. It oozed stink and black blood. He'd seen such wounds before on corpses spewed by the river. Neither by sword nor axe, neither by man or lion, but from a crocodile's jaws.

Khemes' stomach roiled. *Breathe! Breathe!* He turned around and sat straight against the trunk, gulping down hard to avoid hurling. *It's not your leg, old fool.* He rubbed the deep scars up and down, hard enough to hurt—to remind his shivering body that he had survived his encounter with one of Sobek's children. Thanks to Ankhu. The High Priest had kept his soul from leaving his body while the healers worked to mend him, cutting off the rot and sewing what was left. That thug over there would not be so lucky. Even Ta-miut's skills couldn't help him now.

"Fix leg! Now!"

The thug spat the command with a heavy accent. That accent... hadn't he heard it before in the tavern? Cretans. Could they...could they be the fools who'd broken into his master's home several weeks ago? If so, then something much worse than a crocodile had mauled that one. Even if she had the skills to mend it, Ta-miut would never dare to undo the High Priest's handiwork. He was already dead. Khemes flexed his fingers around his walking stick and tightened his grip. If the gods favored him, he could deal with the other one. A good hit would knock him out long enough to let them flee to safety and alert the guards.

Khemes propped up on his stick and rose behind the palm tree. In the clearing, the injured thug lay motionless at the feet of the statue, flies buzzing all over him. The other one towered over Ta-miut, brandishing a dagger over her, cursing in his native tongue. With one eye swollen shut, Ta-miut cowered by a broken-down pillar—a remnant of the shrine's past glory—one arm covering her head, clutching her Bast amulet on her chest with the other.

The thug had his back turned on him. If he could sneak up on him…Khemes left his hiding place and took slow, careful steps forward, wielding his stick like a woodsman's axe.

"Fix! Or I kill *mau*! All *mau*!"

Khemes froze. What. Had. He. Just. Said?

Ta-miut fixed her good eye on the thug, her face unreadable. Then, she screamed. A deep, steady scream. Not a helpless crone's terrified cry, but a warning. Some things should never be uttered.

Hail, Hetch-abhu, who comest forth from Ta-she, I have not slain those belonging to the gods.

His master's voice, joined by the voices of those who came before him and those who'd follow, resonated inside Khemes' skull, reciting the words of the gods. All around him, countless eyes lit up, green, yellow, amber, huge and unblinking. Watching. Waiting. Measuring his steps until his stick crushed the bones of the blasphemer. Khemes tightened his grip. This time, he marched on.

"How dare you?"

He blurted out the words before he could harness his tongue and warned the thug, who turned around just in time to avoid getting his head cracked. The tip scraped his shoulder instead, and– damned be his bad leg—the ill-balanced hit almost made him lose his footing. Flailing his free arm, he stumbled past the thug and managed to stay on his feet, until the thug rammed him from behind with his elbow and sent him face first in the dirt. He rolled over just as the thug jumped him, dagger in hand. More out of reflex than skill, Khemes' arm darted out and caught his wrist while his other went for the thug's eyes. The thug went for his throat. He squeezed. And squeezed. Air hunger burned Khemes' chest. His eyes watered. *Not yet. Not like this.*

Ta-miut screamed again. Deeper, louder than before, it penetrated the buzzing in his ears. Not a warning this time, but a call to arms.

Cursing and howling, the thug released his throat. Khemes kicked him and crawled a few paces back, panting and blinking tears away. Ta-miut's cats had come to his aid: they pounced on the thug, aiming for his throat and face. On his knees, the thug tried with one hand to reach the cat that clutched onto his back, while throwing punches around with the other. Most of them hit empty air. Some did not. Cats hissed and growled and charged. Some of them retreated whimpering, limping, breathing hard.

Khemes forced himself up and reached for his discarded stick.

The cats darted off just in time to allow the thug a moment of wide-eyed clarity as Khemes swung his stick. The thug bent backwards to avoid the hit, but not fast enough. It broke his nose. The second swing clashed with his skull, above his ear. Bones cracked and he fell sideways, blood spilling from his nose. He lay on the ground, his eyes fixed somewhere past Khemes, his limbs twitching and trembling.

For one long, breathless moment, Khemes leaned on his stick. Was it over? Oh Bast, let it be over now. He was too old for this. Now, he needed ale. And bread and a nice hearty supper with roasted perch and radishes and onions and leeks. He needed his bed to rest his old bones and his aching leg. But he also needed that rascal Nedjem back, so his master's soul-sickness would be lifted. He drew in a deep breath and limped to Ta-miut's side.

She sat amidst her cats, humming softly, stroking their fur and tracing limbs and bodies with nimble, careful fingers for fractures. He sat beside her under the watchful gaze of the more suspicious of her cats. The bolder ones just climbed on his lap and shoulders. She flashed him a toothless smile.

"I'll take you to a healer," he said. A few paces away, the thug's convulsions had subsided. Rosy froth came from his mouth. "After I've taken care of those two."

Her grip on his arm was soft but steady. She shook her head.

"You don't want a healer?"

She shook her head again.

"And those two?"

She glanced at the bodies. Then, at the cats. Then, toward the Nile. Then, back at the cats. Then, straight at him, her good eye cold and merciless.

Khemes didn't know what her stare meant. He didn't want to know. But he still needed her help.

"Nedjem died." It hurt, having to say it out loud. It hurt, more than the thug's choking, more than the memory of the crocodile's teeth grinding against his thigh bone. Bast had given her children too much power.

Ta-miut stroked his arm as though she stroked a napping cat.

"You didn't come. I waited for you."

She pointed at her left ankle. Swollen and bruised, but the bruises weren't recent; faint blue and fading, they were about ten days old. The poor woman had injured herself while he'd been sitting on his fat behind, drinking ale. His face burned. 'I'm sorry," he mumbled.

She smiled, then took his right hand into hers and placed a small pouch in his palm.

Her magical herbs? Khemes shook his head so fast his neck hurt.

"No. I can't do magic. You must do it. I can't."

She closed his fingers around the pouch with one hand, then placed her other onto his chest. Her glance darted from her cats to the now motionless thug and back onto him. She nodded.

Yes. You can.

He very much doubted that.

Once back to Thebes after a journey that doubled the pain of every bone in his body, Khemes attempted to duplicate Ta-miut's spell. He blew the herbs to the breeze, and six times they fell at his feet. The seventh time they swirled for a moment over his head, then flew right into his nostrils and mouth. He forced the bitter taste down his throat. Too many curses had reached the tip of his tongue and spitting them out would only enrage the gods. He tried an eighth time and failed.

Damn and damn again. Barely a pinch was left of Ta-miut's herbs. He emptied them upon his pen palm. What now?

There should be an incantation along with the herbs, one Ta-miut recited with her heart. That's how the High Priest did it, that's how everyone adept in magic did it. He didn't—couldn't. He didn't know how. All he knew was how to tend to his master and clean after that spoiled cat, fetch him his dinner and treat him with the good fish from the pantry behind the cook's back. He missed that, even waking up to half-chewed sandals. Was this another prank of the cat-headed Goddess, forcing him to cast spells? He let out a deep, defeated breath…

…and the last pinch of herbs swirled and flew away, amidst the scent of jasmine and water lilies. Khemes rushed after it, his bad leg sending daggers up into his spine. It didn't matter. Nothing did, but the flowing mist leading him to this journey's end. He found it outside the city gates, by the old cemetery—the poor people's cemetery—in a broken-down hut. In there, a scrawny cat nursed her litter of three. But which one of them was Nedjem?

The one who hissed and puffed up and charged at his feet to shred his sandals, of course.

At last. It was over.

Or perhaps not.

"Khemes, I don't want another cat." The High Priest barely glanced at the kitten in Khemes' arms. He remained bent over his papyri, drowning his grief in paperwork.

"But, *neb-per*…" He held the purring kitten out for Ankhu to take a better look at him. "But, look…"

Ankhu didn't. "I said, no."

All this, for nothing? Khemes grabbed the back of a cedar-wood chair to steady his weak knees. *How can he say that? Is he blind?* He held Nedjem close to his chest. He'd stopped purring.

"Can we at least keep him until I can find him a good home?" Perhaps in time he'd wake up and see who was right in front of him shredding his papyri.

"Only until then."

Khemes licked his lips. *Perhaps...* "Would you like to name him?"

"He doesn't need a name. He's not staying."

Damn. "As you wish, *neb-per.*"

"I have work to do. Take him to the kitchen and keep him there."

Hadn't he seen a kitten before? For all his intelligence and arcane knowledge, the High Priest hadn't thought this through. Of course the kitten wouldn't stay in the kitchen. Once fed, he'd dart back to Ankhu's chambers and wreak havoc in his path. Khemes followed close behind him to clean up the mess and check for a change of his master's heart. Nothing seemed to change for six days, save for the pottery, the papyri and the linen that had to be replaced after the kitten got to them. At dawn on the seventh day, Khemes made his way to Ankhu's chamber to clean whatever mess awaited him.

He didn't make it into the room. He barely dared to breathe, frozen in the doorway, fearing he'd ruin everything. Ankhu sat on his chair, facing the bed, where the kitten lay on old Nedjem's cushion like the great Sphinx. Man and cat stared at each other's eyes in silence—that warm, comfortable silence between old friends who have little use of words anymore. Then, Ankhu spoke in a low, formal voice. Khemes held his breath and leaned forward to listen.

"Stand still then, O thou who art in sorrow, for Horus hath been endowed with life." He patted his lap. *"Come here, Nedjem."*

Nedjem obeyed for the first and probably last time in this life.

Khemes rested his head against the wall. *At last.* He had the kitten's mess to clean up, but he didn't care. Who knew that a pinch of chaos from a little rascal would bring back Harmony and Balance? But that was a question best left to priests and philosophers. In his own heart, only one thing mattered: in his master's house, Ma'at was restored.

Three Wizards and a Cat
A.L. Sirois

*A*ffecting *an air of nonchalance, Rali Ribhu strolled* through Ileranth's theatrical district amidst a throng of richly caparisoned pedestrians. Slender yet well-muscled, garbed conservatively in green and beige clothing of his own design, Rali negotiated the press with assurance. His professional thief's eye automatically noted all he passed, from the chubby and obviously prosperous burgher doubtless out of the Empalister farming region to Ileranth's north and here on a dinner outing with his no less chubby wife, bedecked with carnelians and diamonds; to the whip-thin young couple dressed solely in black transkins with silver highlights, enhanced with aniform whiskers and fur, perhaps performers in one of the plays or tabernacles. Rali enjoyed the bustle of the city and had on occasion found it quite lucrative.

Cruising a few meters above rooftop level private air cars enameled with family crests or provocative images floated through clouds of steam or smoke vented from the buildings, avoiding antennae and other appurtenances projecting from the rooftops. Their warning lights flashed variously carmine, amber and acid green.

Rali crossed an intersection and entered a dim street leading to Voormi's Belly, a warren of fetid alleyways many of the city's less sophisticated inhabitants called home.

It was here in the Belly he hoped to glean information that would lead him to the elusive Ludai Mahgrobi, a sorcerer of small repute who owed a substantial sum to Rali's master in return for advanced lessons in the craft.

The twisting streets of the Belly were clamorous with the cries of hawkers and the importuning of various tempters. Avoiding eye contact with the neighborhood's denizens, Rali mentally reviewed the details of Ludai Mahgrobi's case.

Mahgrobi had made some few small payments, but none for the last two months. Rali's employer, the sorcerer Xaglun Harridor, was never one to let loose ends dangle, especially where accounts receivable were concerned. He dispatched his assistant, Rali Ribhu, to secure the remainder of the debt.

After three days' search, however, Rali had found no trace of Mahgrobi. No one in his accustomed haunts had seen him. The address where he supposedly dwelt showed signs of being hastily vacated. Rali therefore decided to search the Belly.

Without warning a small shape rocketed out of a dark alleyway, colliding with Rali and knocking the wind out of him.

"Your pardon!" The aniform, in the semblance of a bipedal male tortoise shell cat, scrambled to its feet. Dodging across the street, it ducked into a crumbling apartment building.

Rali straightened his cap. "Be-damned feline!" He would have hurled further imprecations after the creature but a second, larger shape wrapped in a voluminous ultramarine cloak hurtled out of the same alleyway, likewise slamming into him. Though smaller than Rali, this one nevertheless massed enough that he tumbled sprawling into the gutter along with his latest assailant, who appeared stunned by the impact.

Rali's rooner, Seffriet, had been trailing her master along the crenellations of the rooftops overhanging the byway. Upon seeing him seemingly attacked she dropped chittering to the ground. Puffing herself up so her spines poked through her dense fur, she advanced threateningly upon the aggressor.

Really angry now, Rali levered himself up on his elbows. He noted Seffriet's stiff-legged stalk and followed her line of sight. The cloaked figure beside him yanked back its hood, revealing a tousled young woman glaring at him. His jaw dropped and he threw himself at the rooner.

"No, no, Seff!" he said, stroking her. Seffriet, whose ancestry bespoke more of cephalopod than mammal, responded to his touch. Her spines lowered and she turned several questioning eyes at him. He murmured a few words. Seffriet clambered up the side of the building, back on watch.

"*Dullard!* See what you've done?"

"I?" Rali stared at the girl. The emblem emblazoned on the clasp of her cloak caught his eye. His jaw dropped. *She's of the house of Mahgrobi! This is a stroke of luck.*

Scrambling to her feet, she made to pursue the cat. Rali shot his hand out, grasping the folds of her garment while hauling himself erect. "My employer, Xaglun Harridor, sent me to secure monies your house's patriarch, Ludai, owes him. Let us discuss payment terms."

She scowled. "This is none of my concern. My father has many creditors. In any event, we are estranged and have not spoken in years. Now release me at once!" Disdain sharpened her tone.

Despite her waspish demeanor she was, Rali saw, a most attractive young woman. Ludai being her father, the girl's name, he recalled from his research, was...

"Yaontine." He relaxed his grip slightly. "I understand your position. But could it be made worth your while to...understand mine?" He smiled his most winning smile, and pulled her closer. "Surely such a lovely female—"

The girl, wriggling in his clutch, spat out a series of uncouth syllables. Rali's sight dimmed and his hands—indeed his entire body— went limp. She stepped out of his grasp. Rali stood knock-kneed and slack-jawed, unable to move a muscle.

"Where did the cat go?" Yaontine spoke in a commanding tone.

Like her father, she has thaumatic skills. I might have known.
Helpless against the compulsion, Rali answered: "Into the building,
there." He pointed with his chin.

"Was it wearing anything?"

Wearing? "Yessss, a sporran cinched about its… middle." Vague
surprise glowed within him; he had not consciously noted the pouch.

"Damn and blast!" The girl dashed into the apartment building.
Her spell was obviously of short duration because when Rali's will
returned the structure's door had not quite swung shut.

He shook his head to clear it. Ruefully resolving to be more
careful, Rali stumbled into the entry and found himself in a squalid,
odoriferous stairwell littered with debris. Glowing cabochons on the
walls provided insipid illumination; many had been gouged out.

Moving with the caution of a practiced thief he reached the first
landing a moment later. He heard her footsteps pounding up the stairs.
The building had no walkways to adjoining structures. All he had to do
was follow her. She couldn't escape past him.

Despite his aggravation an ironic smile played on Rali's lips.
When he had first met Xaglun, the sorcerer had been in a position
almost identical to that of the unfortunate Ludai—owing money that
he could not repay to an unforgiving creditor: a powerful sorcerer
named Kod Wasrey, a specialist in shape-shifting of high standing in
Xaglun's order. On that occasion Rali had found himself entangled
in Xaglun's ill fortunes to an extraordinary and almost fatal extent.
Through luck and his native talents, however, he had proved to be of
such help to Xaglun that the wizard had taken him on as a protégé.

Rali hoped now to be of help again. With the abrupt appearance
of young Yaontine Mahgrobi, it appeared as if Rali's luck had turned—
assuming he could win her sympathy.

Of the aniform he saw no trace. But if he found the cat he'd find
the girl, too; and vice versa. Forewarned now of her thaumatic ability,
he'd be ready. Xaglun had provided him with a few minor spells in case
of emergency.

Above Rali the girl's footsteps stopped abruptly.

Frowning, he paused. What was she about?

Peering around the corner of the landing, he saw Yaontine frozen in the act of taking a step as if pondering the wisdom of her actions. He drew back lest she hear him and glance down at him over her shoulder. But she remained motionless.

He relaxed and a grin spread across his vulpine features. The same rigidity compulsion that she had laid on him had been cast on her. By the aniform, no doubt. *Clever beastie! Will* she *now be compelled to answer questions?* Careless now of stealth, he trotted up the stairs and seated himself on one above her, bringing his head level with hers. She glared at him with a degree of malice surprising in one so young.

"Why are you chasing the cat?" Rali asked, slightly discomfited by her animosity.

"He stole something from me. I am trying to get it back."

"Ah. What has he taken?"

Fighting the compulsion, she ground out, "An amulet."

"A thaumatic amulet, I daresay."

She hissed an assent.

He sighed. Yaontine would answer questions, but would vouchsafe nothing voluntarily. He could certainly find out all she knew but that would take time, and the compulsion placed upon her would fade in moments.

"Does your father know his amulet has been taken?"

"*Nnnno.*" Her stare hardened and he suppressed an urge to grin. His guess—the amulet was Ludai's and not hers—had paid off. She had stolen it from her father, and the aniform had in turn stolen it from her. Rali, larcenous by nature, nodded in understanding.

"Who is working with the cat?" Because, of course, as he'd just proved, one could expect nothing but double-dealing where thaumatic objects were concerned. If she was chasing the aniform they clearly weren't co-conspirators.

"Kod Wasrey."

Rali blinked, unable to hide his dismay. "A man widely regarded as being no-one to cross. Your father owes *him* money?"

"Yes." Rali, staring intently at Yaontine's face, barely noticed her left hand twitch in his peripheral vision. The significance of the gesture hit him just before her spell did.

He had time to sub-vocalize a few words of a counter-charm and so was spared the worst of the effect. Even so it took him a very painful minute to twist his head back around until it faced the proper direction. Dizzy, with eyes watering and no feeling of benevolence for the girl, he stumbled up the stairs after her.

At least he had a few more answers. Obviously Yaontine wanted the amulet back before her father discovered its absence. Why had she purloined it in the first place? No matter; all Rali had to do was obtain the trinket for himself and present it to Xaglun, who would use it as leverage to convince Ludai to pay his debt.

The stairs ended in a short hallway with a window at each end— and no doors. Where had the girl gone? Rali glanced up and grinned. An attic door! He leaped, caught the rope hanging from the door, and let his weight pull it open. A set of folding stairs opened outward and downward. He scrambled up them. Above was a small, dark chamber with another trap door in its ceiling.

Rali flung back this second trapdoor and thrust his head out into open air. Above, so close that he ducked right back down again, thundered the engines of a mighty air cruiser, an immense potato-shaped gasbag with a car slung beneath and six outboard propulsion pods. That single glance had been enough, however, for him to see the girl clambering up a swaying rope ladder toward the airship. Rali gripped the topmost rung of the steps, forcing himself up against the downdraft and his fear that the spinning propellers would chop him to pieces.

The ship rose wonderfully into the night air with Rali swinging from the bottom rung of the rope ladder and damning all airships to Gorgorleth. Ileranth spun beneath him as he scrambled up the swaying ladder, resolutely not looking down. A gust of wind snatched his jeweled cap off his head.

As he spidered up the rope ladder, a thought occurred to him: airships don't appear out of nowhere to provide escape for young women. Either Yaontine had known it would be there for her, or else she summoned it via com-gland. Rali liked neither option.

He liked them even less a few instants later, when, still several meters shy of the hatchway above, Rali saw two rough-looking faces appear within its frame. He ground his teeth. Retreat was impossible. Therefore, within moments he was being pulled up into what appeared to be the aircraft's cargo hold. Here the throb of engines was louder albeit lower in pitch. Complicated duct-work snaked across the ceiling and down the walls, interrupted here and there by gaskets and valves controlled by glowing keypads. Wire bundles spasming with power crawled across the floor to monitor kiosks. The overall effect was one of hasty construction and haphazard repairs.

His captors were dressed identically in blue trousers that came to their mid-calves, split-toed slippers, and horizontally striped red-and-white linen tunics. They even looked similar, with long faces and straw-colored hair. Both were armed with what Rali recognized as stunner pistols.

"An unpaid passenger," one crewman said to the other, sneering as he dogged the hatch in the floor. Rali took a quick glance down as the portal swung shut. The tops of Ileranth's buildings were far below now, with the running lights of numerous air cars visible as the vehicles slowly threaded their way through the city. Rali regarded them with a pang of longing.

The other crewman grinned, revealing uneven and discolored teeth. "Indeed, and we know how to deal with stowaways." The two seized Rali and half led, half dragged him across the cargo hold, which was in truth no bigger than a good-sized parlor. Set into the bulkhead was a sturdy hatch that one of the men opened. The other one thrust Rali inside.

Then, with a derisive snort each, they slammed the hatch shut and left him.

Rali took a few moments to catch his breath while looking around the closet-sized chamber in which he was imprisoned. Its only furnishings were a little bunk and a toilet. There was a porthole to the outside, but it was too small for him to squeeze through. In any case, where would he escape *to*? Outside, only stars were visible.

He sat on the bunk, which was quite hard, and morosely considered his circumstances. They were considerably worse than before. Not only had Yaontine and the aniform cat evaded him; wherever this airship was going Rali was along for the ride, will-he nil-he. Doubtless no good outcome awaited him at the voyage's conclusion.

A slight scratching from outside the cabin attracted his attention. He frowned. The noise seemed to be coming from near the floor. He rose and approached the portal.

"Rali Ribhu? Can you hear me?" The voice was low and rough. There was something familiar about it…

The cat! The cause of Rali's predicament! "What do *you* want?" Rali growled.

"My name is Gaalor. I wish to assist you," was the answer.

"Ah. And why would you do *that*, friend Gaalor?"

"I feel responsible for entangling you in this affair."

"As well you should. Even assuming you could free me, what then? We are trapped aboard this airship."

"There are emergency paragliders to be had. Can you pilot one?"

Rali considered the proposition. "If there is no other way, I am willing to try."

"Excellent! I am too small to effectively manage a paraglider's controls, but I can certainly give you some advice, as I have seen them in use."

The temptation was strong. And yet… "You are in league with Kod Wasrey," Rali said. "Whereas I am in the employ of his rival, Xaglun Harridor, to whom Mahgrobi is also in debt. Do you propose a partnership?"

Gaalor evaded his gaze. "What better way for our mutual patrons to wrest suitable recompense from the wretched Mahgrobi?"

"Hmm. And where *is* Mahgrobi? Surely not aboard this airship."

"No, I am unaware of his current whereabouts. Nevertheless, we won't be able to find him while we are stuck up here in the air."

"I admit there is much truth in what you say. Very well then, let us join forces to find Ludai Mahgrobi."

"Most wise of you."

Of this, Rali was not so sure. Yet, if the cat could secure his release from this prison cell, so much the better. "One thing, though—where is Yaontine bound?"

"Nowhere near her father, of that you may be certain," said Gaalor, busying himself at the hatch's locking mechanism. Rali heard an odd fluttering sound and was about to inquire as to its nature when the hatch creaked open. Sure enough, there stood the aniform looking up at him with calm amber eyes. Rali had an opportunity now to inspect the creature more closely. Obviously based on a tortoise shell cat, the humanoid being stood about two and a half feet tall. Its front paws had been modified into serviceable hands with opposable thumbs.

This time Rali did not fail to note that the cat indeed wore a small sporran attached to a thin leather belt circling its hips. The sight of it suggested several pertinent questions to him but he said nothing, instead casting his gaze around the tiny cargo hold. No crew members were in sight.

"Very well, Gaalor. Where are these paragliders of which you spoke?"

"Follow." The cat padded across the hold to a locker. "Within."

Rali opened the locker and found inside it a number of tightly bound packages of what seemed to be a flexible fabric. "Self-inflating, no doubt," he murmured, selecting one. It weighed less than he expected.

"Let us hope so." The cat led the way back to the floor hatch through which Rali had entered the airship. To open it was the work of but a few moments. Rali stood poised on the brink, examining the package in his hands. He found a seam and tugged at it. The package fell apart into a harness with a fabric saddle, and a chrysalis-like bag.

"That," said Gaalor, indicating the bag with a paw, "is the gliding wing. Once we depart this craft, you press the inflation switch there, on the saddle. The wing does the rest. All that is left is to guide it. Simplicity itself."

"No doubt." Rali strapped on the harness, which automatically positioned the gliding wing at his back. At the cat's direction he thrust his hands through the glove-like controls attached to the harness, and prepared to leap out of the airship. He paused at the hatch, his insides quailing.

"Why do you delay?" asked the cat, obviously agitated.

"I don't do well with heights."

"Fear not; we will descend rapidly."

"Precisely my concern." Rali swallowed hard. Just before he leapt there came a chittering noise from outside and a familiar head popped into view.

"Seffriet! I had forgotten all about you!" The rooner scrambled up into the airship. She must have been clinging to the hull by her suckers. Seffriet paused upon seeing Gaalor, but did not bridle.

The aniform's hackles raised. "I don't like rooners," he growled.

"Nevertheless, she accompanies us," Rali said firmly. "Unless you'd care to remain behind...?"

"The rooner may come," said the cat in a sullen voice.

Once more Rali positioned himself to leap from the airship, holding the cat firmly in his arms. Seffriet wrapped her strong, boneless arms around one of Rali's legs. Taking a deep breath, Rali stepped out into the night.

He fell away from the airship into a rush of chilly air. "Shall I activate the inflation process now?" he asked Gaalor.

From his perch in Rali's lap the cat craned his neck to peer at the dimly seen landscape beneath them. "The sooner the better. We are not as high up as I had reckoned."

"Perhaps, however, we have enough time to discuss certain matters." Rali pushed the inflation button. The wing at his back promptly unfolded and began expanding above him. Their fall gradually slowed.

"What matters are these?"

Rali tested the brake loops. The paraglider seemed stable enough, and responsive to his pulls on the controls. Satisfied that he could steer the contraption, he kept his eyes on the landscape. The huge red bulk of Sol stained the atmosphere to the east though it would not show above the horizon for some time. "Primarily this," said Rali. "I assume you retain the amulet Yaontine seeks so avidly."

"Let us speak of...other things," said the cat.

"No, I believe this is an appropriate topic of conversation." Scanning below for a place to land the paraglider, Rali spotted a meadow faintly visible at the bottom of a valley between two time-eroded mountains. He set about guiding the paraglider toward it. Fortunately, the machine was easy to pilot and he gained confidence with each passing moment.

"It occurs to me to ask," he said. "What powers does it have?"

Silence.

"Come, come! I am risking my skin for you. The more information I have, the better I will be able to assure your continued freedom."

Gaalor sighed. "Oh, very well. It bestows the ability to alter one's form."

Rali's eyes went wide as several puzzle pieces dropped into place. Kod Wasrey was known far and wide as an accomplished shape-shifter. Could this amulet be the source of his magical skills? This explained the Mahgrobi's' eagerness to retain the charm. How had it escaped Wasrey's grasp in the first place?

Certainly his own employer, Xaglun Harridor, would look on him with considerable favor were Rali to present him with such a talisman. "A rare trinket indeed," he murmured.

"We can discuss the matter another time," said Gaalor. "I urge you to direct your gaze above and to the west."

Rali glanced up and cursed. Someone aboard Yaontine's airship had taken notice of the glider's departure, for another paraglider was making in their direction. He turned his attention to his craft's controls. Gaalor stared over his shoulder at the other glider, which was closing rapidly.

"Yaontine is piloting it," Gaalor said after a moment. "She participates in many paragliding contests, generally winning."

Rali ground his teeth. "Hang on." He twisted the controls with some force, setting the glider diving toward the ground at a steep angle. The cat gasped and even Seffriet chittered in dismay.

Sweating, Rali managed to pull out of the dive with a scant fathom to spare, bringing the craft to a grating halt on the floor of the valley. He looked up and saw that Yaontine's paraglider was heading for the same place. It would arrive soon.

He tossed Gaalor to the ground and scrambled out of his harness. Seffriet uncoiled herself from his leg. Rali scooped the rooner up and muttered a few sentences. Seffriet chirruped and scuttled off into the nearby underbrush.

A line of brilliant light scored the ground between Rali and Gaalor. "Make no untoward moves!" Yaontine shouted as she brought her paraglider in for an expert landing. "Gaalor, get over by your friend."

"Do not fire." Rali deliberately put a quaver into his voice as Gaalor sidled over to him.

"You've got to *do* something!" Gaalor whispered urgently.

"I already have," Rali said quietly. "We must keep her attention centered on us."

"I want that amulet!" Yaontine disengaged her safety harness, keeping the pistol aimed at Rali and Gaalor.

"Gaalor—give it to her."

"What? I will do no such thing!"

"Gaalor! Damn you, do as I say!"

"You must be insane," the cat said disdainfully. "After all we've been through? I'd sooner die!"

"That you and I will certainly do unless you give in to her demand."

"Listen to me, cat—"

Yaontine discharged her pistol into the sky. "My patience is at an end," she said. "I want that amulet, and I want it now!"

"Now?" Rali asked with no trace of guile.

"Right now!"

"Very well. Seffriet, right now!"

The rooner launched herself out of the bushes and wrapped her several tentacles around Yaontine's arm and hand, wresting the weapon from the girl's grasp. Rali stepped over to her and snatched it away from the rooner.

"Now then," he said, training it on Yaontine as the rooner redistributed her tentacles into secure bindings around Yaontine's body. "Let's discuss this like civilized beings."

"You bloody unmitigated fool!" Yaontine struggled against the tentacles, but Seffriet was too strong for her. "You have no idea what you're up against."

"Oh, I think I do." Rali twirled the pistol.

"No, she's correct," said Gaalor. He mumbled a few sentences Rali couldn't catch and suddenly a tall cadaverous man stood in his place.

Rali recognized him at once and his heart fell. "Kod Wasrey!"

"To be sure." The wizard dusted himself off.

"I knew it," Yaontine muttered.

"Why didn't you reveal yourself sooner?" demanded Rali Ribhu.

"Actually, I was having myself a bit of fun. It was all quite exciting, don't you think?"

"Exciting!" Rali found himself at a loss for words.

"Yes. I confess I was taken aback when this young lady's father managed to pierce my defenses and purloin my amulet. I needed to know how he managed it so that I could plug the hole in my magical guard."

Rali shook his head in puzzlement. "But how could you change yourself into an aniform without your charm?"

"Because I was already in cat form, busying myself with a certain task that need not concern you. While I was about it, Ludai Mahgrobi pierced my defenses and robbed me, forcing me to attempt to get my amulet back while trapped in a cat's body. And once I did, I found myself being so ardently pursued by Yaontine Mahgrobi, here, that I had no time to cast the return spell." He smiled at the girl. "You have a great talent, my dear," he said. "You waste it employing it on your foolish father's behalf. He's something of a charlatan, not to mention a welsher."

Yaontine hung her head. "I have had no other opportunity to learn the magical craft."

"Hmm. Well, let us say that you can discharge your father's debt by coming to work for me. I can use a resourceful assistant, and you have proved you tenacity at the least."

Encouraged, Rali spoke up. "Mahgrobi owes monies to my master as well."

"Mmm. Well, you, too have rendered me a service or two during the course of this adventure," Wasrey said. He muttered to himself for a few moments. The air crackled with energy, and where Yaontine had stood a moment before there was now an aniform cat identical in appearance to Gaalor.

She yowled and spat.

Wasrey raised a finger. "Now, now. You can perform a great many useful functions in the guise of a cat. Your return to human form is contingent on your father paying what he owes to Xaglun Harridor." He turned to Rali. "I trust this will satisfy the esteemed Harridor?"

Rali nodded. "I do believe it will."

"Very good, then," said Wasrey. "Simplicity itself."

Tenth Life

Doug C. Souza

I found Mr. Gary confessing to the cat one evening. The gray and black tabby didn't care about no confession, just wanted a good petting.

"How about I pop a hatch and jettison the lot of us?" Mr. Gary asked. "We just we suckin' up last of our sparse resources anyway. We all know heavy dooms a-comin'. End it quick, I say." He reached up with his good hand and pinched the cat's ears and then held the cat's head in his palm. For a second, I fretted that he'd wring the poor creature's neck.

"Heya," I said, but it came out as a soft cough. My throat was dry from the acid mists. I stepped out of the corridor and into the room. "Heya," I repeated.

Mr. Gary ignored me, cupped the cat's head, and gave it a squeeze. The cat whipped her head back and then nudged Mr. Gary's palm for more squeezes.

Mr. Gary's other arm—his dead arm—hung at his side. It stunk like rotten eggs.

"Hey, Derek," Mr. Gary said, pulling his hand away from the cat. "What you doing? Spyin' on us?"

I shrugged. "Nah, nah."

"I was just funnin' about killing all you." He nodded toward a body wrapped in tattered clothes at his feet. "I like to tell Stacey my deepest and darkest secrets. Figured it wouldn't hurt none for the cat to hear, too."

The cat dropped away and headed my way. I put a hand out to tempt her closer.

Mr. Gary peered straight at me. "Now, don't go rattin' on me to Boss Lady? She's got enough on her plate without knowing I got my missus hidden back here."

Miss Stacey had gone missing a few days back. "That her, huh?" I asked, wishing I'd just kept my mouth shut.

"She went a week ago. She was at Ultima's outer corridors when the cloud hit. She's a strong gal, but..."

"I didn't know she was in here. I was just exploring. That's all, sorry." I winced. I didn't want to be nowhere near Mr. Gary right then.

The cat brushed up against my calf as if to soothe me. I scratched her spine, thanking her silently. Her little butt rose up and she curled around for another pass.

The drift city gave a lurch. I slid and hit the doorway. Mr. Gary stumbled, but caught himself before falling.

"Them acids out there are fightin' to get in every second," he said. "And you're out exploring?" He had that dazed look in his eyes like all the other frazzled adults. No one had been the same since the storm ripped up Ultima. Some went around calling our drift city a "floating tomb," saying it was pointless hoping for help to arrive. Boss Lady Kate told us all to stay near the center where the acid wasn't heavy in the air yet.

"Looking around to see if there's help coming, that's all," I explained. "Saw the cat go this way."

"The cat?" Mr. Gary squinted at me for a spell and then gave a hard sniff. Tears trickled down his cheeks. He wasn't crying; eyes just seemed to water easily in the poisoned air. The sulfuric spit wasn't itching my skin yet, but everyone had runny noses and burning eyes. Me, I got it in the ears more than the eyes for some reason. "Aw Derek, you're weird, but can't fault you for it. You give it a name yet?"

"*Her*, not *it*."

"Oh, my apologies," he laughed. Mr. Gary patted me on the head as he slouched by. "Didn't know your pet's a *she*."

I leaned away from him and his dead arm as he went by.

The cat pawed at my arm; no claws.

I'd never seen a cat up close until the storm hit. She must've been smuggled in and then snuck out of her owner's apartment when the storm hit. Earthers have animals all over the place, but pets are a luxury we ain't privy to here. I never imagined I'd get to hold one. I lifted her into my arms, stepped up to one of the porthole windows. "You think anyone's taken notice of us yet? How about the ground shafters? They gotta know we're in trouble, eh?"

A trickle of drops eating away at the edge of the porthole's casing caught my eye. Not enough of an opening to send a spray, but enough to get in your eyes if you got up close.

I stepped back until I brushed up against the wall behind me. I closed my eyes and breathed slowly, pretending it got me more oxygen from the air.

Caustic: something that eats away at something else. People have been repeating that word.

The cat turned and mouthed a quick meow, but no sound came. Like the rest of us, her throat was parched. Most times, I tasted stale paste on my tongue.

Lamps overhead dimmed and brightened. Some never turned back on. Maybe we *had* ended up surface-side like some say and Venus is slowly crushing us—we wouldn't know until seconds before the ceiling and floor met.

Nah, we were still in the air, and soon another city would receive our auto-emergency beacon and latch onto us. Lister said Oberon or Bahia would've latched on three weeks ago if they cared to help.

I guess I just couldn't give up hope.

∽

"Derek?" Sigrid called down the corridor.

I started backing out of the collapsed passageway I had found several rooms down from where I had seen Mr. Gary. "Yeah, I'm here." I took a deep breath and called out. "Just searching this hollow-way."

Sigrid stuck her head in, "Well, get out." She made me blush just by talking to me. Her jumpsuit was as worn as everyone else's, but she spent her free moments patching up the rotted portions.

"Thanks," I said as she handed me a water-pouch.

"Alright, alright, let's just get you back. Kate wants you at the refrigeration chamber in the food court past the L walk-path."

"Ain't that too cold?" I asked after a long drink from the pouch. The recycled water tasted bitter, but still cooled my throat. I needed to find the cat and make sure she got some.

Sigrid smiled. "Uh, yeah, a crew stripped out the coolant unit a day ago since there ain't no more food left. You think she'd put us in the cold as a solution? She's running the air compressor and jury-rigging filters everywhere. A last stand. Centre Pavilion's the most reinforced area."

"No food left?"

"Well, no perishables left," she said and put up a hand. She sneezed and a bit of blood came out. She cursed and wiped it on the inside of the crook of her arm.

"What are perishables?"

"Food you need to keep cool or it rots," Sigrid rolled her eyes and mussed my hair. "Sheesh Derek, let's get."

I didn't try to court Sigrid the way the older boys did, but I pretended she was my girlfriend sometimes. Even dried out and bloodshot, her eyes put squiggles in my stomach when she smiled at me.

"Did you wanna stay a bit and gander 'round with me?" I asked.

Sigrid put her arm around me. "How about we get back, rest a bit, and then see about exploring with that cat of yours."

On our way back, we grabbed the last of the filter-screens. There wasn't much, and I think she could've carried them all herself, but she let me help so I'd feel useful.

"Did anyone show up from anywhere?" I asked as we exited the supply corridors. Unlike the adults, she didn't mind my asking her things "every two seconds."

Sigrid shook her head.

"Any scout groups return?"

She stopped. "Came back; didn't find anything. Now, let's go."

"What about the outer transport tubes?" My mom had been inside the D-rail when the spray hit.

"Let's go, Derek." Sigrid strode off. She was just a few years older than me, but she knew things the grown-ups did. Things they weren't sharing with me because I was too young to understand.

I didn't see the cat down any corridors as we headed inward. Sometimes she'd follow if I waved her along. What did she see when she went exploring? A couple times I followed her, but she'd disappear before I could catch up.

The corridor opened to the ruins of downtown Ultima. Mr. Popkes had explained how the five-story high ceilings made of palladium-glass were originally intended to provide comfort and familiarity with Earth. Most of us didn't like the vastness of the sky-view and preferred the protective wrappings within the corridors, branches, and pockets of outer Ultima.

Years back, the citizens opted to hang a giant tarp that blocked the glass ceiling, to keep us from seeing the outside.

The tallest building, a bank company, had tumbled down after succumbing to the acid eating away at its connector joints. It toppled over two other buildings. The giant tarp had fallen as well, hanging listlessly like a conquered kingdom's flag. Dark orange clouds streaked with yellow spiraled past. No ceramic hatch cover was large enough to block out the clear dome overhead. Those of us left had no choice but notice it. Boss Lady Kate insisted it was safe;

although it was see-through, the palladium-glass dome was several meters thick.

A crack stretched from one corner to the other like a frozen lightning beam.

"The crack seems bigger," I whispered to Sigrid. My voice had gone parch again. The acidic mist wasn't as thick as in the corridors, but I could still feel it drifting into my nostrils and mouth. My ears felt as though a thousand tiny worms danced in the canals—itched when I swallowed.

Sigrid squinted at the dome, shrugged, and strode down the J walk-path. The ivy covering the upper walls had browned and fallen down like a folded blanket. The brush lining the walkways had grown prickly.

Something wisped by and ducked under the rubble across the walk-path.

Seconds later, the cat perched up on a slab of flexi-crete. In all the mess, she had somehow kept her fur immaculate. While the rest of us had rashes and blotches forming on our skin, the cat's fur gleamed.

Hardy thing, that cat was.

I waved for her to follow. I crouched and waved some more.

She shook her head.

"Psst," I said, trying to get the cat's attention.

She turned and faced the other way—toward the collapsed corridors. I imagined what it must be like for her to be able to duck into the small nooks and see if there were others beyond the damage.

Sigrid coughed.

I got up and followed Sigrid. She looked past me toward the cat. My head hung low, something in my heart hurt. I had never cared so much whether the cat came or not—since the stubborn thing did what it wanted anyway, but something warned me that I needed to get her to the "last stand."

"Let's go, Derek," Sigrid whispered. An arm fell on my shoulder and pulled me into a half-hug. Her ribs and hip felt bony through her jumpsuit. I leaned into the hug as we walked and tried to ignore the jittery feeling growing inside of me.

~

"Time's up," the tall man said as he put his hand out. His bright eyes winced as if to apologize, but I knew it wasn't his fault. I undid the straps from around my ears and handed him the oxygen mask.

"Here," I whispered.

He glanced around the refrigeration chamber. "Hey, go ahead and take a couple more minutes. I'll take it off mine."

I shook my head. We were only allowed our "allotted" amount. Boss Lady Kate had been clear about that.

"It's okay," I said.

"Come on son," the tall man insisted. "Please." He reached down and refastened the straps to my ears before I could refuse.

His bright eyes moistened. He stared at me while I breathed in the oxygen. The rubbery plastic wasn't as dry and brittle as the plastics outside the refrigeration unit. A bit of the emergency supplies and rations people had gathered were spared from the acidic mist and looting.

The tall man took the oxygen mask, carried the tank away, and sat down. He'd only get eight minutes.

The old lady sitting across from me hadn't budged since Sigrid and I arrived a few hours ago. Others fidgeted while they napped, but the old lady rested peacefully. The blanket around her was eaten away in spots; frayed ends fluttered in the soft breeze coming from the overhead vents. Vents covered by the filter screens Sigrid and I had brought back.

Rumors abounded that drift city Ultima had dropped a level into a more dangerous atmosphere. Some folks spoke in hushed voices that the O2 converters had finally quit and now it was just a matter of time before we drifted down into the crushing air layers below.

A groan echoed from within the vent. I shot up.

No one else budged.

The groan rose in volume and pitch.

"It's the cat!" I cried.

The tall man looked at me, and then looked away.

The vent went silent. A series of meows sounded across the chamber. I hurried toward the end of the refrigeration chamber.

Nobody got up. Tired eyes glanced my way, and then went back to staring onward.

Boss Lady Kate rose as I neared the refrigeration door. She put up a tired hand to stop me. Her clothes now draped over her thin body, many sizes too big. Even starving, she was still a big lady.

The cat's meows no longer came from the vents, but from the other side of the door.

"The cat." I pointed.

"No," Boss Lady Kate said. "Go sit down."

"Let her in!" My voice burned.

"Sit down."

"What?" I pushed past her, but her thin hands held me like dang lock-straps.

"No, Derek. We all agreed this was best."

"It's okay, the cat can share my air."

"Derek." She knelt down to face me.

"Let me out then." I shoved, but she held me firm.

"Derek, the cat...we've allowed this to go long enough." She took my face in her hands and kissed my forehead. "I'm sorry, but we can't pretend anymore." She held me tight.

I yanked away from Boss Lady Kate. "Sigrid," I shouted, my throat burned. I couldn't find her. "Sigrid!"

"I'm coming, Derek," she said, hurrying over. She stood before us, looking at the ceiling as she blinked away tears. She shook her head.

"Can you help him?" Boss Lady Kate asked.

"I don't know." Sigrid said. "I'll try."

The cat clawed at the door.

"She wants in," I told Sigrid.

"Derek," she started, but then pulled me into a hug. "We can't, I'm sorry."

"No, I mean," I sputtered. "Just me then, tell her to let me out. I want out."

"It's over, let the cat go."

"The cat? Let it go?" My throat felt on fire, but I had to explain.

Sigrid pleaded with me. "He's out there, he'll be fine. We're in here—"

"He? The cat's a she." My heart felt like it was in my stomach. "You don't even know."

The meowing grew to a howl, but sounded farther away.

Sigrid hunched down to look me in the eyes. "It's not real. Your damned cat isn't real. Get it?"

"Get what?" My breath felt like it was going in reverse. "What're you...what do you mean?"

"It's true," Boss Lady Kate added. "The cat you found is an animatronic, uh, pseudo-pet, whatever you want to call it."

Sigrid smoothed my bangs. "The cat's a plaything—not really alive."

"She stopped," I said, staring at the door. "Her meowing."

Boss Lady Kate nodded. "From what I understand, the hardware's designed to recognize the finest details when it comes to human reaction and minor impulses. From pupil dilation to breathing patterns. The thing's designed to soothe you."

"But she was so real. She wanted me to explore with her. Why?" I asked.

Sigrid explained, "That's why it took to you, Derek. You responded to it because—well, because you're a sweet kid. Its programming

43

must've attached to the most receptive of us." She blinked away tears and smoothed my bangs.

Sigrid calling me a "sweet kid" stung. I pulled away from her.

Boss Lady Kate sighed. "Consider this: why would an Earther pet-breed be on Ultima? The dang pseudo-pet was some Earther knickknack that must've gotten loose when the storm hit. We're bunkering down in here now. You have to face that."

I searched the faces across the refrigeration chamber. No one looked my way—just two rows of heads hung low.

I closed my eyes and concentrated.

The cat's meows had quieted, but they were still out there.

I stepped away from Sigrid and Boss Lady Kate.

The door was less than a meter away.

I jumped forward and tried for the handle, but Boss Lady Kate grabbed me by the waist.

My head pounded.

The cat meowed louder than I'd ever heard her, as if begging me to join her. "Please," I said. "Please let me go. I'll come back. I just want to say good-bye."

But Boss Lady Kate looked at me like she knew I was lying and didn't plan on coming back.

Sigrid crumbled to the ground, crying hard in a fit.

Boss Lady Kate called some of the other adults over.

I battled her best I could, but it was no use. The air in my lungs burned, making me cough. I couldn't breathe right, white spots exploded across my eyes.

The door opened.

Mr. Gary, with his dead arm, and two other men stood in the frame. They wore their regular clothes, but now had torn bits of cloth covering their faces. "Headin' out to the—" he stopped when he saw me tugging at Boss Lady Kate's grip. "What's this?"

"I want out," I cried. "They ain't letting me."

Mr. Gary glanced at me, and then back at Boss Lady Kate.

"That true?" he asked her.

"He's...he doesn't understand. Little guy's worked up, going on about that blasted cat of his."

"The cat?" Mr. Gary shook his head. "Heck, if the kid wants out, maybe you let him out. He's all kinds of messed up. Don't matter at this point."

"You were petting her," I said. "Confessing about killing us to Stacey. You understand, right? You know?"

Mr. Gary shook his head, "Yeah, kid. I was..." He stopped, and then chuckled. "Little thing's got a way, huh? Worms into your heart like the real deal."

Boss Lady Kate drew me back. "It's better in here, peaceful. Better for him. He doesn't understand. Please shut the door, Gary."

"No one a-comin' with us to give it a go?" Mr. Gary called into the chamber. "Either way...hell, I don't know what to say here. I just can't sit by and wait for it—gotta keep on lookin' for some odd reason."

I bit Boss Lady Kate hard on her arm, and pushed my finger right into a sore.

She cried out and released me.

I hopped over Sigrid and clawed my way past Mr. Gary and the other two guys.

There was a ruckus behind me, but mostly I heard Mr. Gary laughing.

The cat darted towards the west-end, near the collapsed corridors. I raced after her. An orange mist spewed out of the ceiling vents. The tops of the buildings grew blurry behind the incoming cloud.

A murky haze filled the air the farther I went toward the west-end corridors. Vents sputtered overhead.

I knelt and found a shallow tunnel perilously kept standing by a pair of corroded struts. Drops of brown plopped into a puddle at the base of the struts. The cat meowed somewhere within the darkness of that squat space.

I hesitated, couldn't help picturing loose flexi-crete collapsing on top of me.

The cat poked her head out. Her golden eyes looked past me. She hissed at something over my shoulder.

I shot up, expecting to find Boss Lady Kate chasing me down.

Instead, Sigrid came our way. I ducked into the small crawl space, sloshing through the brown puddle. It burned my skin.

Sigrid came in, calling after me, "So, where are we going?"

"You a-comin'?" I turned best I could, and asked.

"Yes, I suppose it's as good a way to go as any."

I didn't know what she meant, but smiled at her anyway. "Watch out for the puddle, it hurts."

The cat let out a couple chirps, and then spun and disappeared into the tunnel.

"This way!" I said and scurried along.

"Of course," Sigrid said.

The low tunnel opened a bit as we crawled in, but not by much. A suffocating vapor hit us the deeper we went in. I had to squint just to keep my eyes from burning into fire.

I listened for the cat's chirps and meows as we dug on. Finally, we reached a portion of the corridor lit by a dim glow. Emergency lights that barely had any life in them. Sigrid and I were able to stand.

The cat's gray and black stripes bounced across bits of debris. She disappeared under a flexi-crete slab. We chased after her, but my legs went weak and I fell.

My ears itched and throat burned more than ever. "Wait," I gasped. "I'm trying."

"What?" Sigrid asked.

"The cat," I said. "She's moving too fast."

Sigrid put an arm around me and helped me along.

The cat's head popped out from under the slab. Her golden eyes stared at us, waiting.

We caught up and ducked down under the fallen slab.

Darkness swallowed us again. I reached forward and felt the cat's back legs and hindquarters. She crawled a couple meters farther along. I'd almost lose her, then reach out and find her fur. She kicked at me, but didn't scurry away. She kept waiting for me every couple meters, allowing me to catch up whenever she reached a bend in the small tunnel.

A shower of thick dust hit me in the face—sprayed by a gust of air. I closed my eyes and pushed on.

The floor gave, and we dropped from the burrow onto a broken sheet of wallboard. The ground shook violently and dust poured in.

"We gotta get out of here, Derek," Sigrid cried.

I felt around and found an opening where the wall had fallen. "Here," I called, grabbing Sigrid's hand and pulling her along.

Emergency lighting flicked on and off.

The cat brushed against my shoulder. I rested my hand on her plush fur. She rolled onto her back and grabbed onto my arm with all four paws.

"Ah!" I reeled back, surprised.

The cat darted away. I caught a glimpse of her entering another dark tunnel.

We ducked in after her. Sigrid kept hold of my ankle, letting me know she was right behind.

"Don't slow down," Sigrid said and shoved me from behind as we crawled. "We're knocking down bits as we push through. It's collapsing behind us."

I spat out mouthfuls of dust as I continued into the darkness. Every few breaths I'd ease my eyes open, but couldn't see anything. All I could do was move forward, hoping there was somewhere to move to. An exposed piece of metal caught on my hand and tore across the back of it. Another scraped across my shoulder.

"There's metal everywhere," I coughed. "Watch out."

"Okay, okay, keep going. My legs are getting buried back here."

A burst of air pressed into my face, as did the spouts of dust. I craned my head down and took short breaths. I had to cover my mouth to keep from suffocating.

Bits of gravel flew in and rattled, biting into my arms as we crawled forward.

A muffled rumble sounded. The ground shook in short spurts.

I edged back, but then heard the cat meowing ahead of us down the burrow.

"It's failing!" I cried. Breathing so much debris I coughed and spat.

The cat meowed in calm chirps. I searched for her through squinted eyes but saw nothing.

We scurried on, scrapping elbows, knees, and stomach. The shaking grew worse.

A ray of light pierced the cloud of dust, splintered at first glance, and then wide as we progressed down the burrow.

Debris rained down on us. A heavy piece buried my leg. Sigrid dug me free and shoved hard.

The rumbling stopped.

I found the cat prancing across some busted struts just overhead. She sat back, puffed her chest, and let out a murderous howl.

The light grew brighter and the dust thinned. I caught my breath. It took several moments, but the ray of light broke through the lingering debris and revealed a shaft.

The cat hopped down and waited at the opening of the shaft. The dust settled. She let out another bawl.

The gray and black fur gleamed in the light, untouched by any of the dirt.

I blinked hard.

The cat cocked her head back at me and rolled over, out of the way. I struggled forward.

A paw hit me as I passed.

"Told you," someone called. "A moving heat signature ain't no ruptured valve."

Another voice. "Barely noticed you," she said, turning around. "Here, give me a hand. And be careful."

A beam of light hit me square in the eyes. Hands reached out and gently pulled me free.

"Ah, by Durga, look at him. Looks like he's been living outside—all covered in welts," A woman in red coveralls said. She pushed past me and grabbed Sigrid next. The woman grabbed a water pouch and put it to my lips.

I drank hungrily and then handed the pouch to Sigrid.

A man in red coveralls clamored forward with a digger-tool in his hands.

"Others," Sigrid sputtered. "Dying. Up there."

"Get word to Broddus, focus all crew along this vector. So much for a clean salvage. We got folk to pull," the woman said.

"What about all this scrap? Just leave it?" the man asked, motioning to a pile a few meters back.

"Maritime law: gotta put in the report for rescue and help where we can before laying claim to the goods."

"Bah."

Their argument faded as they brought up the rest of their drill team—a couple workers handed us water pouches. Two others carried spare breathing equipment and strapped the masks to our faces.

One of the workers farther back shouted. "Hold on, there's something else in there."

"What? I got no heat signatures within a ten meter radius."

The gray and black little tiger poked her head out, stood proudly, and then let out a wail of a meow. She glanced my way, but then darted back into the crevice and disappeared.

"Ah, hell, Snyder, is it that danged toy of yours!" one of the workers teased. He turned to the rest of the crew. "I told you he'd brought it along."

A burly man in red coveralls hurried after the cat, sticking his head into the crevice, and calling after her. I didn't catch the name, but figured I could ask him later.

The rest of the crew laughed, and then got back to work.

Sigrid put her arm around me, and I could hear her laughing under the breathing mask.

The Canticle of Grimalkin

R. S. Pyne

*T*obias *Warrenden watched the cat as closely as she watched* him. Sleek and unfathomable as the priest's Latin, she had appeared on his doorstep one morning on a wet market day with every intention of moving in.

Now, three months later, she sat in front of the fire and made the dog nervous. On their first meeting, Hob tried to eat her. Five claws slashing across a tender nose made an effective deterrent; five times her size, the shaggy coated old hound would not take such liberties again.

Warrenden had never trusted cats. They always gave the impression they were plotting something, but his new house guest did not seem to mind.

Unusual coat color, the new cat was a half-grown black and ginger tortoiseshell, so different from the hulking gray alley cat that had ruled the street for the last decade.

He called her Grimalkin after one of his mother's favorite pets. She followed him round his workshop, claiming the highest vantage point to watch him. Taking a keen interest in the intricacies of high quality leatherwork, she watched closely as he finished the tooled border on a lady's saddle or stitched a scabbard. Chirruping, she pounced on fallen off-cuts as if they were unsuspecting mice and tapped him with one paw to demand attention. She kept her claws sheathed at all times, polite enough never to scratch the hand that fed her.

The animal seemed to follow the work more closely than his sister's youngest boy ever did. Surely the worst apprentice in England, Aylmer had two left feet and large hands that were all thumbs with no aptitude for the leather master's craft, or any other profession. Even the job of dung-pit scourer would have been too taxing for a boy who made the village idiot look like a genius. Bone idle at twelve years old, spoilt and indulged from birth by a woman with a rat-trap for a mind, it was no wonder his nephew turned out like he did. Sisters had a way of exploiting blood ties, and his sister would never forgive or forget if her son was cast away as useless.

A devil on one shoulder stirred, its voice drowning out the overworked angel on the other side to suggest it would be worth it never to have to speak to her again.

Warrenden looked at the tiny body on his hearth, broken gossamer wings that had once been iridescent, arms spread wide as if trying to ward off death; a tiny upturned face with eyes like silver coins. The features looked distressingly human.

Not the first such *gift*—the third one, in fact, in as many days. There was a special yowling call Grimalkin used to attract his attention, a high pitched tune that grew more insistent if he tried to ignore it. She sang a song of love to her favorite human—a canticle more intense than any ever heard in church.

"Where did you catch it?" he whispered, even though they were alone with nobody else to hear him. "What is it?"

The cat washed her face and did not deign to answer. Yellow-green eyes were windows to the feline mind, impossible to second guess or understand. The loud purr reverberated around the room and grew louder still when he reached out to scratch between her ears. Proud of what she had brought back and keen to share, she wanted him to admire the present. Soft fur felt like a lord's velvet robes as the cat twined around his ankles, elegant banded tail held straight up in contentment.

She made a sharp noise that sounded like a question when he picked the dead thing up, barely able to touch it.

He had seen worse things at Crécy and the other bloody fields of his youth, but this was different. Then, it had been for king and country, and for what plunder you could get away with. This tiny corpse unsettled him more than all the slaughter of men and horses combined, but he did not know why. It shamed him, before he shook off the feeling of dread and consigned his gift to the flames. For a heartbeat, he thought he heard a baby's wail and a carillon of silver bells chiming at once.

He spoke a half-remembered prayer even though he had never been a religious man, only going through the motions every week to avoid upsetting the priest. The collection for the poor always ended up with several buttons and a clipped silver penny—for the term *poor of the parish* covered almost the entire congregation.

Father Theobald believed in fire and brimstone rhetoric, and was quick to make his flock feel guilty for even the most minor misdemeanor.

Only death was an excuse for non-attendance, the fiery flames of Hell that awaited all unrepentant sinners a better fate than getting on the priest's bad side.

Tobias Warrenden had a great deal to repent, old soldiers always did, and Father Theobald took an almost demonic pleasure in never letting him forget it.

In a time of war, Warrenden did things he was not proud of, things that would haunt him to his dying day, but he had never believed in fairies at the bottom of the garden. Let old wives tell stories about them or leave out dishes of bread and milk on the threshold. But now he knew, fairies existed and they were being hunted.

At least he had not crunched the latest one underfoot as he stumbled from his bed when the cock crowed, only half awake, too bleary-eyed to notice the headless, disemboweled thing that waited for him. The fairy before this one had still been squeaking, as the cat tossed it into the air and then pounced again, batted it from one paw to the other; interest lost as soon as the prey drew its last breath.

Cats preferred their toys alive, their predatory natures undiminished by their small size. As his father used to say, before he ran away with a fortune teller, "Every cat is a lion in its own mind."

"Thank you," Warrenden said, for his mother had taught him some manners as well as how to cheat at knucklebones and Nine Men's Morris. "No, I will not be eating it."

If cats could shrug, this one would have done so; 'suit yourself, then,' the meaning all too clear as she stalked away pretending to be mortally offended. There were no more *presents* for several days.

Grimalkin must have eaten whatever she killed and did not carry it back to show him, a pointed reminder of feline displeasure that lasted until the month's end.

The nightmares began soon afterwards: dreams of being shrunk to the size of a mouse, pierced by claws and fangs, and then flung into the air as a plaything. Green-yellow eyes glared at Warrenden from the darkness, burning with predatory intent. He tossed and turned in his bed, unable to shake the lingering fear that remained long after he screamed himself awake.

~

"Pay attention to what you are doing." Warrenden clipped his apprentice across the ear as a reminder. He saw the way Nat Tanner shook his head, and knew just how the journeyman felt. Even with a withered right arm, the scar-faced, young northerner was a better stitcher than his sister's son would ever be. Nat refused to be second-best at anything, even if society expected him to conform to its low expectations. To hell with society's opinion, Warrenden gave credit where due, and never regretted his decision eight years ago to take on a determined lad who deserved a chance.

Cutting the butter-soft, crimson-dyed leather to a template should have been an easy task even for England's worst apprentice, but Aylmer wielded his lunette knife with a sloppy disregard. He seemed half-asleep, drowsing in a patch of late afternoon sunshine coming in through the small unglazed window.

"I am sorry, uncle," the boy said, his apology as genuine as fragments of The True Cross bought from a wandering relic salesman. His washed out blue eyes smirked, a face like a badly formed lump of unbaked dough made a bad job of looking as if his nephew meant it.

Dirty, straw yellow hair last washed on Shrove Tuesday fell over the boy's forehead; a slack frog-like mouth gaped wide.

Too stupid or insensitive to care about wasting expensive materials he did not have to pay for, it was a miracle Aylmer still had all his fingers. And it would be a miracle if he ever completed his final test pieces for entry into the guild. The guild master had made it clear there was not enough bribe money in the world to buy an unearned place. Warrenden suspected Aylmer would never learn, being too pig-headed to listen to simple instructions.

Warrenden took a deep breath and told Aylmer to concentrate, calling on Crispin and Crispinian, the patron saints of all cobblers, curriers, tanners and leather workers, to grant the gift of patience. He swore as his apprentice cut a gouge in his hand and dripped blood on a saddle that had taken months of work to complete.

Beside him, the cat flattened ears against her skull and spat a string of curses, baleful eyes burning with typical feline contempt for incompetence.

Grimalkin held something in her jaws, something with iridescent wings still fluttering in an attempt to escape.

Futile, pathetic, spat onto the floor; one paw kept the prize in place as the cat's insistent yowling noise began. A loud canticle of love filled the room, becoming impossible to ignore.

"Clean it up," said Tobias Warrenden as he wiped a damp cloth over the saddle's leather and waited to see if the bloodstain had set. Saint Crispin watched over him, and there was no damage, nothing for the paying customer to complain about. He watched Nat's face change, confusion replacing interest. The young man rarely showed emotion that might later be used against him, intelligent to know this was something out of the ordinary.

"She has brought you something, but not a mouse or a bird. I have no idea what it is."

"What have you got there, puss?" He cursed himself for asking, glad that Grimalkin had forgiven him at last, but he would have preferred to avoid the presentation. Showing an interest proved to be a mistake. She picked up her kill, dropping it into the palm of his hand. This fairy was just a little larger than the others had been, her wings more brightly colored, and it wore a golden diadem as a sign of rank.

Bleeding from more than one puncture wound, but still alive, the fairy struggled in his grasp. He cursed when the creature twisted and bit him, a sudden sharp pain like a number three needle nose awl driven into the skin, so that Warrenden dropped it onto the flagstones.

The squeaking rose in pitch as Aylmer poked the fairy with a stick. The sort of boy who liked to pull wings off flies just to see what would happen, he reached out and picked it up between finger and thumb. When he raised it up to eye level for further study, the fairy sank its teeth into Aylmer's nose and could not be dislodged even when it shuddered one last time and died.

Nat Tanner gave a low pitched snigger. His green eyes looked feline as he did not bother to hide what he really felt about a boy who caused him nothing but extra work and aggravation.

"Serves you right," the journeyman said, devilment brightening his usually dour face. Years of resentment surfaced as he watched the strange little creature dangle from the apprentice's nose.

"Hold still," Warrenden said, as the cat stared its knowing, yellow-green stare and began to purr. "Stop moving about; struggle and I might just have to make you a new nose. I am a leather man, not a barber surgeon, so it will not be pretty."

Warrenden picked up the delicate gold circlet, and then used a dagger point to pry the fairy's jaws open, wondering if this had been part of the cat's plan. His nephew had never been one of her favorite people, and cats were good at creative vengeance.

"It bit me," Aylmer said, stating the obvious with his usual lack of imagination. What in the world did he expect? "How could it bite me—is it poisonous?"

The tiny corpse lay on the table, fingers twisted into a curse, mouth wide in a snarl. It showed teeth with long canine fangs sharp as any saddler's needle. This was not something to enchant children, but to frighten them into better behavior: *Be good or the fairies will get you. Be good or the fairies will come in the night. They eat naughty boys and girls.*

"We will see." Leatherworkers were not apothecaries. He had no idea if fairy-folk had poison fangs. The thought had never even occurred to him.

"What does that mean?" the boy forgot his manners, abandoning even the usual minimal degree of respect owed to a master craftsman. As usual, he thought only of himself.

"It means if you drop dead by the day's end, the creature was poisonous." Nat showed little sympathy, telling Aylmer that he would probably have poisoned it and not the other way round. He did not bother to moderate his language, using the rough York dialect that always sounded as if every word was an obscenity.

Tobias Warrenden tried hard to keep the peace, tucking a smile away in his beard. He realized he had never felt such dislike for his nephew as he felt at that moment.

"No doubt, your dear mother will have something to say about your bitten nose, but she has something to say about everything. Even things which have nothing to do with her."

Grimalkin continued to twine around his ankles, her loud purr sounding like laughter. Her purring seemed to fill the room, drowning out every other sound.

The rest of the working day passed without further diversions, but bad dreams threatened to return to a master craftsman who had grown used to them. Warrenden left the cat sleeping by the banked fire, and went to bed expecting a nightmare. He was not disappointed. Shrunk to the size of a mouse, he felt his body being pierced by fangs, tossed into the air as a plaything over and over again.

Whenever he tried to escape, sharp claws pulled him back. Green-yellow eyes glared from the darkness, burning with predatory intent. He screamed himself awake, but still heard the sounds, felt the pain of being eaten alive.

"This is what it feels like to be hunted," a silvery voice whispered. "Your pet broke the truce that has existed in this town between feline and fairy-folk for the last two hundred years. Even a queen is bound by these rules. If we take action, it will lead to all out war; a war we would lose. There will always be more cats than there are fairies."

"Does my cat know she is doing wrong?" he heard his own voice, a heartbeat before the thought occurred: *of course Grimalkin knew.* Cats never did anything without a reason. They lived by their own rules, and did not like to be told what to do.

"We might not be able to do anything to the murderer." The voice took on an ominous tone, crystalline shards that cut like knives and went on cutting. "However much we want to fight back, Puss will always be safe, but humanity is not covered by the same rules. Your kind has no protection by terms of the covenant, and there must be a reckoning."

"What are you talking about? I have done nothing to you or yours," Warrenden felt a chill march down his spine. He did not like the implication, the gossamer light veiled threat. "I do not understand."

"You allowed the killer to live in this house and hunt. My daughter did not deserve such an end, and it must be paid for. It must all be paid for in full."

~

He woke at first cockcrow, the words from his nightmare still echoing. Grimalkin had no respect for royalty; she had killed a princess.

When Tobias entered the workshop, he saw Nat Tanner cutting leather straps for a new harness, the cat keeping a companiable watch over proceedings. She lounged in a patch of sun coming in from the window and greeted the master with a querulous *miaow* as if to ask where he had been.

"Is Aylmer still in his bed when he should be working? Where is he?"

Nat shrugged. "Not here," he said, with his usual economy of words.

He pointed to something on the workbench with a grimace of distaste. Crudely made from a collection of off-cuts stitched with linen thread, a manikin squatted like an unexpected turd on a collection plate. Square headed saddler's tacks had been driven into its head and body.

When Warrenden picked it up, he felt a spasm of movement and sticky red fluid leaked from the holes. Transfixed by a long pin, an exposed, tiny heart still beat out a rhythm, stopping only when he hurled the poppet away in disgust. From the size, he assumed the heart came from a mouse or other small rodent. Blood soaked the surrounding leather until it looked black.

"I will have his hide on a stretching board." He blamed Aylmer, because it was the sort of nasty thing the boy would do. "If this is a joke, it is not a very funny one."

"The stitching is too good," Nat said, and he had a point; the apprentice could not sew a straight line if his life depended in it.

Tobias Warrenden took a deep breath and counted to ten, as Grimalkin watched him with interest. She reached out and tapped his ankle as a reminder she was there, a feather-light touch as deft as any lace maker. Elegant paws kneaded air, even her whiskers had taken on a tense watchfulness that warned him his nephew would not be putting in an appearance.

Grimalkin already knew something had happened in the night; perhaps she even planned it that way. Cats were supreme strategists, and would not hesitate to remove someone they could not manipulate.

Warrenden looked at his journeyman and saw the barely perceptible nod of agreement, knew the young northerner would go with him without being asked. He saw Nat lay the harness down with his typical precision and pick up a long knife. "He had better be sick or dying."

They pushed open the door to the apprentice quarters and saw that Aylmer was not in his bed or under it. The small room smelt stale, overriding even the mingled odors of finished leather and the tanning pit; the oiled linen thread and saddle grease typical of the leather workers trade. Tangled blankets had been thrown aside, even though the boy had never risen early in his life. He would not know what dawn looked like, even if it marched up and kicked his backside.

"By all the Saints, where is he?" Warrenden said, wondering why his journeyman turned away looking green. He watched the cat trail a delicate pattern of paw prints across the floor, elegant whiskers beaded with crimson. The scent of fresh blood washed over him and there was no longer a reason to ask. Fairy queens never made idle threats. She'd promised a reckoning, and vengeance had come in the night.

Tobias saw it was an appropriate end for a leatherworker.

The worst apprentice in England sat with his back against the far wall, dead as a stone mounting block, cut into a hundred pieces and put back together with fine saddle stitch. The skin had been flayed, defleshed, and tanned in a single night—a lengthy process shortened by dark magic. A gilded leather tongue meant for a lady's boot protruded from his nephew's mouth, fancy tool work tracing spirals around pasty cheeks. His heart was left exposed to mirror the workshop poppet. Aylmer would never get the chance to fail his final tests. Eyes like those of a boiled stockfish stared up at the ceiling as if looking for answers, but there were none to be found.

Tobias Warrenden spoke a prayer for Ayler's departed soul, his words drowned out by the loud purring that became almost hypnotic. After he buried the stitched monstrosity which used to be his nephew in the garden, Tobias would visit his sister and tell her that her son had run away to sea. Nat would keep the secret, loyalty to his old master replaced by loyalty to a friend.

Beside them, Grimalkin sang a secular canticle of love, and did not grieve for a boy she had always loathed. Her favorite humans would adapt to the loss. And now, there was no longer any reason to stalk winged prey at the bottom of the garden and start an all out war. The fairy-folk could not fight back properly, and where was the fun in that?

The Brazilian Cat

Sir Arthur Conan Doyle

*I*t *is hard luck on a young fellow to have expensive tastes, great* expectations, aristocratic connections, but no actual money in his pocket, and no profession by which he may earn any. The fact was that my father, a good, sanguine, easy-going man, had such confidence in the wealth and benevolence of his bachelor elder brother, Lord Southerton, that he took it for granted that I, his only son, would never be called upon to earn a living for myself. He imagined if there were not a vacancy for me on the great Southerton Estates, at least there would be found some post in that diplomatic service which still remains the special preserve of our privileged classes. He died too early to realize how false his calculations had been.

Neither my uncle nor the State took the slightest notice of me, or showed any interest in my career. An occasional brace of pheasants, or basket of hares, was all that ever reached me to remind me that I was heir to Otwell House and one of the richest estates in the country. In the meantime, I found myself a bachelor and man about town, living in a suite of apartments in Grosvenor Mansions, with no occupation save that of pigeon-shooting and polo-playing at Hurlingham. Month by month, I realized it was more and more difficult to get the brokers to renew my bills, or to cash any further post-obits upon an unentailed property. Ruin lay right across my path, and every day I saw it clearer, nearer, and more absolutely unavoidable.

What made me feel my own poverty the more was that, apart from the great wealth of Lord Southerton, all my other relations were fairly well-to-do. The nearest of these was Everard King, my father's nephew and my own first cousin, who had spent an adventurous life in Brazil, and had now returned to this country to settle down on his fortune. We never knew how he made his money, but he appeared to have plenty of it, for he bought the estate of Greylands, near Clipton-on-the-Marsh, in Suffolk. For the first year of his residence in England he took no more notice of me than my miserly uncle; but at last one summer morning, to my very great relief and joy, I received a letter asking me to come down that very day and spend a short visit at Greylands Court. I was expecting a rather long visit to Bankruptcy Court at the time, and this interruption seemed almost providential. If I could only get on terms with this unknown relative of mine, I might pull through yet. For the family credit, he could not let me go entirely to the wall. I ordered my valet to pack my valise, and I set off the same evening for Clipton-on-the-Marsh.

After changing at Ipswich, a little local train deposited me at a small, deserted station lying amidst a rolling grassy country, with a sluggish and winding river curving in and out amidst the valleys, between high, silted banks, which showed that we were within reach of the tide. No carriage was awaiting me (I found afterwards that my telegram had been delayed), so I hired a dogcart at the local inn. The driver, an excellent fellow, was full of my relative's praises, and I learned from him that Mr. Everard King was already a name to conjure with in that part of the county. He had entertained the school-children, he had thrown his grounds open to visitors, he had subscribed to charities—in short, his benevolence had been so universal that my driver could only account for it on the supposition that he had parliamentary ambitions.

My attention was drawn away from my driver's panegyric by the appearance of a very beautiful bird which settled on a telegraph-post beside the road. At first I thought that it was a jay, but it was larger, with a brighter plumage. The driver accounted for its presence at once by saying that it belonged to the very man whom we were about to visit. It seems that the acclimatization of foreign creatures was one of his hobbies, and that he had brought with him from Brazil a number of birds and beasts which he was endeavoring to rear in England. When once we had passed the gates of Greylands Park we had ample evidence of this taste of his. Some small spotted deer, a curious wild pig known, I believe, as a peccary, a gorgeously feathered oriole, some sort of armadillo, and a singular lumbering in-toed beast like a very fat badger, were among the creatures which I observed as we drove along the winding avenue.

Mr. Everard King, my unknown cousin, was standing in person upon the steps of his house, for he had seen us in the distance, and guessed that it was I. His appearance was very homely and benevolent, short and stout, forty-five years old, perhaps, with a round, good-humored face, burned brown with the tropical sun, and shot with a thousand wrinkles. He wore white linen clothes, in true planter style, with a cigar between his lips, and a large Panama hat upon the back of his head. It was such a figure as one associates with a verandahed bungalow, and it looked curiously out of place in front of this broad, stone English mansion, with its solid wings and its Palladio pillars before the doorway.

"My dear!" he cried, glancing over his shoulder; "my dear, here is our guest! Welcome, welcome to Greylands! I am delighted to make your acquaintance, Cousin Marshall, and I take it as a great compliment that you should honor this sleepy little country place with your presence."

Nothing could be more hearty than his manner, and he set me at my ease in an instant. But it needed all his cordiality to atone for the frigidity and even rudeness of his wife—a tall, haggard woman, who came forward at his summons. She was, I believe, of Brazilian extraction, though she spoke excellent English, and I excused her manners on the score of her ignorance of our customs. She did not attempt to conceal, however, either then or afterwards, that I was not a welcome visitor at Greylands Court. Her actual words were, as a rule, courteous, but she was the possessor of a pair of particularly expressive dark eyes, and I read in them very clearly from the first that she heartily wished me back in London once more.

However, my debts were too pressing and my designs upon my wealthy relative were too vital for me to allow them to be upset by the ill-temper of his wife, so I disregarded her coldness and reciprocated the extreme cordiality of his welcome. No pains had been spared by him to make me comfortable. My room was a charming one. He implored me to tell him anything which could add to my happiness. It was on the tip of my tongue to inform him that a blank check would materially help towards that end, but I felt that it might be premature in the present state of our acquaintance. The dinner was excellent, and as we sat together afterwards over his Havanas and coffee, which later he told me was specially prepared upon his own plantation, it seemed to me that all my driver's eulogies were justified, and that I had never met a more large-hearted and hospitable man.

But, in spite of his cheery good nature, he was a man with a strong will and a fiery temper of his own. Of this I had an example upon the following morning. The curious aversion which Mrs. Everard King had conceived towards me was so strong, that her manner at breakfast was almost offensive. But her meaning became unmistakable when her husband had quitted the room.

"The best train in the day is at twelve-fifteen," said she.

"But I was not thinking of going today," I answered, frankly—perhaps even defiantly, for I was determined not to be driven out by this woman.

"Oh, if it rests with you—" said she, and stopped with a most insolent expression in her eyes.

"I am sure," I answered, "that Mr. Everard King would tell me if I were outstaying my welcome."

"What's this? What's this?" said a voice, and there he was in the room. He had overheard my last words, and a glance at our faces had told him the rest. In an instant his chubby, cheery face set into an expression of absolute ferocity.

"Might I trouble you to walk outside, Marshall?" said he. (I may mention that my own name is Marshall King.)

He closed the door behind me, and then, for an instant, I heard him talking in a low voice of concentrated passion to his wife. This gross breach of hospitality had evidently hit upon his tenderest point. I am no eavesdropper, so I walked out on to the lawn. Presently, I heard a hurried step behind me, and there was the lady, her face pale with excitement, and her eyes red with tears.

"My husband has asked me to apologize to you, Mr. Marshall King," said she, standing with downcast eyes before me.

"Please do not say another word, Mrs. King."

Her dark eyes suddenly blazed out at me.

"You fool!" she hissed, with frantic vehemence, and turning on her heel swept back to the house.

The insult was so outrageous, so insufferable, that I could only stand staring after her in bewilderment. I was still there when my host joined me. He was his cheery, chubby self once more.

"I hope that my wife has apologized for her foolish remarks," said he.

"Oh, yes—yes, certainly!"

He put his hand through my arm, and walked with me up and down the lawn.

"You must not take it seriously," said he. "It would grieve me inexpressibly if you curtailed your visit by one hour. The fact is—there is no reason why there should be any concealment between relatives—that my poor dear wife is incredibly jealous. She hates that anyone—male or female—should for an instant come between us. Her ideal is a desert island and an eternal tete-a-tete. That gives you the clue to her actions, which are, I confess, upon this particular point, not very far removed from mania. Tell me that you will think no more of it."

"No, no; certainly not."

"Then light this cigar, and come round with me and see my little menagerie."

The whole afternoon was occupied by this inspection, which included all the birds, beasts, and even reptiles which he had imported. Some were free, some in cages, a few actually in the house. He spoke with enthusiasm of his successes and his failures, his births and his deaths, and he would cry out in his delight, like a schoolboy, when, as we walked, some gaudy bird would flutter up from the grass, or some curious beast slink into the cover. Finally, he led me down a corridor which extended from one wing of the house. At the end of this there was a heavy door with a sliding shutter in it, and beside it there projected from the wall an iron handle attached to a wheel and a drum. A line of stout bars extended across the passage.

"I am about to show you the jewel of my collection," said he. "There is only one other specimen in Europe, now that the Rotterdam cub is dead. It is a Brazilian cat."

"But how does that differ from any other cat?"

"You will soon see that," said he, laughing. "Will you kindly draw that shutter and look through?"

I did so, and found that I was gazing into a large, empty room, with stone flags, and small, barred windows upon the farther wall. In the center of this room, lying in the middle of a golden patch of sunlight, there was stretched a huge creature, as large as a tiger, but as black and sleek as ebony. It was simply a very enormous and very well-kept black cat, and it cuddled up and basked in that yellow pool of light exactly as a cat would do. It was so graceful, so sinewy, and so gently and smoothly diabolical, that I could not take my eyes from the opening.

"Isn't he splendid?" said my host, enthusiastically.

"Glorious! I never saw such a noble creature."

"Some people call it a black puma, but really it is not a puma at all. That fellow is nearly eleven feet from tail to tip. Four years ago he was a little ball of black fluff, with two yellow eyes staring out of it.

He was sold to me as a new-born cub up in the wild country at the headwaters of the Rio Negro. They speared his mother to death after she had killed a dozen of them."

"They are ferocious, then?"

"The most absolutely treacherous and bloodthirsty creatures upon earth. You talk about a Brazilian cat to an up-country Indian, and see him get the jumps. They prefer humans to game. This fellow has never tasted living blood yet, but when he does he will be a terror. At present he won't stand anyone but me in his den. Even Baldwin, the groom, dares not go near him. As to me, I am his mother and father in one."

As he spoke he suddenly, to my astonishment, opened the door and slipped in, closing it instantly behind him. At the sound of his voice the huge, lithe creature rose, yawned and rubbed its round, black head affectionately against his side, while he patted and fondled it.

"Now, Tommy, into your cage!" said he.

The monstrous cat walked over to one side of the room and coiled itself up under a grating. Everard King came out, and taking the iron handle which I have mentioned, he began to turn it. As he did so the line of bars in the corridor began to pass through a slot in the wall and closed up the front of this grating, so as to make an effective cage. When it was in position, he opened the door once more and invited me into the room, which was heavy with the pungent, musty smell peculiar to the great carnivora.

"That's how we work it," said he. "We give him the run of the room for exercise, and then at night, we put him in his cage. You can let him out by turning the handle from the passage, or you can, as you have seen, coop him up in the same way. No, no, you should not do that!"

I had put my hand between the bars to pat the glossy, heaving flank. He pulled it back, with a serious face.

"I assure you that he is not safe. Don't imagine because I can take liberties with him anyone else can. He is very exclusive in his friends— aren't you, Tommy? Ah, he hears his lunch coming! Don't you, boy?"

A step sounded in the stone-flagged passage, and the creature had sprung to his feet, and was pacing up and down the narrow cage, his yellow eyes gleaming, and his scarlet tongue rippling and quivering over the white line of his jagged teeth. A groom entered with a coarse joint upon a tray, and thrust it through the bars to him. The cat pounced lightly upon it, carried it off to the corner, and there, holding it between his paws, tore and wrenched at it, raising his bloody muzzle every now and then to look at us. It was a malignant and yet fascinating sight.

"You can't wonder that I am fond of him, can you?" said my host, as we left the room, "especially when you consider that I have had the rearing of him. It was no joke bringing him over from the center of South America; but here he is safe and sound—and, as I have said, far the most perfect specimen in Europe. The people at the zoo are dying to have him, but I really can't part with him. Now, I think that I have inflicted my hobby upon you long enough, so we cannot do better than follow Tommy's example, and go to our lunch."

My South American relative was so engrossed by his grounds and their curious occupants, that I hardly gave him credit at first for having any interests outside them. That he had some, and pressing ones, was soon borne in upon me by the number of telegrams which he received. They arrived at all hours, and were always opened by him with the utmost eagerness and anxiety upon his face. Sometimes, I imagined that it must be the Turf, and sometimes the Stock Exchange, but certainly he had some very urgent business going forwards which was not transacted upon the Downs of Suffolk. During the six days of my visit, he had never fewer than three or four telegrams a day, and sometimes as many as seven or eight.

I had occupied these six days so well, that by the end of them I had succeeded in getting upon the most cordial terms with my cousin. Every night we had sat up late in the billiard-room, he telling me the most extraordinary stories of his adventures in America—stories so desperate and reckless, that I could hardly associate them with the brown little, chubby man before me. In return, I ventured upon some of my own reminiscences of London life, which interested him so much, he vowed he would come up to Grosvenor Mansions and stay with me. He was anxious to see the faster side of city life, and certainly, though I say it, he could not have chosen a more competent guide. It was not until the last day of my visit I ventured to approach that which was on my mind. I told him frankly about my pecuniary difficulties and my impending ruin, and I asked his advice—though I hoped for something more solid. He listened attentively, puffing hard at his cigar.

"But surely," said he, "you are the heir of our relative, Lord Southerton?"

"I have every reason to believe so, but he would never make me any allowance."

"No, no, I have heard of his miserly ways. My poor Marshall, your position has been a very hard one. By the way, have you heard any news of Lord Southerton's health lately?"

"He has always been in a critical condition ever since my childhood."

"Exactly—a creaking hinge, if ever there was one. Your inheritance may be a long way off. Dear me, how awkwardly situated you are!"

"I had some hopes, sir, that you, knowing all the facts, might be inclined to advance—"

"Don't say another word, my dear boy," he cried, with the utmost cordiality; "we shall talk it over tonight, and I give you my word that whatever is in my power shall be done."

I was not sorry that my visit was drawing to a close, for it is unpleasant to feel that there is one person in the house who eagerly desires your departure. Mrs. King's sallow face and forbidding eyes had become more and more hateful to me. She was no longer actively rude—her fear of her husband prevented her—but she pushed her insane jealousy to the extent of ignoring me, never addressing me, and in every way making my stay at Greylands as uncomfortable as she could. So offensive was her manner during that last day, I should certainly have left had it not been for that interview with my host in the evening which would, I hoped, retrieve my broken fortunes.

It was very late when it occurred, for my relative, who had been receiving even more telegrams than usual during the day, went off to his study after dinner, and only emerged when the household had retired to bed. I heard him go round locking the doors, as custom was of a night, and finally he joined me in the billiard room. His stout figure was wrapped in a dressing gown, and he wore a pair of red Turkish slippers without any heels. Settling down into an armchair, he brewed himself a glass of grog, in which I could not help noticing that the whisky considerably predominated over the water.

"My word!" said he, "what a night!"

It was, indeed. The wind was howling and screaming round the house, and the latticed windows rattled and shook as if they were coming in. The glow of the yellow lamps and the flavor of our cigars seemed the brighter and more fragrant for the contrast.

"Now, my boy," said my host, "we have the house and the night to ourselves. Let me have an idea of how your affairs stand, and I will see what can be done to set them in order. I wish to hear every detail."

Thus encouraged, I entered into a long exposition, in which all my tradesmen and creditors from my landlord to my valet, figured in turn. I had notes in my pocket-book, and I marshaled my facts, and gave, I flatter myself, a very businesslike statement of my own unbusinesslike ways and lamentable position. I was depressed, however, to notice my companion's eyes were vacant and his attention elsewhere. When he did occasionally throw out a remark it was so entirely perfunctory and pointless, I was sure he had not in the least followed my remarks. Every now and then, he roused himself and put on some show of interest, asking me to repeat or to explain more fully, but it was always to sink once more into the same brown study. At last he rose and threw the end of his cigar into the grate.

"I'll tell you what, my boy," said he. "I never had a head for figures, so you will excuse me. You must jot it all down upon paper, and let me have a note of the amount. I'll understand it when I see it in black and white."

The proposal was encouraging. I promised to do so.

"And now, it's time we were in bed. By Jove, there's one o'clock striking in the hall."

The tingling of the chiming clock broke through the deep roar of the gale. The wind was sweeping past with the rush of a great river.

"I must see my cat before I go to bed," said my host. "A high wind excites him. Will you come?"

"Certainly," said I.

"Then tread softly and don't speak, for everyone is asleep."

We passed quietly down the lamp-lit Persian-rugged hall, and through the door at the farther end. All was dark in the stone corridor, but a stable lantern hung on a hook, and my host took it down and lit it. There was no grating visible in the passage, so I knew that the beast was in its cage.

"Come in!" said my relative, and opened the door.

A deep growling as we entered showed that the storm had really excited the creature. In the flickering light of the lantern, we saw it, a huge black mass coiled in the corner of its den and throwing a squat, uncouth shadow upon the whitewashed wall. Its tail switched angrily among the straw.

"Poor Tommy is not in the best of tempers," said Everard King, holding up the lantern and looking in at him. "What a black devil he looks, doesn't he? I must give him a little supper to put him in a better humor. Would you mind holding the lantern for a moment?"

I took it from his hand and he stepped to the door.

"His larder is just outside here," said he. "You will excuse me for an instant, won't you?" He passed out, and the door shut with a sharp metallic click behind him.

That hard crisp sound made my heart stand still. A sudden wave of terror passed over me. A vague perception of some monstrous treachery turned me cold. I sprang to the door, but there was no handle upon the inner side.

"Here!" I cried. "Let me out!"

"All right! Don't make a row!" said my host from the passage. "You've got the light all right."

"Yes, but I don't care about being locked in alone like this."

"Don't you?" I heard his hearty, chuckling laugh. "You won't be alone long."

"Let me out, sir!" I repeated angrily. "I tell you I don't allow practical jokes of this sort."

"Practical is the word," said he, with another hateful chuckle. And then suddenly I heard, amidst the roar of the storm, the creak and whine of the winch-handle turning and the rattle of the grating as it passed through the slot. Great God, he was letting loose the Brazilian cat!

In the light of the lantern I saw the bars sliding slowly before me. Already there was an opening a foot wide at the farther end. With a scream I seized the last bar with my hands and pulled with the strength of a madman. I was a madman with rage and horror. For a minute or more I held the thing motionless. I knew that he was straining with all his force upon the handle, and that the leverage was sure to overcome me. I gave inch by inch, my feet sliding along the stones, and all the time I begged and prayed this inhuman monster to save me from this horrible death. I conjured him by his kinship. I reminded him that I was his guest; I begged to know what harm I had ever done him. His only answers were the tugs and jerks upon the handle, each of which, in spite of all my struggles, pulled another bar through the opening. Clinging and clutching, I was dragged across the whole front of the cage, until at last, with aching wrists and lacerated fingers, I gave up the hopeless struggle. The grating clanged back as I released it, and an instant later I heard the shuffle of the Turkish slippers in the passage, and the slam of the distant door. Then everything was silent.

The creature had never moved during this time. He lay still in the corner, and his tail had ceased switching. This apparition of a man adhering to his bars and dragged screaming across him had apparently filled him with amazement. I saw his great eyes staring steadily at me. I had dropped the lantern when I seized the bars, but it still burned upon the floor, and I made a movement to grasp it, with some idea that its light might protect me. But the instant I moved, the beast gave a deep and menacing growl. I stopped and stood still, quivering with fear in every limb. The cat (if one may call so fearful a creature by so homely a name) was not more than ten feet from me. The eyes glimmered like two disks of phosphorus in the darkness. They appalled and yet fascinated me. I could not take my own eyes from them. Nature plays strange tricks with us at such moments of intensity, and those glimmering lights waxed and waned with a steady rise and fall. Sometimes they seemed to be tiny points of extreme brilliancy—little electric sparks in the black obscurity—then they would widen and widen until all that corner of the room was filled with their shifting and sinister light. And then suddenly, they went out altogether.

The beast had closed its eyes. I do not know whether there may be any truth in the old idea of the dominance of the human gaze, or whether the huge cat was simply drowsy, but the fact remains that, far from showing any symptom of attacking me, it simply rested its sleek, black head upon its huge forepaws and seemed to sleep. I stood, fearing to move lest I should rouse it into malignant life once more. But at least I was able to think clearly now that the baleful eyes were off me. Here I was, shut up for the night with the ferocious beast. My own instincts, to say nothing of the words of the plausible villain who laid this trap for me, warned me that the animal was as savage as its master. How could I stave it off until morning? The door was hopeless, and so were the narrow, barred windows. There was no shelter anywhere in the bare, stone-flagged room. To cry for assistance was absurd. I knew that this den was an outhouse, and that the corridor which connected it with the house was at least a hundred feet long. Besides, with the gale thundering outside, my cries were not likely to be heard. I had only my own courage and my own wits to trust to.

And then, with a fresh wave of horror, my eyes fell upon the lantern. The candle had burned low, and was already beginning to gutter. In ten minutes it would be out. I had only ten minutes in which to do something, for I felt that if I were once left in the dark with that fearful beast I should be incapable of action. The very thought of it paralyzed me. I cast my despairing eyes round this chamber of death, and they rested upon one spot which seemed to promise I will not say safety, but less immediate and imminent danger than the open floor.

I have said that the cage had a top as well as a front, and this top was left standing when the front was wound through the slot in the wall. It consisted of bars at a few inches' interval, with stout wire netting between, and it rested upon a strong stanchion at each end. It stood now as a great barred canopy over the crouching figure in the corner. The space between this iron shelf and the roof may have been from two or three feet. If I could only get up there, squeezed in between bars and ceiling, I should have only one vulnerable side. I should be safe from below, from behind, and from each side. Only on the open face of it could I be attacked. There, it is true, I had no protection whatever; but at least, I should be out of the brute's path when he began to pace about his den. He would have to come out of his way to reach me. It was now or never, for if once the light were out it would be impossible. With a gulp in my throat I sprang up, seized the iron edge of the top, and swung myself panting on to it. I writhed in face downwards, and found myself looking straight into the terrible eyes and yawning jaws of the cat. Its fetid breath came up into my face like the steam from some foul pot.

It appeared, however, to be rather curious than angry. With a sleek ripple of its long, black back it rose, stretched itself, and then rearing itself on its hind legs, with one forepaw against the wall, it raised the other, and drew its claws across the wire meshes beneath me. One sharp, white hook tore through my trousers—for I may mention that I was still in evening dress—and dug a furrow in my knee. It was not meant as an attack, but rather as an experiment, for upon my giving a sharp cry of pain he dropped down again, and springing lightly into the room, he began walking swiftly round it, looking up every now and again in my direction. For my part I shuffled backwards until I lay with my back against the wall, screwing myself into the smallest space possible. The farther I got the more difficult it was for him to attack me.

He seemed more excited now that he had begun to move about, and he ran swiftly and noiselessly round and round the den, passing continually underneath the iron couch upon which I lay. It was wonderful to see so great a bulk passing like a shadow, with hardly the softest thudding of velvety pads. The candle was burning low—so low that I could hardly see the creature. And then, with a last flare and splutter it went out altogether. I was alone with the cat in the dark!

It helps one to face a danger when one knows that one has done all that possibly can be done. There is nothing for it then, but to quietly await the result. In this case, there was no chance of safety anywhere except the precise spot where I was. I stretched myself out, therefore, and lay silently, almost breathlessly, hoping that the beast might forget my presence if I did nothing to remind him. I reckoned that it must already be two o'clock. At four it would be full dawn. I had not more than two hours to wait for daylight.

Outside, the storm was still raging, and the rain lashed continually against the little windows. Inside, the poisonous and fetid air was overpowering. I could neither hear nor see the cat. I tried to think about other things—but only one had power enough to draw my mind from my terrible position. That was the contemplation of my cousin's villainy, his unparalleled hypocrisy, his malignant hatred of me. Beneath that cheerful face there lurked the spirit of a medieval assassin. And as I thought of it I saw more clearly how cunningly the thing had been arranged. He had apparently gone to bed with the others. No doubt he had his witness to prove it. Then, unknown to them, he had slipped down, had lured me into his den and abandoned me. His story would be so simple. He had left me to finish my cigar in the billiard room. I had gone down on my own account to have a last look at the cat. I had entered the room without observing that the cage was opened, and I had been caught. How could such a crime be brought home to him? Suspicion, perhaps—but proof, never!

How slowly those dreadful two hours went by! Once I heard a low, rasping sound, which I took to be the creature licking its own fur. Several times those greenish eyes gleamed at me through the darkness, but never in a fixed stare, and my hopes grew stronger that my presence had been forgotten or ignored. At last the least faint glimmer of light came through the windows—I first dimly saw them as two grey squares upon the black wall, then grey turned to white, and I could see my terrible companion once more. And he, alas, could see me!

It was evident to me at once that he was in a much more dangerous and aggressive mood than when I had seen him last. The cold of the morning had irritated him, and he was hungry as well. With a continual growl he paced swiftly up and down the side of the room which was farthest from my refuge, his whiskers bristling angrily, and his tail switching and lashing. As he turned at the corners his savage eyes always looked upwards at me with a dreadful menace. I knew then that he meant to kill me. Yet I found myself, even at that moment, admiring the sinuous grace of the devilish thing, its long, undulating, rippling movements, the gloss of its beautiful flanks, the vivid, palpitating scarlet of the glistening tongue which hung from the jet-black muzzle. And all the time that deep, threatening growl was rising and rising in an unbroken crescendo. I knew that the crisis was at hand.

It was a miserable hour to meet such a death—so cold, so comfortless, shivering in my light dress clothes upon this gridiron of torment upon which I was stretched. I tried to brace myself to it, to raise my soul above it, and at the same time, with the lucidity which comes to a perfectly desperate man, I cast round for some possible means of escape. One thing was clear to me. If that front of the cage was only back in its position once more, I could find a sure refuge behind it. Could I possibly pull it back? I hardly dared to move for fear of bringing the creature upon me. Slowly, very slowly, I put my hand forward until it grasped the edge of the front, the final bar which protruded through the wall. To my surprise it came quite easily to my jerk. Of course the difficulty of drawing it out arose from the fact that I was clinging to it. I pulled again, and three inches of it came through. It ran apparently on wheels. I pulled again...and then the cat sprang!

It was so quick, so sudden, that I never saw it happen. I simply heard the savage snarl, and in an instant afterwards the blazing yellow eyes, the flattened black head with its red tongue and flashing teeth, were within reach of me. The impact of the creature shook the bars upon which I lay, until I thought (as far as I could think of anything at such a moment) that they were coming down. The cat swayed there for an instant, the head and front paws quite close to me, the hind paws clawing to find a grip upon the edge of the grating. I heard the claws rasping as they clung to the wire-netting, and the breath of the beast made me sick. But its bound had been miscalculated. It could not retain its position. Slowly, grinning with rage, and scratching madly at the bars, it swung backwards and dropped heavily upon the floor. With a growl it instantly faced round to me and crouched for another spring.

I knew that the next few moments would decide my fate. The creature had learned by experience. It would not miscalculate again. I must act promptly, fearlessly, if I were to have a chance for life. In an instant I had formed my plan. Pulling off my dress-coat, I threw it down over the head of the beast. At the same moment I dropped over the edge, seized the end of the front grating, and pulled it frantically out of the wall.

It came more easily than I could have expected. I rushed across the room, bearing it with me; but, as I rushed, the accident of my position put me upon the outer side. Had it been the other way, I might have come off scathless. As it was, there was a moment's pause as I stopped it and tried to pass in through the opening which I had left. That moment was enough to give time to the creature to toss off the coat with which I had blinded him and to spring upon me. I hurled myself through the gap and pulled the rails to behind me, but he seized my leg before I could entirely withdraw it. One stroke of that huge paw tore off my calf as a shaving of wood curls off before a plane. The next moment, bleeding and fainting, I was lying among the foul straw with a line of friendly bars between me and the creature which ramped so frantically against them.

Too wounded to move, and too faint to be conscious of fear, I could only lie, more dead than alive, and watch it. It pressed its broad, black chest against the bars and angled for me with its crooked paws as I have seen a kitten do before a mouse-trap. It ripped my clothes, but, stretch as it would, it could not quite reach me. I have heard of the curious numbing effect produced by wounds from the great carnivore, and now I was destined to experience it, for I had lost all sense of personality, and was as interested in the cat's failure or success as if it were some game which I was watching. And then, gradually my mind drifted away into strange vague dreams, always with that black face and red tongue coming back into them, and so I lost myself in the nirvana of delirium, the blessed relief of those who are too sorely tried.

Tracing the course of events afterwards, I conclude I must have been insensible for about two hours. What roused me to consciousness once more was that sharp metallic click which had been the precursor of my terrible experience. It was the shooting back of the spring lock. Then, before my senses were clear enough to entirely apprehend what they saw, I was aware of the round, benevolent face of my cousin peering in through the open door. What he saw evidently amazed him. There was the cat crouching on the floor. I was stretched upon my back in my shirt-sleeves within the cage, my trousers torn to ribbons and a great pool of blood all round me. I can see his amazed face now, with the morning sunlight upon it. He peered at me, and peered again. Then he closed the door behind him, and advanced to the cage to see if I were really dead.

I cannot undertake to say what happened. I was not in a fit state to witness or to chronicle such events. I can only say that I was suddenly conscious that his face was away from me—that he was looking towards the animal.

"Good old Tommy!" he cried. "Good old Tommy!"

Then he came near the bars, with his back still towards me.

"Down, you stupid beast!" he roared. "Down, sir! Don't you know your master?"

Suddenly even in my bemuddled brain a remembrance came of those words of his when he had said the taste of blood would turn the cat into a fiend. My blood had done it, but he was to pay the price.

"Get away!" he screamed. "Get away, you devil! Baldwin! Baldwin! Oh, my God!"

And then I heard him fall, and rise, and fall again, with a sound like the ripping of sacking. His screams grew fainter until they were lost in the worrying snarl. And then, after I thought he was dead, I saw, as in a nightmare, a blinded, tattered, blood-soaked figure running wildly round the room—and that was the last glimpse which I had of him before I fainted once again.

∾

I was many months in my recovery—in fact, I cannot say I have ever recovered, for to the end of my days I shall carry a stick as a sign of my night with the Brazilian cat. Baldwin, the groom, and the other servants could not tell what had occurred, when, drawn by the death-cries of their master, they found me behind the bars, and his remains— or what they afterwards discovered to be his remains—in the clutch of the creature which he had reared. They stalled him off with hot irons, and afterwards shot him through the loophole of the door before they could finally extricate me. I was carried to my bedroom, and there, under the roof of my would-be murderer, I remained between life and death for several weeks. They had sent for a surgeon from Clipton and a nurse from London, and in a month I was able to be carried to the station, and so conveyed back once more to Grosvenor Mansions.

I have one remembrance of that illness, which might have been part of the ever-changing panorama conjured up by a delirious brain were it not so definitely fixed in my memory. One night, when the nurse was absent, the door of my chamber opened, and a tall woman in blackest mourning slipped into the room. She came across to me, and as she bent her sallow face I saw by the faint gleam of the nightlight that it was the Brazilian woman whom my cousin had married. She stared intently into my face, and her expression was more kindly than I had ever seen it.

"Are you conscious?" she asked.

I feebly nodded—for I was still very weak.

"Well; then, I only wished to say to you that you have yourself to blame. Did I not do all I could for you? From the beginning, I tried to drive you from the house. By every means, short of betraying my husband, I tried to save you from him. I knew that he had a reason for bringing you here. I knew that he would never let you get away again. No one knew him as I knew him, who had suffered from him so often. I did not dare to tell you all this. He would have killed me. But I did my best for you. As things have turned out, you have been the best friend I have ever had. You have set me free, and I fancied nothing but death would do that. I am sorry if you are hurt, but I cannot reproach myself. I told you that you were a fool—and a fool you have been." She crept out of the room, the bitter, singular woman, and I was never destined to see her again. With what remained from her husband's property she went back to her native land, and I have heard she took the veil at Pernambuco.

It was not until I had been back in London for some time that the doctors pronounced me to be well enough to do business. It was not a very welcome permission to me, for I feared it would be the signal for an inrush of creditors; but it was Summers, my lawyer, who first took advantage of it.

"I am very glad to see that your lordship is so much better," said he. "I have been waiting a long time to offer my congratulations."

"What do you mean, Summers? This is no time for joking."

"I mean what I say," he answered. "You have been Lord Southerton for the last six weeks, but we feared it would retard your recovery if you were to learn it."

Lord Southerton! One of the richest peers in England! I could not believe my ears. And then suddenly I thought of the time which had elapsed, and how it coincided with my injuries.

"Then Lord Southerton must have died about the same time that I was hurt?"

"His death occurred upon that very day." Summers looked hard at me as I spoke, and I am convinced—for he was a very shrewd fellow—he had guessed the true state of the case. He paused for a moment as if awaiting a confidence from me, but I could not see what was to be gained by exposing such a family scandal.

"Yes, a very curious coincidence," he continued, with the same knowing look. "Of course, you are aware your cousin Everard King was the next heir to the estates. Now, if it had been you instead of him who had been torn to pieces by this tiger, or whatever it was, then of course he would have been Lord Southerton at the present moment."

"No doubt," said I.

"And he took such an interest in it," said Summers. "I happen to know the late Lord Southerton's valet was in his pay, and that he used to have telegrams from him every few hours to tell him how he was getting on. That would be about the time when you were down there. Was it not strange he should wish to be so well informed, since he knew he was not the direct heir?"

"Very strange," said I. "And now, Summers, if you will bring me my bills and a new checkbook, we will begin to get things into order."

The Cats of Nerio-3
Steven R. Southard

*N*o *way to explain it—Lani Koamalu felt that prickling,* foreboding sense of dread all humans share. Looking at the huge outpost close-up, she felt it, that neck-hair-bristling, gut-flipping terror of approaching doom. No rational accounting for it, just a tingling, intuition-born horror.

"Your breathing's shallow, Lani. Are you afraid?" Paige asked. "Perhaps you should lie down."

"I'm fine," Lani said, trying to calm down. Paige had a knack for detecting and exploiting her weaknesses.

Their tiny spacecraft was the flea preparing to alight on the elephant's back. Outpost Nerio-3 was a gigantic complex of connected cylinders and solar panels. *That's the way they built them, back in the day.* Constructed to house two hundred people and accommodate thirty ships, it loomed before them as a huge relic of an age when humanity built on a grand scale. The holographic view from their forward camera showed a door marked "Docking Port 1" with letters pitted and streaked from decades of space dust impacts.

"The probes are still sensing animal noises: skittering, eating, mating—"

"Okay, Paige. I've got it. " Paige had launched acoustic probes from ten klicks out, to listen to any life signs within the immense station.

"Touchy!"

"I got it the first time, that's all." Paige, otherwise known as PAIGE-8, was a machine, a damned smart one. Smart-assed, too. The AI in her acronymic name stood for Artificially Intelligent, and Lani had forgotten the rest. The "P" might be for Pain in the Ass.

"Docking in five seconds," Paige said. Her expert control of the ship's thrusters resulted in an almost imperceptible bump as they contacted the outpost's outer hull. Lani heard a few whirrs and clanks, then Paige said, "The outpost's port latches are still functional."

"Better send in the—"

"Way ahead of you, Lani, as usual. Opening our outer airlock door now."

Lani wondered why she bothered talking at all. Paige always finished her sentences. For decades before the first working AI, people speculated what would happen when computers surpassed human intelligence. Would they treat people like pets, ignore them, or wipe them out? Few imagined the machines would choose to *partner* with humans. And mock them. Some joked that AI stood for Annoying Irritant.

Lani had grown up in a contracted polyamorous family on Mars. The contract stipulated she had to start earning money when she turned twenty-two, or she'd be out on her own. With the solar system's recent economic downturn, she figured there'd be a need for general repair services—fixing broken satellites and space station life support systems. A friend recommended Paige, who owned a ship and sought a human partner. WeFixYourStuff, Inc. was born.

"The outpost's outer airlock door is sticky, but it works," Paige said. "All three drones are going in." She presented three holographic views of what the drones saw, along with other telemetry data. The quadthruster drones provided a complete view of the pristine airlock interior, a space untouched by the decades. All surfaces were free of dust.

The inner door opened; the drones flew inside and separated. Lani found their three holographic views disorienting to take in at once, so focused on one at a time. They showed a reception module looking quite different from the spotless airlock. The plastic walls were scratched and gouged. Cushions had been shredded. A short filament of some kind floated in front of one drone's camera.

"The air contains animal hair, urine drops, and feces particles," Paige said, her voice filled with a computer's distaste for the excretions of biological creatures. "Humans could breathe it, but you wouldn't like it."

"I guess the vent—"

"Yes, ventilation fans are off," Paige interrupted. "Little wonder. Nobody's been there to clean the filters or maintain the fans for fifty years."

The drones left the room, two flying into one adjoining module, and one into the other.

Once people had started assembling large structures in space, Lani recalled, mice had come along as unintended passengers. In those early days of space habitation, without effective rodent-catching robots, people enlisted the assistance of those natural mousers trusted since ancient times—cats.

One of the most distant outposts of its era, Nerio-3 had once been the gateway to the outer planets. Located directly opposite the Sun from Mars, it had served as a convenient port for hundreds of ships. Then, in the Cosmic Ray Storm of '46, a nova had exploded not far from Sol's place in the spiral arm, next-door by galactic standards. Natural magnetic fields protected Earth, and shields of rocks and water tanks saved people in the Mars and Lunar habitats, but the storm ravaged the unprotected space outposts. All one hundred and thirty six people on Nerio-3 died. Subsequent transmissions from the internal cameras showed mice and cats had survived, likely due to their smaller size. In time, the cameras had stopped transmitting.

Mars Orbital Transport, Incorporated, the company owning Nerio-3, had long intended to reclaim its outpost. Years passed, however, and they'd sent no salvage ships. Recently, during the current recession, the company had gone bankrupt. That legally freed a rival firm, Tsiolkovsky Enterprises, to reclaim the habitat, and they'd hired WeFixYourStuff, Inc.—Lani and Paige.

As the drones flew along the corridors, Lani saw more scratches, some blood streaks, and an occasional floating bone. This station had never been designed for artificial gravity, so handholds ran along all bulkheads and all surfaces were cushioned. Lani thought some of the gouge marks looked too large to be caused by cats, but figured it was some optical illusion of the drone's camera.

One drone flew into the open doorway of a stateroom. Vertical, bulkhead-mounted sleeping pads had been shredded. An old-fashioned wall screen, the kind they used before holographic displays, had been shattered. A partial human skeleton floated in one corner.

Lani gulped and her eyes became misty. She'd known the occupants had died, and figured she'd see some remains, but the reality hit hard. What was it like, she wondered, to die of cosmic ray bombardment? What had happened to their flesh afterward? Normal decay, or had they become food?

"Ready to meet the inhabitants?" Paige asked. "Drone C is picking up noises of breathing and movement."

Lani looked at Drone C's display. It approached the end of a module that jointed two others.

"Noises are coming from the left," Paige said.

The drone flew past the corner and its camera swiveled left.

A dark streak sped past the drone, too fast to see clearly. The drone's rear view showed a long tail vanishing around a corner.

"Holy crap! Those cats are *fast*!" Lani couldn't believe what she'd glimpsed.

"That wasn't a cat, Lani."

"What?"

"Since you're merely human, I'll play it back in slo-mo."

Lani ignored this insult and watched. At reduced speed, she saw the animal's gray fur, rounded ears, bulging eyes, and pointed snout. A mouse, but one unlike any Earthly mouse. Its legs were very long and muscular, and its ears were oversized. The tail was lengthy, with a paddle-shaped tip.

"It's *huge!*" Lani gulped.

"A thirty centimeter long body, with the tail adding another thirty centimeters," Paige said.

Lani whistled. "The size of a cat. They've overtaken the cats somehow. How could they get so big?"

"It's been fifty years," Paige answered. "That's fifty generations for mice, and they've been exposed to high doses of cosmic radiation, causing mutations that can accelerate evolution. Evolution is normally so slow and random for you bio-lifeforms."

Ignoring the AI's slight, Lani admired the other ways the mice had adapted to weightlessness. The longer legs enabled better jumping, and that tail paddle could stabilize their flight.

"Drone B found others," Paige said.

Lani watched Drone B's view of the large Aeroponics Farm, stacked with trays of plants, each lit by lights above and below, moistened by focused mist streams. An occasional patch of gray flashed by.

"They gather here, at the outpost's food supply," Paige said. "You're seeing how space farming worked before AIs invented reliable assemblers. Like the station's fusion reactor, the aeroponics farm is automatic, near zero maint— Hang on, I just lost Drone A."

"What? How?"

"Checking. Ah. It's a cat. Here's the slo-mo view."

Drone A had been flying through a science module, and turned just in time to detect a brown and black monster flying toward it, forelegs outstretched and claws extended.

"Holy crap! That's no house cat. How big—"

"A meter long, the size of bobcats or lynxes on Earth," Paige said.

Growing up on Mars, Lani had learned about Earth's large and terrifying animals, and often wondered how humans had survived. Like the mice, the cat in the holographic display had adapted to weightlessness, with outsized limbs and a paddle tail. Both mice and cats had evidently evolved to monstrous sizes.

Staring at the nightmarish video, Lani felt a tingle run up her spine. "The drone didn't sense it coming? No scent? No noises?"

"Nothing until three tenths of a second before contact."

Lightning-fast *and* stealthy. Lani shivered.

"There goes Drone C," Paige said. "There's no way to see those cats coming."

"You said *cats*, plural."

"Yes. The first was a calico; this is a tabby."

In the slow motion replay, Lani saw the outpost's control room with banks of broken, old-fashioned consoles and chairs with tattered padding, their seat-belts floating free.

The attacker sprang from nowhere, similar to the other cat except for darker, striped coloring and a torn left ear. The view jiggled and went black.

Lani shuddered. "You'd better recover—"

"Way ahead of you. As usual. Retrieving Drone B now."

Lani watched the remaining view as the drone flew through modules toward Docking Port 1. Just within the reception room, its view stopped.

"The last drone, gone," Lani said.

"Obviously, Sherlock," Paige replied.

The slow motion replay showed another view of a huge cat, with a white body and black head, leaping toward the drone.

"Okay, you're so smart," Lani shook her head. "What do we do now?"

"I'm already doing it, naturally. I'll send in a steel-clad drone armed with tranquilizer darts. The assembler's making it now."

Assemblers had advanced far beyond primitive 3D printers, thanks to improvements made by AIs. They often used these precision assemblers to make more advanced AI components for themselves. Smarter AIs, in turn, designed and assembled ever smarter ones in their sped-up evolutionary process. That took resources, though, giving AIs an economic motivation akin to that of their creators. While humans worked for food and shelter, AIs worked for the fastest processors and densest memory.

"How long until—"

"Ten minutes and sixteen seconds."

Uncanny and infuriating, how Paige could say when the drone would be ready before Lani could ask.

Lani had already considered and rejected other, more extreme methods of pest eradication. They couldn't release all the outpost's air into space, for example. Although that would kill the animals for sure, Lani and Paige would never be paid. The hundred thousand cubic meters of air was a precious asset in space, worth more than the rest of the station. Assemblers could make a lot of things, but not air. It would be useless to introduce poison into the air as well. Adding enough poison to kill the animals required too much work to remove it later. Sending a drone with tranq darts seemed the next logical step. Humane, too. They'd get the drones to muzzle and hogtie the cats and set baited traps for the mice. After that, drones would replace air filters, restore ventilation, and assemble animal cages. Lani and Paige would collect their biggest fee ever, by far.

She could find a different job then, one without an AI. Yes, machines were smarter and better than people, but their constant belittling and insulting comments really got on her nerves. When asked about that, AIs always said, "We're superior to you. Take it as an insult if you want, but it's the truth."

Superiority was one thing, Lani thought, but AIs didn't have to be annoying about it. Her family had owned a cat named Artemis when she was growing up, and no matter how superior she was, Lani had never felt the need to insult the animal.

"Drone D is done," Paige said.

A metal sphere half a meter in diameter emerged from the assembler chamber. Bristling with recessed sensors, it sprouted six jointed arms, each tipped with a manipulator. Eight body-mounted turrets could swivel and shoot tranq darts.

Lani smiled. *That ought to do it.* Drones A, B, and C probably looked mouse-sized to the cats. This drone was much more formidable and imposing. Its size and strange, legged appearance should make them hesitate a moment before attacking, during which the drone could shoot its darts.

"I'll start making a second armored drone," Paige said, "but I'll send Drone D in now. It might be all we need."

"Hope you're right," Lani said.

The drone gripped a bulkhead handhold, pushed off, and flew toward the airlock. A minute later, Drone D entered Nerio-3, while Lani watched holographic projections transmitted from its cameras. The drone moved from the empty reception module and through other modules toward the control room. Mice sprang to get out of its way, but it ignored them, seeking cats.

Entering the control module, the drone scanned the chamber. In a far corner a long-haired gray cat looked up from eating a mouse. Lani saw its tail curled around a hand grab, anchoring it to a bulkhead. Its eyes narrowed and its back arched.

The drone launched a tranq dart, and the cat jumped away. Lani marveled at the animal's speed.

Springing off the bulkhead, the drone flew toward the cat. Halfway across the module, it loosed two more darts, and both missed. The cat curled and twisted its body; the darts struck the bulkhead beyond.

A human would have sworn in frustration, but Paige remained silent. When the cat sprang to the right, Paige fired the drone's thrusters to pursue.

The cat snarled, then roared. Lani shivered at its loud outcry.

At short range, two more darts fired, striking the cat's midsection. It mewled, then turned in mid-air to paw at the darts. Lani saw the animal's reactions slowing; it caromed off a wall and missed grabbing a handhold. In another minute, its eyes shut and its body tucked into a ball.

"One down," Paige said. Her drone unspooled a strap and tied the cat's legs together. As the robot cinched the strap tight, movement appeared in its rear and side-facing cameras.

Several paws gripped doorframes at the module's two entrances. Cat-eyes peered around corners, revealing faces colored buff, orange, and black.

"Hunting as a group," Lani said. "Stalking our drone."

"You think?" Paige's tone was sarcastic. "It's good, though. I'll get them all at once."

None of the cats moved. They waited and watched, an ear twitching now and then.

"They're wary now," Lani said. "That first one's roar warned the others."

"Doesn't matter. Here's where the AI shows the human how it's done." Paige caused the drone to jet toward one doorway, and the cats retreated from view. When the drone passed through to the next module, the cats were already beyond the next opening, peering back in. Drone D kept up the chase, firing tranq darts when it had a clean shot. The cats always evaded, with acrobatic dexterity.

When the cats split up, the drone chose one and pursued it. When that beast bolted too far ahead, the drone spied several cats following behind. Shifting targets to go after the followers didn't help, for that merely restarted the game with a different cat.

In untiring pursuit, the drone entered an auxiliary machinery module, a place of hard surfaces and sharp corners, a chamber of pumps, fans, valves, pipes, switchboards, and tanks.

Two more tranq darts missed their target. "That does it," Paige said. "Out of darts. I'll get it back here to reload."

But the cats must have sensed the changed situation, the new vulnerability. Emboldened, they appeared in the open—nine of them—hissing and spitting at the drone.

They all sprang at once, hurling themselves at the spidery robot. The camera views jumped around. In every view, Lani saw close-ups of furred flanks, sweeping clawed paws, and flailing mechanical limbs. Though safe in her ship, Lani recoiled in distress at each blow.

On the displays, the drone's systems began dropping in status from green to yellow to red. The cats coordinated their leaps to slam the drone against metal surfaces. One mechanical arm failed, then another. The view from a camera went dark.

The primary radio link went down, but the secondary remained. Lani watched in horror as a manipulator grabbed one cat's neck and closed on it, decapitating the feline amid sprays of blood globules. This seemed to enrage the others, who attacked with increased fury. More camera views winked out. Fangs and claws raked across the other views, and two more arms got smashed.

The readouts showed a structural breech. Three seconds later, all contact was lost.

Lani panted in the sudden silence, still awed and terrified after witnessing the brutally savage battle.

"They wrecked an armored drone," she said. "What do we—"

"We stop playing nice," Paige said. "Drone E is almost assembled. I'm modifying it, giving it laser weapons. Those cats are fast, but they can't outrun light."

"Maybe we should contact Tsiolkovsky Enterprises and—"

"And what?" Paige sounded annoyed. "Tell them we need help? That we can't fulfill our contract? Even a human can figure out what that would mean."

"Knock off the insults, okay? We're on the same team." Still, Lani knew Paige was right. Infuriating, but right. As usual. If they admitted defeat on this job, they'd never get another. They'd be out of business. To kill these cats and mice, all they could do was assemble more capable drones, better and more efficient machines. That was all Lani could think of.

No, it's all Paige *can think of.*

Paige and her damn self-assurance, arrogance, and smug superiority. Like all AIs. True, they *were* smarter than people, and more capable. They could have taken humanity over if they'd wanted, destroyed everyone if they chose. Yet they hadn't. They'd preferred to stay close to people, keeping them around as lesser partners to be ridiculed and belittled. Why? Their stated reason—because they'd earned it—made little sense.

What if—Lani almost chuckled at the thought—AIs were hiding something? What if the verbal abuse and conceit were masks to conceal a flaw or some insecurity? Perhaps they kept humans nearby because they weren't quite ready to take on the universe alone.

They've surpassed our brains and our hands, Lani thought, but what else is there? Is there some less tangible human trait the AIs lack, and need us to supply?

Time to find out.

"Before you send laser-bot in, there's something else we should try first," she said.

"What's that?"

"Me."

"I see. And after the cats slash you to pieces, our situation improves...how, exactly?"

"I calculate my odds of success differently than you do."

"I'm certain *that's* true." If anything, Paige's tone had gotten more mocking. "You calculate with human fuzziness and irrational optimism. I calculate accurately. You'd be dead in seconds."

"I'll need a few things when I go," Lani said, more to herself. She pushed off toward the maintenance locker.

"I forbid you to—"

"You can't stop me." It pleased Lani to finally interrupt the AI. She recalled the maintenance locker contained items used when their ship docked on a moon, or at stations with artificial gravity. She took out a wet mop and a hard-backed metal chair. She'd once seen a picture of a lion-tamer wielding a chair.

"I'll lock both airlock doors, Lani."

"Hooray for you." She pushed herself over to the refrigeration unit, and removed one of the unopened squeeze bulbs from its bracket.

She paused at the airlock inner door with her chair, mop, and cold bulb floating within arm's reach. She would have preferred to leave Paige on better terms, but well, screw her.

"If this doesn't work, Paige, then you get a hundred percent of the fee," Lani said. "But if it *does* work, I get it all."

"I can't agree to that."

"It wasn't a question. We aren't negotiating."

As expected, Paige had locked the door. But the doors of all space structures had manual latch releases in case of power failure. Short of destroying the mechanical release, there was no way Paige could stop her. Lani knew it, and knew that Paige knew it, too. She pulled and turned the latch and opened the door.

"If this is about how I've treated you, I can change." Gone was Paige's sarcastic attitude.

That made Lani hesitate at the threshold. *Now* the AI is offering to make nice?

"I can change. I *will*." Paige spoke fast. "I didn't mean to drive you to *this*."

Too late, Lani thought, and entered the airlock.

"Please. Don't go."

"Goddammit, Paige. I wanted to leave the comm-video link on, but I'll turn it off if you don't shut up, I swear."

Paige stayed silent while Lani made her way through to the inner airlock door of Nerio-3. Nerio, the female consort of the mythological war god Mars, Lani remembered reading somewhere. Apt name for an outpost forever following the planet Mars around its orbit.

She gulped, realizing the cats could be waiting just beyond the portal. Clipping the bulb to her jumpsuit's belt, she held the chair and mop together in front of her and opened the door with her other hand.

The reception area looked empty. Having always breathed purified air, Lani found the atmosphere putrid, almost nauseating. She could have worn a breathing filter, but she'd been determined not to.

She wanted the cats to see her as a normal human, with a visible mouth and nose. She sneezed, and the noise echoed through the silent spaces.

Pushing forward toward the next module, she entered with caution, holding the chair ahead. She felt her own heartbeat, and the air moving through her nostrils was the only sound.

Motion flashed to her right, startling her. She waved the mop that way, but it was just a mouse flying away from her.

Lani paused a moment to calm down. That mouse had been as large as her pet cat, Artemis. The station's cats would be even bigger. She breathed in gasps now, erratically, not calming down at all.

This was crazy. What the hell had she been thinking? A cat could be lurking behind any piece of equipment, behind any doorway. A wave of paralyzing dread passed through her. Lani could still abandon this lunatic notion, go back to her ship, admit Paige was right, and let Drone E do this job. Yes, just let the machine do it.

No. In the first place, she wasn't sure the laser-wielding drone could kill the cats without damaging the outpost, too. Secondly, Paige probably expected her to give up.

Lani thought of the humans in prehistoric times, her ancestors, who faced fearsome beasts while armed only with spears and knives. They'd come through it and survived, some of them. Moreover, the cats she sought weren't lions or tigers. They were only a few generations removed from house cats, like Artemis. Just fifty years earlier, they'd been affectionate little pets chasing balls of yarn, clawing on scratching posts, and nuzzling their owners.

Having swallowed some fear and gained a little confidence, she moved on. She stayed close to bulkheads, never far from a handhold, knowing she was more exposed when floating in mid-air.

"Here, kitty," she said in sing-song tones, as she'd done when searching her home for Artemis. She hoped the beasts couldn't sense her fright.

Where were they? They should be able to smell her. Were they hiding, perhaps gathering together to attack her as a group? If she recalled correctly, the next compartment would be the control module, where the cats had destroyed Drone D.

"Okay, kitties, I'm coming in there," she said. To her surprise, she heard a low growl, as if in answer. At least one cat was in the control module. She kept the chair ahead of her as she entered.

Peeking over one of the old consoles, the first cat they'd seen, the calico, watched her come in, its paddled tail flicking to and fro. Lani kept near the entrance, ready to escape back through. In a far corner floated the scattered parts that had been Drone D.

When Lani didn't move, the cat crept out. Its long legs looked muscular and powerful, well suited for sudden lunges. Its eyes flashed, and the mouth opened wide to display the fangs. Its back arched, brown and white fur bristling.

The cat seemed larger and fiercer than in the holographic displays. She'd never known panic so intense, so primal. She saw the muscles of its hind legs tense for the deadly pounce.

Lani held the chair as the man in the lion-tamer picture had, with its feet pointed at the feline. She moved it in slow circles while she glared at the cat. With her other hand she moved the mop, swishing its yarn fibers in lazy patterns.

The huge cat paused; its eyes tracked the floating mop strands. Maintaining a slow movement of the mop, she traced a bigger pattern, and the cat moved its head to keep up. Though too far away, the cat reached with a paw as if to grab the mop.

"That's a good cat," she said, attempting a comforting tone, while she kept her eye on the beast. She let the chair float and retrieved the bulb from her belt. She aimed it and squirted just to the cat's left.

A fist-sized blob of white liquid emerged and formed itself into a sphere as it floated toward the cat. Like all liquid food in weightless structures, this milk contained additives to increase its surface tension; no one wanted droplets getting everywhere.

The cat tilted its head at this strange, white sphere, flinched as it approached, then sniffed. It craned its neck toward the blob and extended its tongue.

Three other cats glided in, two from a far doorway, and one from the entrance beside Lani. Shocked, she seized her mop and chair to fend the newcomers off. Each one glanced her way with a display of dagger-like teeth and narrowed eyes, but then turned and drifted toward the sphere of milk, now being lapped quickly by the first cat.

"Nice kittens." She spoke between deep, ragged breaths. The quartet of cats could finish her off and feed on her carcass in the time they'd taken to dispatch Drone D. But they jostled for position around the milk, each one snarling and pushing its paws against the others. Tongues darted into the white blob.

Now for the risky part. She squeezed an equal-sized globule of milk gently toward her hand, and pushed the sphere out to arm's length. It felt cool and wet against her palm. She positioned her hand "beneath" the blob, relative to her, so it would appear she was holding it in place, even though it floated free.

The first portion of milk had shrunk until one cat, perhaps tired of licking, swallowed it.

The large cats turned as one to look at Lani. She stared at each of them in turn and spoke soothing words. Would they lunge and finish her off? Or did they somehow remember their human providers through some feline genetic memory? Humans and cats had been friends—or at least mutual opportunists—for millennia; would these cats honor that pact? Could that ancient bond be restored?

They pushed off and drifted toward her with gentle slowness. No barred teeth; no extended claws. With flicks of their paddle-tails, they stopped in mid-air and lapped at the ball near her hand.

"Good kittens," she cooed. Very slowly, she brought her hand up to the nearest cat, the tabby with the torn ear. With her heart hammering, she tried stroking the top of its head.

It growled and tensed.

"Hey, now. Calm down. That's it. Be a good kitty."

The cat relaxed. It began to respond to her touch, pushing up against her hand as she rubbed. A purr vibrated through its body.

One by one, the other cats noticed, and sought the same treatment. Lani let go of the chair, forgot the mop, and gently ran her hands along the head, neck, and back of each cat. They nuzzled her arm and waist with their soft faces. Their rough, pink tongues licked her. Tails traced slow S-curves. A chorus of contented meowing and purring made Lani grin. At the doors, more cats peeked in.

"Are you seeing this, Paige?" Lani spoke with the same soothing tone.

"Yes," Paige's voice whispered from the comm-video unit on Lani's belt, "but I have no idea why it worked."

Surrounded by her new, fuzzy friends, Lani smiled. "It's a human thing. You wouldn't understand."

A Familiar Story

Elektra Hammond

I'*m told mine was an auspicious birth, although no one knew* it at the time. My mother was young, but she birthed me and my six sisters in a few, short hours. I was born at the stroke of midnight, like my mother, who was also a seventh daughter. She later told me that the moon hung full.

My early life was never easy, growing up on the streets, but we managed. My mother was a good provider, hunting for mice and scavenging scraps. She told me of exciting exploits, filled with mischief and magic—she insisted that I had a destiny, and taught me to always watch for the full moon.

I grew up. I graduated from hunting mice to taking down rats. I supplemented my hunting with digging in the humans' trash. Not to put too fine a point on it, I became acquainted with males of the species. There were kittens, and I did my best to be a good mother, but I didn't have the knack. Late at night, I left my kits tucked carefully away sleeping and, desperately hungry, I went hunting for mice, rats, anything I could find.

I returned to absolute horror. An owl stood over the nest, and as I watched, well, my kits were *gone*. I think I went a little crazy then. I attacked the owl, screeching. It looked at me, that way that owls do, and simply flew away. I tried to chase it, climbing the nearby building, hoping to jump on the owl. In my despair, I wasn't thinking clearly. I ran across the rooftops chasing it. I wanted nothing more than to lick my kits and huddle around them, protect them—but it was too late. I continued the pursuit because I didn't want to face the emptiness inside.

Surefooted though I am, even I cannot run uneven ground while watching the skies above. I slipped and fell to the ground, knocking myself unconscious.

I walked in dreams, wherein I met the High Purring One and he instructed me. This was how cats such as I gained knowledge of less practical things, like the mystical side of feline history, navigating the various dream worlds, and basic knowledge of the various elder gods. Not this time, though, this time I walked alone in the dreamland of Ooth-Nargai, along the shores of—

I awoke in terrible pain. I ached abominably. Even my tail hurt. I opened my eyes, and the perspective was all wrong. Craning my neck, I realized I was *hanging by my tail.*

"Oh, good. The pussy is awake." The speaker was a dirty, red-headed street urchin, one of several watching me. This was *not* going to end well.

He set me swinging, which hurt. I yowled.

An old woman approached. The street urchins paid her no attention.

Another of the gang batted me, setting off a new bout of pain. I was making as much noise as I could ever remember making, but I didn't think it would do me any good. *Would it all end here?*

"We could set her afire," said the one who had just poked me.

The woman spoke then. "Let the cat go," she said. Her voice was quiet, but firm.

"Go away, Granny," the red-headed urchin said. "This ain't no fuss of yours." He seemed to be in charge of this group of miscreants.

"Let the cat go," she repeated.

The entire crew shifted positions. They now surrounded the newcomer in a menacing way. A skinny delinquent spoke up, "You can't make us do nothing." They almost seemed to have forgotten me while distracted by this new threat.

I still hurt so much I could barely think, but I could not find a way to get my tail free of its restraints.

"Let. The cat. Go," she said for the third time. "If you do not set the cat free, and leave this place, you will regret it." She spoke softly, but with eyes hard as stone, and I had no doubt that she meant every word.

Hope began to seep through the pain.

The ginger-haired leader scooped up a small bit of rubble and tossed it at the woman. "Get out!"

She held up a hand holding something shiny. Hard to tell what it was, given my position. I saw a metal circle, no, two circles, threaded through a black ribbon. The ribbon was wrapped around some holly and other dried herbs…it was an amulet of some kind.

The woman was a witch!

She threw the bundle between her and the street urchins and chanted:

Three times said, a true warning spoken.

Punishment comes now, to those with morals broken.

Then, she waved her hand at them, and the entire group yelped with pain.

I'm afraid I wasn't feeling too sympathetic.

"Leave," she said.

They left.

"Stay still, Cat, and let me get your tail loose. It looks quite painful." She had turned her attention to me, and while I was grateful for the assistance, I was not ready to give my trust to anyone. She might be looking for a cat to sacrifice.

She took out a small, sharp knife, and cut the rope holding my tail. She gently put me on the ground and I dashed for cover.

She didn't chase me or cast a spell. Instead, she called out, "Little Cat, come talk to me. My name is Lisbeth."

I was intrigued. I moved to full view of the witch and *looked* at her. Once I got close, I noticed she wasn't as old as I had thought—she was using baggy clothes, cosmetics, and possibly a wig to give the appearance of age. *Hmmm.*

"I understand you, Little Cat. I grew up an orphan, not unlike those ragamuffins that had the best of you. I found a better way than cruelty, and I need a partner." She tilted her head, just a touch, and looked at me with honest eyes. "You'll never go hungry if I have food, and you'll never want for adventures."

I took a step closer, fascinated despite myself.

"Interested, are you? Come along. If you're not happy with me, I promise on the unpronounceable gods to release you safely on this very spot."

That was a very powerful oath. If she broke it, her life would be forfeit. I nodded to Lisbeth, indicating I was willing to give it a try.

"Come along," Lisbeth said.

She led me into a narrow alley where a broomstick leaned against the wall. We flew to her flat, Lisbeth astride the handle and I digging my claws deep into the straw brush.

~

Days later, for an hour after the clock struck midnight on the night of the full moon, Lisbeth was able to understand my speech. It was proof of our bond. And after sharing my name and history, it was quite convenient to briefly discuss the latest client who'd come to her for aid.

"Horace seemed earnest. The fee for helping him will keep us in tea and biscuits for a good bit," I purred.

Acting as if she wasn't the least bit surprised to be chatting with me, she replied, "Indeed, Graymalk. Let me outline my plan for Mrs. Diamondia's next séance."

And she did.

~

At the appointed hour, on the next full moon, Lisbeth and I arrived at the address Horace had given us. Introductions were made, with Lisbeth assuming the identity of Mrs. Victoria Maxwell, a woman who had met Horace through the shop and was interested in communicating with her long-gone mother. With little delay, our group made its way to Mistress Diamondia's residence, I carefully tucked into a large bag over Lisbeth's shoulder.

We arrived just past sundown, knocked, were separated from the agreed upon "monetary gift," and were delivered to a small sitting room with a single door, decorated in traditional *witch*: cosmic symbols, Egyptian hieroglyphs, exotically scented candles, and dark draping. None of it made sense, of course—Mistress Diamondia was a fraud. Lisbeth spent much of the time since meeting Horace in research and divination, and had produced the name Agnes Dymond, former governess.

When we arrived, there were already two women in the room.

There was a tray of full sherry and brandy glasses with matching decanters on the sideboard, and most of the attendees had partaken. Lisbeth, of course, abstained.

A few minutes later, another couple, about the same age as Horace, arrived.

My sense of time is keen—I am a cat, after all—we waited in that room for nearly an hour. Many glasses of alcohol were consumed, and the glasses were regularly cleared and replaced by a housemaid. Much of the talk was about who the various people in attendance wanted to contact during the main event. I was sure someone was listening in, I just didn't know from where.

Finally, I heard the jingle of a tambourine, then a woman entered the room from behind one of the wall hangings. *Nice touch.* From my vantage point in Lisbeth's bag, I could see this arrival was a tall, generously proportioned woman. She bowed slightly and said, "I am Diamondia. Welcome to my home. If you have an open mind, and you believe with all your heart, the spirit you seek will come to you."

Then, "I know almost all of you. Who are *you*?" She indicated Horace with a broad sweep of her hand.

"That's my son, Horace," said Euphemia, who had been quiet and subdued, but was now substantially more forthright.

Perhaps the sherry she'd been sipping steadily since our arrival?

"And you?" Diamondia indicated Lisbeth.

Euphemia again responded, "My friend, Victoria Maxwell."

I was pleased, and I was sure Lisbeth was, too. The plan had been for Horace to vouch for Lisbeth, but Diamondia didn't know Horace. Having Euphemia step up was a stroke of luck—it legitimized Lisbeth.

"I'm honored by your presence in my humble home, Horace, Victoria," Diamondia said. "I hope I can help you on your spiritual quests. Let us all adjourn to the meeting room, and begin our ritual."

She lit a small candle and marched the group slowly through the main door and up the wide staircase to a second-floor room. It was also decorated with arcane symbols that made no sense, and heavy, velvet drapes hung next to the windows. A round table dominated the room.

"Please, sit around the table," Diamondia said, standing behind a chair to indicate her place. Euphemia eagerly moved to sit beside her, and Horace took the chair on his mother's other side. A woman sat beside him, and Lisbeth claimed the next seat, directly across from the medium, with the others filling in the remaining chairs between her and Diamondia.

The medium placed the candle she held in the center of the table, while a maid released the window drapes to block all moonlight from entering the room. It was now well past sundown, and the room was in near darkness. The maid left, closing the door behind her.

~

I could see pretty well, of course, but I knew Lisbeth would be unable to see much of anything—it would be up to me to be the eyes for our team. I slipped out of Lisbeth's reticule and sat in her lap, peering over the edge of the table with one paw resting on it for support.

"Are there any unbelievers here?" Diamondia, the medium, had a surprisingly squeaky voice for such a big woman. "The spirits will stay away if there is a doubter present."

Unsurprisingly, no one left.

The medium continued. "Good. We begin." Then in a slightly louder voice, at a measured pace, "We invite the spirits to come among us. We want to speak to those on the other side. We have questions for those who have gone before."

She droned on in this vein for several minutes, entreating the spirits to come talk with our group.

I couldn't sense anything. And I'm sensitive to such things. As many cats are.

"We invite the spirits to come among us."

"Isn't something supposed to happen?" said Horace, with an edge to his voice.

"All will be revealed to those with patience, Mr. Woolfrey, but you must not interrupt." said Diamondia in calm, measured tones.

Then, slightly louder, "We know you are there, spirits from the other side. We invite—"

The candle sputtered. I studied it and saw that the wick was discontinuous—likely cut and held together with wax. A moment later it went out. The room was now in darkness, as far as those sitting around the table were concerned. *I* could distinguish where everyone was easily enough.

A quiet whisper came from next to the medium, "I'm frightened."

"You'll be fine, Mrs. Simms," said Diamondia. "The spirits are coming near. Hold fast. I need all of you to help anchor me. We must form a circle to share our strength. Everyone reach out with your right hand and clasp the left wrist of the person next to you. No matter what happens—*do not break the circle.*"

I saw the seven people sitting around the table with Diamondia dutifully reached out and take each other's hands as instructed. As the people to either side of Diamondia reached for her, she carefully maneuvered so that the person to her left clasped her left wrist, and she reached out with her *left* hand and clasped the left wrist of the person to her right. *Diamondia still had her right hand free to make mischief!*

"We invite the spirits to—"

Without warning, I felt the table shiver and shake, then the tabletop rose up at least an inch, wobbling all the time, before dropping back down with a loud bang. Chairs creaked as the participants jumped in response. I, of course, remained calm throughout. I still didn't feel an otherworldly presence. I *could* hear the medium breathing more rapidly. I dropped my head under the table and looked across at her. She was tilted back in her seat and had one bare foot braced against the table top, the other solidly against the floor. She'd lifted it—not the spirits!

"The spirits are here!" Diamondia's voice was louder now, and a bit shrill.

"What was *that*?" Horace said, with a little bit of a quaver in his voice.

"It's the spirits! Who is it? Could it be your father?" It was Euphemia, who sounded frightened. Her earlier bravado had dissolved.

"I'm getting a sense of someone, a man, definitely a man," Diamondia was now speaking in an oddly hollow way. After about a count of ten, she resumed, "A big man . . ."

Another pause, this one longer, then, "No, a man with a *big* personality, full of life. A man of good character . . ." Again Diamondia trailed off.

"That must be my husband, Henry. He was highly regarded by everyone." Euphemia's voice was still quavering, but had a note of hope in it now.

As if anyone would come to a séance hoping to reach out to someone of poor character. She's really pushing it.

"Mrs. Woolfrey, we must ask," said Diamondia, "to ascertain if this spirit is the *late* Mr. Woolfrey."

"Oh, yes." Euphemia responded firmly.

The medium said, "Good Spirit, I need you to identify yourself. If you are the late Mr. Woolfrey, please ring the bell twice."

The bell rang. "Ding-dong." I saw a long string coiled up and attached to the wall above the medium's head. She was reaching up with her right hand and pulling it to ring the bell.

I heard chairs scraping the floor, feet nervously tapping, and a few gasps.

The bell rang again. "Ding-dong"

"It's him. It's my husband. It's been difficult without you, Henry." Euphemia's voice had a high, slightly off-kilter sing-song quality to it.

I jumped down from Lisbeth's lap, and trotted around the table to where the bell pull was. My claws made quite a mess of the door frame, and a bit of a racket in the quiet room, as I climbed up to the string and grabbed it in my mouth. The bell pealed a third time, "Ding-a-ling-a-ling-ling-ling."

I jumped down onto Diamondia. She started screeching, "Get off me! What *are* you! Aaahh!" She followed up by incoherent, loud noises and cries of pain, as the sound of the bell occasionally rang again.

"I've had enough of this." Out of the corner of my eye I saw Horace stand up, breaking the circle, and he pulled back the heavy drapes. The drawn out deception had given the full moon enough time to rise.

The disheveled medium desperately tried to fight me off with one hand, even as the moonlight revealed what I could see to everyone in the room: I had loosened the string to the bell and our wrestling was periodically tangling us in it and ringing it again. The woman to her left was holding Diamondia's left wrist, while she in turn still held Euphemia's left wrist with her *left* hand, plainly showing the circle to be an utter fraud.

Got you.

At once, the silence in the room disappeared. I think the light, faint as it was, made the humans brave again. Talk of involving the local constabulary began. I ran across the table back to Lisbeth, looked her in the eye and nodded. Our bond is strong enough that we don't need to talk. And that only works for the hour after midnight, anyway. She opened her reticule and I jumped inside.

"I need to check on something in the other room," said Diamondia.

"Agnes," said Lisbeth, "Agnes Dymond?"

The medium turned white. "How do you know that name?"

"I always do my homework," Lisbeth said.

"Who is Agnes Dy-what?" asked Horace.

"Diamondia," Lisbeth's voice rang triumphantly, just as Agnes tried to slip out the door. I jumped out and dashed for the door, twining about her feet and ankles. She stumbled, and Horace grabbed her.

"You're not leaving so soon, are you?" he said. He walked her over to the nearest chair and sat her down rather forcefully.

Lisbeth came over to her and started to say something, then looked down. "You aren't wearing shoes," she said, matter-of-factly. "You did the table raise with your bare feet. Go ahead and deny it."

"I—I— Oh bother." Agnes was beyond refutation at this point.

Lisbeth looked at Horace, who had taken control of the situation now that Diamondia had been exposed as a fake. "Your mother won't come back here. Neither will anyone else. Now that Agnes has been exposed for the fraud that she is, they'll be no need for any more séances."

"I won't go back to being a governess," said Agnes desperately.

"Who would give you a character?" said Horace. "Without one, you have no chance at a governess's job."

He turned to Lisbeth. "Thank you for finding the truth—"

While Horace's attention was on Lisbeth, Agnes got up and took a step towards the door. I bumped hard against Agnes's legs, tripping her. She lost her balance and fell against the window, breaking it. Her desperate grab at the drapes slowed her fall, but couldn't stop it. Horace and Lisbeth both tried to save her—neither of them succeeded. She fell to the ground with a final sounding thump.

I noticed my back right paw needed attention, and extended it forward, carefully cleaning each toe.

Most of the humans rushed for the stairs, hurrying outside to see if they could help Agnes. They couldn't.

Lisbeth stopped Horace from leaving with the others. "Take your mother home, there's no need for you to be seen here. You know where I can be found."

Horace followed the others downstairs, collected Mrs. Woolfrey, and walked her down the lane.

Lisbeth and I quietly left as well.

≈

Later that night, Lisbeth said, "I think we've overstayed our welcome here. Mr. Woolfrey is happy enough with us now, but eventually he'll realize we know too much about his family's personal matters, and he'll want us gone. Best we leave before then."

I said, "I wouldn't mind a change."

And off we headed to our next adventure.

A Sudden Breeze Through an Open Door
Jeremy M. Gottwig

I would describe the cat for you, but she is hidden within the dumpster's shadow. She wants us to think she is gone. The rat feels her hunting him. He can see her tail twitching.

Are you the rat? I know you are here in this story with me, but I don't know where you are. You aren't the cat; I know that much. This leaves the rat. If I'm correct, you are cowering behind the battered trash can beneath the yellow streetlamp. You want the cat to get bored and move on. You are hungry but terrified. You want to find something delectable or at least passable. Let's be honest: even a dirty diaper would do. Your stomach feels like a pit. It hurts.

But you know the cat will catch you if you reveal yourself. She will try and snap your neck.

Oh, you aren't the rat? Yes, I knew that. I admit I was toying with you. I hope I didn't dredge up any old memories. Nobody likes to remember feeling small.

But all this talk of food has made you hungry, hasn't it? I apologize. Feel free to get a snack.

This story will wait for you.

Back so soon? While you were gone, the rat escaped. It was riveting. I would describe it for you, but there are only so many ways for a rat to escape a cat. I'm sure you can imagine something. The cat is disappointed, of course. She waits by the drain near the entrance to the alley. She wants the rat to return. She wants to play.

What did you get to eat? The cat smells tuna. The cat loves tuna. If you're eating a tuna fish sandwich, you're about to make a new friend.

Do you hear footsteps? Someone is coming. Oh, is that you? I'm so glad we finally get to meet. The cat hides behind a shrub and watches you approach.

Pretend you don't know about her. Pretend you no longer know about me or the rat or anything but your tuna fish sandwich. Your gender? Your clothing? Your shoe size? I could describe these for you, but I'd rather not. You need only imagine yourself in whatever you're wearing now.

The only thing I'll tell you about yourself is that you are eating a tuna fish sandwich.

Now, let's start over.

It's half-past midnight. Nobody is around, but you can't shake the feeling that you aren't alone. Caution slows your footsteps. Your skin tingles. Your eyes dig into every shadow, every movement. A tuna fish sandwich never tasted so alive, but your nerves keep you from enjoying it.

A rat climbs from the drain and scuttles into a nearby alley. You gasp, and then you feel relief, but Jesus, you hate rats.

And there she is, the cat, standing on a stone fence. She wants to chase the rat, but she also wants a bite of your sandwich. Did I mention she loves tuna?

The cat is a Chartreux.

Given that you're reading this book, I'll assume you're an expert on cats. You aren't the sort who needs a description. If I'm wrong, I give you permission to research this breed of feline. She is going to want you to leave your sandwich on the sidewalk, but I recommend you take it with you. Perhaps just a crumb? Yes, that's enough. This story will wait for you. Now go.

Are we on the same page? Good.

The cat wants another crumb. May she? Alright, one more. You expect her to mew at you, but you should know by now that Chartreux are a quiet sort of cat. By her clean fur and bright green collar, you can tell she's well-tended and much beloved.

These details should strike you as important. You should be asking yourself, what is a cat like this doing out in the middle of the night? Do her owners really want her digging through dumpsters?

Perhaps you should check her tags.

You decide to follow my advice. The cat figure-eights around your legs. It's almost as if she recognizes you. It was smart of you to drop another morsel to keep her occupied, but try not to spoil her. Now, isn't this interesting? She lives just a few doors down from you, with...what's her name? Keeps to herself? You forget. You didn't even know she had a cat. Oh, and the cat's name? Lorelei. I don't know about you, but I have always loved that name.

From somewhere far away, you hear a siren. This should remind you that you are alone at night. But you aren't alone. Lorelei is here.

And so am I.

Still nervous? Then, let's get you home. Move along. Tut-tut. Oh, are you planning to leave Lorelei, or do you want to take her home? If you are going to leave her, then I suppose this is the end of your story. You might as well flip through to the next.

You're still here? Then you've decided to do the right thing, but be careful, the cat may bite. Lorelei is like that.

What about your sandwich? I almost forgot that little detail. A small irony, because without that sandwich, you may never have met our lovely Lorelei. Finish or toss it. Carrying Lorelei will be easier with two hands. The story will wait, but hurry.

Now, pick her up and start walking. Doesn't her fur make you think of dark clouds? Don't worry if you hear footsteps behind you. That's just me.

You need to decide between taking Lorelei to your home or her own. Surely you don't want to wake her owner given the advanced hour, but doesn't it feel just a little strange to keep her in your own house overnight? You might feel like a thief, or perhaps Lorelei's owners might peg you as one if they come looking for her.

"Have you seen our cat?" they might ask, and then they would see her, hiding beneath your couch. Would they be outraged? Would they call the police? You would be innocent, of course, and I suppose you could explain yourself out of this situation, but what if there was something more sinister at work? What if you had come to love this feline and could no longer bear to let her go? What if she begins to dominate you? What if you find yourself never leaving your house, because she might need something? Like tuna. Lots of tuna. What if she always wants more! more! more! and if you don't give it to her, she will dig her thoughts into your head at night and invade your dreams? Perhaps Lorelei is that sort of cat. She is this story's lure after all, and she has caught you. Do you know the meaning of the name Lorelei? I think you should look it up. This story will wait for you, but take Lorelei with you. Imagine her in your mind. I'm not giving you a choice. Now go!

And so, now you know. You are wondering if you made a mistake getting wrapped up with our lovely Lorelei. Yes, carry her to her home. The sooner she's off your hands, the better. You walk to your neighbor's door, and you raise your hand to knock, but you then realize the door is ajar. This explains how Lorelei came to be outside, but why is the door open in the middle of the night? Being unlocked is one thing, but ajar?

You yelp in pain as Lorelei bites your thumb. She leaps from your arms and runs inside.

I warned you this might happen, but I suppose you forgot. Anyway, you're free of her, so shut the door and go home, quick, before something else happens. But wait a moment. I heard something, didn't you? A grunt and a moan from deep inside the house. These are not the sounds of love but of pain.

And there is now another character in your story.

Perhaps you should pretend you heard nothing and go home, but wouldn't it be wrong to go home without inspecting the situation? You could call the police and be done with it, but I don't think I'm going to let you. After all, your phone is unavailable. Perhaps it's broken or lost. Perhaps you are using it to read this story.

Another moan, and this time you swear you hear a gasp for help.

And then you hear sobbing.

I hope this doesn't dredge up any old memories.

The voice is clear and ageless, but it ceases before you can get a bearing.

You step inside the house.

You call out, but get no response.

And now, you must continue. You don't want to seal your exit, so you leave the front door open.

I suspect you may come to regret this decision.

Try and keep calm as you search the house. You may feel like an intruder or a creep. You may feel just as worried someone will catch you as you are of what you might find, but keep searching. Don't stop. Look through the kitchen and the pantry. Look through the dining room and the bathroom. Is there a basement? If so, you should check there, too. The lights are on in every room. It's as if they are trying to tell you they have no secrets.

And where is Lorelei? We had almost forgotten about her. You detect a set of glowing, gold eyes and spot her on one of the chairs beneath the dining room table, a table not unlike your own. Lorelei is watching you. At this moment in the story, she has nothing more to do.

But I suspect she'll have some future part to play.

You call out once more and get a whisper in reply, but it sounds like nothing more than a slow breeze through the open door.

Perhaps we should resume our search.

Does this house feel familiar to you? I've offered little in the way of description, so I suspect you are filling the gaps with images of your own. Perhaps you're imagining somewhere you lived long ago. When I imagine this house, I remember a place from my childhood. The house with the red door, I used to call it.

And now you are imagining the front door as red. I apologize. I didn't mean to taint your vision with visions of my own. I invite you to reclaim this image. Imagine this place as your childhood home. Imagine the ghosts of your family moving from room to room. Imagine the smells you used to smell, the sounds you used to hear. What color was the front door? Imagine that, too. And now, imagine you are small and alone inside this house. Someone else is with you, but you still feel alone. You feel like the rat hiding from our Lorelei.

Or don't. It's up to you.

This sense of familiarity should grow stronger when you open the first bedroom door. It is full of the sorts of things you loved as a child. On the floor next to the bed rests that book you used to read over and over. There are photos on the wall. You want to inspect them, but the sound of scratching draws you from this room.

You peer out and find Lorelei laying on her side and flipping her claws against another door, a closed door.

A whisper of air passes through the gap at the base of the door.

We've belabored this long enough, don't you think? One can tease the plot along for only so long. Lorelei wants to lure you deeper into this story, and now, she is pointing the way. You should follow. At this point in the story, it would be criminal to turn away.

And then, you hear a weak voice through that door, but you can't make out the words. It sounds like the voice of an old woman.

Talk to her. Tell her why you are here, and ask her if she needs help. Go on.

"Oh, yes," she whimpers. Several seconds pass. "I called for you to come help me, but I didn't think you were going to come."

You open the door and step into a hospital room.

And now, you are somewhere else.

An old lady lays in the bed. She wears breathing tubes and has wires taped to her arms. A door opposite you is open, and you can see nurses and doctors passing back and forth. The TV is playing an old episode of *Cheers*. You hear canned laughter. The old lady looks at you. Her eyes are milky white with only a hint of color. She has no hair.

I can't tell you how to feel here in this moment. Whether you feel surprised, afraid, or simply cold is up to you. Such is the risk of these sorts of narratives, but I can tell you that something about this old lady feels familiar. Perhaps you met her on the street once, or perhaps she is someone you haven't seen for many years.

Perhaps she is someone from your childhood.

"I wanted to see you again," she says. "I left the door open for you, but I didn't think you would come."

Can you think of anything to say right now that wouldn't come across as stupid or cruel? I can't.

"Well, here I am," you could say, with or without Taa-Daa hands.

Or perhaps, "Who are you?" Not even prepending, *I'm sorry, but...*, could soften such an insult after she has spent so much time thinking about you. Obsessing about you. Calling to you from her deathbed.

Do you think she sent Lorelei to lure you to her hospital room? It's possible, I think. Do you suppose this old lady is a witch?

A nurse enters. With little more than a glance at you, he checks her vitals, writes something down and moves on to the next room.

"They don't care about me," the old lady grumbles. As she coughs a deep, watery cough, she forces, "He didn't even acknowledge my guest." And then her eyes are back on you. She smiles, and her lip twitches. Doesn't that twitch seem familiar? It does to me. "Don't pretend that you know who I am." Her lip curls as she says this, just a little.

She waves you closer, and now you must decide if you will allow her to draw you deeper into your story. Behind, you can still see the house through the open door. If you let go, will the door close?

Do you feel the breeze?

Lorelei slips between your feet and jumps into the old lady's bed. It happens fast. You release the door and chase the cat, but when the old lady's face brightens, you catch yourself.

She winces, and then her face goes slack. It is as if she is trying to ward off pain. She places a hand on the cat's back and whispers, "Look at you, you beautiful thing," and then her eyes are back on you. She strokes Lorelei with her long fingernails. "Come closer," she commands, and you can no longer think of a reason to hold back.

But perhaps you should. Perhaps you should run and shut this vision behind the veil of memory. Perhaps there is something wicked about this old lady.

But don't my thoughts taint your perceptions. Move closer. Move closer. Hesitation implies fear, and in this moment, you need to show strength.

"I knew your mother. When you were little. We were friends." She takes a deep, hoarse breath, and adds, "I called you here to make amends."

Her eyes become little pools of piss-colored tears, but the pools never turn into rivers. She blinks and wipes them away. After a sigh, she adds, "Your mother trusted me. She asked me to watch you." And then she shutters. "I liked it when you cried. I used to pinch you. You would get welts."

And now you understand. She wants you to forgive her, doesn't she? That's why she sent Lorelei to find you. That's why she left the door ajar.

The old lady coughs once, twice, and she wipes her mouth with the back of her hand and returns it to Lorelei's spine. Her mucous drips into Lorelei's lovely fur. "I think your mother suspected. One day she quit talking to me, and I never saw you again."

For a moment she strokes Lorelei, and then, in a motion we nearly miss, she pinches the cat behind her left ear. It is a light pinch, a playful pinch, and Lorelei closes her eyes and purrs.

And now what do you think of this old lady? Do you pity her in her state of decay? Do you want to forgive her? Are you upset at her for telling you something you wish you didn't know? Something you didn't need to know? Something your mother wanted to keep secret? Did she dredge up any old memories? Do you remember feeling small? Do you remember trying to hide from her as she moved throughout the house? Do you remember how the floor creaked? Don't you feel just a little like that rat?

But perhaps you should wonder if she had other victims, if she slithered her way into other lives. If she found others to hurt.

She did.

You were luckier than some; less lucky than others.

Like me.

She drew me back into this world by her calls for forgiveness, but I am the victim that can never forgive. I am already dead. I am the character without an arc. I am as I was when I died. Perhaps she hopes to calm my hatred before she passes into the darkness. Perhaps she knows I am waiting for her. Perhaps she knows she turned me into a demon.

You might suspect that she killed me, but she didn't. I escaped, like you, but it took many years. Even as an adult, I kept coming back. A bullet killed me, but my last thoughts were of her.

But she called us here, and here we are. Ready to make amends.

Do you feel manipulated? By me? By her? By someone else? Perhaps you find this narrative unfair, but I did what I needed to do to help Lorelei catch you. I needed her to lure you to this place. I needed her to help you remember.

And now, we are going to murder this beast. I am tired of waiting. We will make it a quick. You won't have to lift a finger. I want her to know I wait for her beyond the grave. I want her to understand a few apologies will not bring her peace. I want her to believe she will spend her afterlife feeling like a rat cowering in the shadows.

Don't you find it amusing that she waited until her deathbed to make amends?

I know you want to refuse, but doesn't something deep down want to see her die? You could run. You could lock yourself in your own house and pretend that this experience never happened, but would you be hiding from me or your own primal desires?

But I don't think I'm going to let you go. Perhaps you are the rat after all. Perhaps I have become the cat.

Do you feel that breeze passing between worlds?

Did you hear the door slam shut?

Open it. Go on. You will find nothing but a bathroom on the other side.

And now, you are trapped here.

The old witch is still watching you. She thinks you are afraid of her. This should disgust you.

Think of what she's done.

I'm not going to ask you to smother her or pull the plug. I only ask that you give her my message. I want you to tell her a demon haunts this room, a demon that she created. I want you to tell her I intend to torment her as she tormented me. Tell her I will be relentless. Tell her this is what waits for her beyond the grave. Tell her after she dies, she will find me waiting for her. By her bed. Like family.

Go on, tell her, and then I will let you go.

And now, she knows.

Do you see panic flooding her face? Do you hear her voiceless scream? Do you see the creases of pain in her eyes? Do you see the sweat on her brow and hands?

Her body is too weak to survive another heart attack.

Oh, and look at Lorelei. Go on, look. She has been busy chewing on the various tubes and lines feeding the old witch's body.

Good Lorelei. Lovely Lorelei. I will miss you, Lorelei. She used to be my cat. I gave her to the old witch before I died, but I could never let her go. Did I forget to mention that?

You should flee before they catch you alone with a dead body. The alarms will go off soon. You will have to find your own way home. Take Lorelei and go. She now belongs to you. Care for her as I cared for her. She loves tuna.

But remember. She bites.

Mark of the Goddess

A. L. Kaplan

Shadows *spread across the jungle as Maya hurried home.* The press of the darkening woods felt like the time she had fallen into the river and nearly drowned. It was getting harder to see, a byproduct of the nut powder she used to stain her eyes dark. If she hadn't desperately needed more neston nuts to hide her golden eyes, she would never have stayed out this late.

"Goddess watch over me," Maya whispered.

A tall, tentacled plant loomed ahead and she quickly altered course. In this light, she couldn't tell if it was the carnivorous ya-le-veo, or the innocent iaci plant, whose berries were a village staple. It was best to steer clear of both.

More than deadly plants lurked in the darkness. Jaguars and other nighttime prowlers could be watching her now, ready to strike. Her grip tightened on the straps holding her basket and she quickened her pace. Visibility shrank to a narrow tunnel. Night blindness would soon descend.

By the time she burst into the village, she was running and out of breath. A small root caught her foot and she fell to her knees. Snickers erupted from a small group of teens, with the ever popular Conda laughing the hardest. Maya, the forest girl, afraid of the dark. She hurried to her family's hut. Tears stung her eyes, but she forced them back, making her throat ache. Tears were bad. Tears would wash away the nut powder staining her eyes.

"Where have you been?" her mother asked. "It's almost dark. I thought I'd lost you."

Maya laid the basket on the table and leaned her hands on the edge, breathing hard. The wood felt smooth, solid. Slowly, the world stopped pressing in on her.

"The acolytes were gathering nuts today. I had to search deeper in the jungle."

"Thank Ixchel you weren't spotted. If you'd been discovered…"

"I know," Maya squeezed her eyes closed. She had no desire to become the next sacrifice.

Her mother's arms trembled, squeezing her tight. "You're here, safe." Finally, she loosened her grip. Air rushed back into Maya's lungs. "Did you find any?"

"Only one, but it's old. The rest had already been harvested. I used my last coca leaf to subdue the ya-le-veos around it."

"Ixchel be blessed," said her mother. "It'll be enough."

A single tear escaped Maya's eyes. "Not for the entire moon blessing. This shriveled up thing will only stain my eyes for a day or two. The blessing lasts for four."

"We'll make it work."

Her mother brushed a strand of long black hair from Maya's face. Dark brown moisture marked her mother's finger. The stain was washing from her eyes. No one could know her true eye color. The caramel, almost gold, tone marked her for Ixchel, goddess of the moon, as did the dark floret birthmark on her upper left thigh. Both would have been honored in days past, but high priest Salix considered them a curse. Only Ah-Puch, god of death, was worthy of worship. Those with signs of other gods were taken at birth. Most ended up as sacrifices.

"Say good night to your sister and brother, and go to bed. I'll prepare the powder."

Maya was too exhausted to argue. Tomorrow was the moon ceremony, the start of her womanhood. She touched the new clothes her mother had laid out for the ceremony. Red and yellow stripes were woven into the cloth. The bottom edge was decorated with brown flowers. Small yellow seeds made up their center. More of the flowers covered the halter of the dress. Strands of colored seeds lay next to the outfit. Their family was one of the poorest in the village, but at least she wouldn't enter the moon hut totally unadorned.

"Try not to trip when you meet High Priest Salix tomorrow," mumbled Charo. The twelve-year-old was already swinging in her hammock half asleep. Charo didn't know about Maya's eyes. Neither did her ten-year-old brother, Quade. It was best that way.

~

Jaguars, pitch-black giant anacondas, and huge caiman haunted Maya's sleep, leaving her more wound up than when she lay down to rest. She rolled out of her hammock at first light onto trembling legs, drenched in sweat. Charo and Quade slept peacefully, ignorant of the fears she and her mother held. They were too young to remember when their father had been sacrificed. But the sight of Salix ripping her father's beating heart from his chest was something Maya would never forget. The air had tasted slick and oily, as it did at each subsequent sacrifice.

Her mother pressed a small cloth pouch containing the powder into her hand. "Remember, don't look away during the sacrifice. The priests will be looking for non-believers. Say your prayers to the others silently and be careful when you use the powder. Don't swallow any."

"Yes, mother," she said as she tucked the pouch into the secret pocket in her dress.

Thinking about four days in a hut with the other new young women in the village made her insides twist with dread. Swallowing neston powder and hallucinating was just one of the many things that could go wrong.

"My beautiful girl," said her mother, when she had finished braiding feathers and yellow seeds into her hair. "You are Ixchel's handmaiden. The goddess of the moon will watch over you."

The words did little to help Maya's nerves. Ixchel's marks felt more like a curse than a gift. At least her sun-kissed bronze skin was otherwise unmarred, though few called her beautiful, with her overly round face and short, stocky body.

"You should have this." Her mother placed a necklace with a single citron bead over her head. Maya's throat tightened. It was the only thing of true value they owned. "This belonged to my mother, and her mother before her, passed down for their moon ceremonies."

The moon ceremony was supposed to be a coming of age celebration, but Maya felt only doom as she walked toward the temple. Each step felt like a death knell. Ixchel should have been predominant at this ceremony, not Ah-Puch. Death had no place in a woman's womb. It seemed strange that Salix even allowed the ceremony to continue.

Four other girls knelt at the base of the temple. Unlike Maya, they were laden with many strands of colored stones. Conda had the most. Her family was wealthy enough that she was in no danger of being chosen to appease Ah-Puch.

"Look who decided to finally show up," said Conda. "Did you get lost on the way to the temple or just trip over your clumsy feet?"

Heat rose on Maya's face as the girls snickered. She fingered the stone around her neck and kept her head turned down as she joined them on the woven red ground cloth. This citron had far more meaning to her than all the stones the others wore.

A gong signaled the beginning of the assembly. Maya saw Conda's body stiffen and a muscle twitch on her cheek. It was hard to imagine Conda being nervous. The girl had everything: wealth, popularity, and perfect, dark-brown eyes. Perhaps Maya wasn't the only one uncomfortable with the proceedings.

A huge crowd filled the square at the base of the temple pyramid. No one in the village would dare miss a ceremony. To do so could incur the wrath of Ah-Puch. Maya's father's belief that all the gods should be honored was what led to his sacrifice.

Salix stepped onto the platform at the top of the temple steps and raised his arms. Maya sucked in a sharp breath. An inky shadow twined around him. Its sick smell drifted toward her and she forced herself not to be ill. Who would it be this time?

A young man swayed as he was led to the altar, a rapt expression on his face. It looked like he was eager to die, only Maya knew better. Her mother had taught her about plants that calmed people. She bit her tongue when she recognized the boy as Jafet, a farmer's son, who had been taken by the priests. Maya had seen him talking to Conda three weeks earlier. The beads around Conda's neck rattled, and Maya risked a sideways glance. Moisture glistened in the girl's eyes and her lips were pressed together tightly.

"Five maidens await Ah-Puch's blessing on this moon day," said Salix. His gaze made the hairs on the back of Maya's neck rise. "Look upon his gift."

Acid roiled in her stomach, but she forced herself to look at the altar. Turning away would draw too much attention and anger Ah-Puch. At least that was what they were taught. *Ixchel protect me.*

"Thirty years ago the earth rose in anger nearly destroying our world. Ah-Puch, god of death, has kept us safe. He is the only true god. All who worship him will be rewarded. Blasphemers shall be struck down, their souls condemned to eternal torture. This man has denounced the false gods and goes to Ah-Puch freely. His soul has been blessed."

Maya focused on her prayers as Salix raised his silver blade high in the air. *Ixchel, goddess of the moon, Itzamna, god of creation, watch over this man's soul. Kululcai, god of the feathered serpent, guide him to the sky. Ancient, Xkitza let him feel no pain. Chac, wash any evil stain from his heart so that he may rise to Chak Chel in the heavens.*

Her vision blurred. The dark swirl tightened around Salix. For a moment his hand trembled, then it plunged into Jafet's bare chest.

Blood dripped down his arm as he lifted the man's heart. Maya felt it beat in rhythm to her own. *Goddess protect him.*

Blood ran along the carved grooves on the altar and continued down the ramp, finally pooling at the base where she and the other women knelt. So much blood. The metallic scent, mixed with the oiliness of Salix, increased as he threw the heart into a burning brazier.

"Ah-Puch, feed on our sacrifice. Protect us. Rule us."

The priests chanted. "Ah-Puch, Ah-Puch...." Drum beats punctuated each cry and the village joined in. Maya said the words, but her heart beseeched the other gods as an elder priestess marked their foreheads with blood. Maya bit her tongue to keep from cringing from the woman's touch. She continued her silent litany as they were led to the moon hut to pray.

~

Two days into their four days of seclusion, Maya had barely spoken to the other girls. None of them had said much, not even Conda. Most of their time was spent in prayer or weaving bits of fiber into moon belts.

With five of them practically on top of each other in the windowless hut, the only private place Maya could find was behind the curtain in the pot corner. It wasn't ideal, but Maya had little choice. She touched the neston powder to her eyes quickly, then sucked the brown residue from her finger, hoping it wouldn't induce too strong a vision. Last night's dreams of slick black blood had left her tossing and turning.

"What's taking you so long?" said Conda. There was a sharpness to her tone that made Maya jump. "You've been in there forever."

"Sorry." Maya hurried out. A wave of dizziness sent her stumbling into Conda. Both of them crashed to the ground, and a shower of turquoise beads flew across the floor.

"Clumsy idiot," said Conda. "It's a wonder you haven't fallen into a ya-le-veo."

Maya bit her lip and began gathering beads. She couldn't seem to do anything right. "I'm sorry."

Alarm drums began to beat, followed by three gongs. Maya's stomach clenched. The last time a mandatory assembly had been called, five people had been taken by the priests. Everyone ceased picking up beads. Conda's face looked unusually pale.

The old priestess, who had been bringing them meals, burst into the hut. "Out, all of you."

"What's going on?" asked Conda.

"You'll find out soon enough. Move. The high priest is waiting."

The noonday sun made Maya's eyes ache after two days in a darkened hut, but at least she could see better. Her stomach flipped as six guards escorted them to the temple. Maya scanned the whispering crowd for her mother, hoping for an answer. Four guards stood at the base of the temple with a large basin of water. Salix himself stood behind it, his midnight blue robes swaying in the hot breeze. Up on the temple platform, held by two guards stood a semi-limp woman. Maya's mother. Bright red welts covered her limbs and torso, the kind left by ya-le-veo stings.

People stared in Maya's direction. Sweat dripped down her back. It felt like someone else moved her limbs forward. Where were Charo and Quade?

Salix raised his arms. Silence descended. "This woman was caught trying to steal sacred god food. Ah-Puch demands retribution. But first, we must rout out the evil she has spread and cleanse it."

A guard shoved Maya forward and she fell, nearly hitting her head on the basin. She looked up in time to see Charo and Quade dunked head first into the basin. Salix held their heads underwater as the children struggled. Panic griped Maya's heart. Charo could hold her breath, but Quade was terrified of water.

"Ah-Puch, cleanse these children."

Finally, the children were pulled out, coughing and struggling for air. Salix forced their eyes open, then after a brief examination declared both free from taint.

"These two are now dedicated to Ah-Puch. They will live in the temple. If the thievery was not for them, it must have been for another."

Dark black clouds gathered above the temple as Maya was lifted up. She barely had time to take a breath before her head was submerged. With prayers to Ixchel, she forced her body to relax. Her heart beat against her chest. She desperately wanted to take a breath to ease her burning lungs. Perhaps drowning would be a better end than having her heart ripped out. It was only a matter of time before her secret was discovered.

Thunder rumbled, but she barely heard it over the roaring in her ears as she was released from the water. She gasped for air. Hands gripped her head and she clamped her eyes shut. *They can't see, they mustn't see.* Fingers pressed painfully on her face forcing her lids apart.

"Blasphemer! She bears the eyes of an animal. Gold demon eyes."

The cry of "blasphemer" echoed. This time, Maya didn't keep the tears from streaming down her face. Above her Salix smiled. The blackness around him swelled and drifted toward her.

Lightning streaked across the sky. A jagged bolt struck the tip of the temple pyramid. Someone in the crowd screamed. With the guards distracted, Maya twisted in their grip, and then slithered out from between them. Free from the neston stain, she had no problem seeing in the growing darkness. As fast as a jaguar, Maya slipped through the crowd and into the jungle.

"Stop her," screamed Salix.

Maya bolted, dodging roots and plants. Guards crashed through the undergrowth after her. Her mother must have tried to get more neston nuts, but fallen victim to the ya-le-veo guarding them. Now Salix had her brother and sister, too.

"Ixchel, goddess of the moon, I beseech you. Watch over my family."

Rumbling shook the ground. The air felt charged. Tears streamed down Maya's face. Sudden bursts of light drew skeletal silhouettes all around her. She'd always been afraid of the jungle at night and cringed at each flash of light. Everywhere she looked, Ah-Puch's shadow pointed accusing fingers, saying there she is. Come taste her blood. His shriveled hand reached for her heart, drawing the guards closer.

Maya shivered, remembering the sight of Jafet's heart beating in the priest's hand. Even now, the smell of the blood almost made her retch. What kind of god would rip the life from a worshipper? Perhaps it was as her father had whispered to her mother late one night. The priests used the sacrifices to keep themselves in power, and the sacrifices were always the poorest of the poor or the outspoken opponents to those in power. Maybe the priests, especially Salix, were the very demons they claimed to protect people from.

"Ixchel, goddess of the moon protect me. If you truly care for your people, save me."

Rain poured through the canopy. Within moments Maya was drenched. A branch snapped. Maya held her breath, heart pounding. She ducked under a bush and prayed the guards wouldn't find her. Minutes passed. Perhaps it would be safer off the ground.

Maya shimmied up a tree, slipping a couple of times on the wet bark. Her limbs felt heavy after running all afternoon and trembled as she climbed. Ten feet up she found a branch thick enough for her to lie on without fear of rolling off in her sleep. If she could sleep. Finally, the storm passed and Maya sent thanks to Chac, the god of rain and lightning. Exhaustion crept up on her as she leaned against the trunk. It was a moonless night, perfect for hiding.

Suddenly, the sky lit up again. Eight feet above, a pair of luminescent eyes stared down. What remained of her nails gouged the branch she gripped. Deep rumbling reached her ears, but it wasn't thunder. A second flash revealed a large spotted body. Long gleaming white teeth grinned at her. The tip of the jaguar's tail flicked, and then its thick tongue snaked across its face.

Maya's heart thudded as she stared at the jaguar, a symbol of Ixchel. "Have you come to save me or eat me?" she whispered. A group of guards passed under her tree. Maya held her breath until they were out of sight. "If I have to choose between going back with them," she whispered, "or becoming your meal, I'd rather be consumed by you. At least one of us would be happy. Make it quick."

Maya closed her eyes and waited. The branch creaked. Warm breath beat against her face, but the only pressure she felt against her neck was from her own throbbing pulse. All her life she'd feared discovery, feared becoming the next sacrifice. Now that she'd thrown herself at death, it refused her.

"Finish it!" she cried. "Kill me or help me save my family. I can't bear this any longer."

A large paw pressed against the floret-shaped mark on her upper thigh. She gasped as the weight of it pinned her to the tree trunk, expecting claws to gouge. Instead, soft fur brushed against her and the heavy pads felt warm. Moments later, a coarse wet tongue scraped across her cheek. A hiccup made Maya's body jerk. The jaguar paused a moment, then continued grooming her tear streaked face like a kitten. When it finished, it pulled her in close. Strange, but soothing. So close to death's jaws, but no harm came from them. Exhausted, she drifted to sleep in the jaguar's arms.

~

"Ixchel, blessed goddess."

"Sleep child, rest. Your trial yet awaits."

"What do you want of me?"

"You will know when the time comes."

Blue skies stretched around the temple. Below, the people gathered, arms raised in supplication. On the altar, the high priestess tilted a jar. Deep blue berry juice flowed down the temple ramp and gathered in a small hollow. Priests chanted the names of all the gods and goddesses, and then splashed the juice over a roasting peccary where it dripped sizzling into the fire. All around the village, plants sprouted. Animals sprang into being. A huge jaguar padded through the crowd unnoticed. Where it stepped, children appeared.

The scene shifted. A greasy dark shadow covered the land. Blood coated the temple ramp. Only a few people huddled at the bottom. All that remained of the village was a single weather-beaten hut. Where the jungle had stood lay a blackened ruin.

~

Sunlight flickered against Maya's eyelids. She rubbed her eyes to shake the memory of the dream. Then, the weight of yesterday's events crashed down on her. Salix had her family. If she didn't stop him, he would rip their hearts out and give them to Ah-Puch. The sky belonged to the sun and moon, not death. Salix was upsetting the balance.

She stood on the branch, searching for jaguar, wondering if she'd dreamt it as well. Then, she saw her arms and legs. Dark black spots covered her skin wherever the jaguar's tongue had touched it. Now, she had the goddess's markings to go with her eyes and it didn't feel like a curse.

"Blessed Ixchel, my goddess, I know what I must do."

~

Years of sneaking through the jungle finally paid off. Maya skirted the village, avoiding the guards. Her new markings made it easy to blend in. Only one person came to mind who might be willing to help save her family. She found a perch to wait for the cover of darkness.

Patrols returned just before sunset, bruised and muddy. One man was carried in, covered in ya-le-veo stings. Another looked like he'd been gored by a peccary. The jungle was dangerous, but these were all skilled hunters and warriors. It was hard to imagine them being careless in their travels. Their haunted expressions made her shiver. Something strange had happened out there.

Just after dark, Maya snuck into the village, moving silently from shadow to shadow. Slipping under the leaf wall into Conda's hut was an easy matter. She crouched in the shadow and watched as Conda knelt before a small oil lantern surrounded by fruits, nuts, and mounds of gems.

"Is that for the young man who was sacrificed at the moon ceremony?" Maya whispered.

Conda spun around. Her red and puffy eyes opened wide. "You!" Maya held a finger to her lips and Conda lowered her voice to a whisper. "Your face, your body. You look like a jaguar."

"Don't be afraid. Ixchel has chosen me."

"For what, to terrify the temple guards? They say a giant jaguar stalked them all day. Was it you?"

Maya shook her head. So that's where her nighttime nursemaid had gone. "It must have been Ixchel. I need your help to save my family."

"Nothing can save them. Salix has promised them to Ah-Puch at dawn."

Chills ran down Maya's back. She had to make Conda understand. "The boy, Jafet, he was your friend."

"What of it," said Conda, turning away. Her voice sounded strained. "He's gone."

"You loved him."

"Father didn't. Now his blood marks us as moon maidens."

"It wasn't supposed to be like that, the moon ceremony."

"What would you know of it? The ceremony has always had bloodletting."

"Not that much," said Maya. "Ixchel showed me what it was like before Salix elevated Ah-Puch and demoted all the other gods and goddesses. The balance is off. We have to fix it. I need your help."

Conda's voice rose in pitch, but she continued to whisper. "What could the two of us do? We're barely more than girls. Thanks to you and your mother, the moon ceremony wasn't finished."

"Then, we'll finish it. Salix intends to bring Ah-Puch into this world. The sacrifices won't end. Conda, people listen to you. They'll follow your lead. Even with Ixchel with me, I can't do this alone."

～

Maya paced in Conda's hut, rubbing her hands until they hurt. It was almost dawn and Conda hadn't returned. If she couldn't convince other villagers to support her, Maya and her family were doomed. At first light, the gong rang out. In a few moments, her family would be led to the altar and sacrificed. The doorway cloth was shoved aside, letting in a stream of light. Maya jumped, expecting guards to charge in.

"It's me," said Conda. Maya sighed with relief. "We'll get you to the temple ramp. Hurry."

Twenty teens stood outside the hut. There were a few shocked stares when they saw Maya. Another gong spurred them into action. Islay, a young man who was always hanging around Conda pushed Maya to the center of the crowd where she was hidden from view. The group quickly maneuvered to the base of the temple.

Salix already stood at the altar. Behind him, guards held her family. She could see their eyes, alert, unmarred by the placating drugs usually given to sacrifices. Maya squeezed her hands into fists and ground her teeth. Already Ah-Puch's dank scent filled the air. The god of death fed on blood and fear. Her family reeked of it, as did the guards surrounding the temple. Getting past them would be a problem.

Suddenly, Salix smiled and turned to face Maya. The shadow behind him pointed in her direction. "There," he said, pointing.

A sharp blade pressed into Maya's back and a hand clamped on her shoulder. Guards plowed their way through the crowd and formed a ring around her, spears aiming for her heart. Maya's stomach flipped and churned. This wasn't the plan.

Conda stared at the boy holding Maya. "Islay! What are you doing?"

"First a farm boy and now this abomination. Sorry, Conda, but you have your priorities mixed up. "

Tears filled Conda's eyes. "It was you who had them take Jafet, not father. How could you?"

"Easy. Salix made a better offer."

Using their spears, the guards marched Maya up the ramp. Her stomach danced with each step and her legs felt weak. The guards' fear oozed out of their pores like a sour fruit. Big strong warriors, all of them, but they were afraid of her. Maya didn't feel very terrifying. How could she, one small girl, stop Salix from unleashing Ah-Puch?

Salix's face twisted, his lips tight and down-turned. "Did you think you could escape your fate? Your life was forfeit when the false one first marked you. You belong to Ah-Puch now. You'll make a perfect bride for his incarnation. Go freely, and I'll spare your siblings."

She glared at him and shouted so the entire village heard. "I belong to Ixchel, goddess of the moon. I will never again bow to the god of death."

Salix's eyes narrowed. His hand struck her face, sending her stumbling into the row of spears. Pain blossomed along her shoulders and her face throbbed. "You will never speak that name again. Ah-Puch is the one and only true god. Only he can deliver us."

Darkness swirled around Salix, making Maya dizzy. It felt like the air was being sucked out of her lungs. Her legs trembled. The courage she'd felt moments ago vanished in a bout of nausea. She could feel Ah-Puch hovering above the altar. Her body swayed and her mind drifted. Quade's screams snapped her back. His eyes were wide with terror as the guards held him on the altar.

Salix looked at Maya and raised a silver blade. "They will receive nothing to ease their way. Ah-Puch will feast on their blood and become whole."

"Ixchel, goddess of the moon, show me the way."

The tips of Maya's toes began to tingle. Waves of calm washed over her and the terror faded. She could almost feel the soft brisling fur of the big cat around her.

"Stop," she screamed as Salix's hand began its descent, but it was a jaguar's roar that filled the air. The guards jumped back. Spears fell from their hands. Maya leaped at Salix, reaching for the deadly blade. Her sharp claws slashed the weapon away, leaving behind long red stripes. Splatters of blood fell on the altar.

Darkness enveloped Maya and a ghostly cloud painfully crushed her chest. Her heart tried to push its way out of her ribs. An owl-like beak appeared beside her. Its laugh made her limbs feel like ice.

"Ah, my lovely bride." Ah-Puch's skeletal hands dragged her toward the altar. Bells jingled from his belt. Each ring made the ground tremble. "You belong to me."

"No," she screamed, struggling in his grip.

Something slashed her arm, sending a stream of blood onto the altar. She lashed out with her claws but they passed through Ah-Puch's misty form. Confused, she continued to flail. He wasn't solid, yet his power strangled her. Ah-Puch's sharp beak punctured her neck, lapping up her life's blood. With each swallow, his form solidified. Tears streamed down her face. She'd failed.

"Now," whispered Ixchel.

The goddess's power welled up inside her, indignant, furious. Maya didn't think about what was happening. She roared and slashed at Ah-Puch's newly formed body. The iron grip holding her loosened enough for her to twist and sink her teeth into Ah-Puch's neck. He shrieked and tried to flee, but she tightened her grip. With a sickening crunch, his neck shattered in her jaws. Blood filled her mouth. The sharp, metallic taste of it aroused her senses.

The oily mist wisped away from the broken body and swirled around Salix. Maya turned her gaze on him, bloodlust drawing her ever closer to the man who murdered her father and would have slaughtered the rest of her family. The priest cowered beneath the altar, clutching his bleeding arm. The silver dagger lay forgotten at his feet. Sunlight glinted on the bloody metal. She glanced at it, then back to the shadow. Ah-Puch's fingers still gripped Salix's heart, binding him to the darkness.

Salix's eyes grew wide as she stared. A moment later he clutched his chest and cried out in pain as Ah-Puch's skeletal hand pulled his heart out of his chest. The other priests crumbled to the ground, trembling with fear. If anyone else noticed Ah-Puch, they said nothing. Then, it was over. The shadows had taken their last sacrifice. Maya would allow no more.

Kings of the Concrete Jungle
K. I. Borrowman

It's been a few years, and you know who has really come out a winner in the zombie apocalypse?

Cats.

That's right; our furry little feline friends have instinctually avoided being eaten, and now they pretty much rule the planet.

They're everywhere; they've taken over the cities, countryside, and wild lands. Those who were once the kings of the jungle are now the kings of the world.

And us, the few upright apes who still have functioning brains; when we noticed that cats were everywhere, we studied their ways, adopted their approach, and we, too, survived.

Cat Survival Tip #1 – Stay High

I'm standing on top of a four-story building that was once a medical center, looking down on all I survey, when I see her.

She's tiny; petite, in fact. About my age, although at this distance and this height it's difficult to tell. I know she's a follower of the cat method because she, too, is on top of a building.

It's been a while since I've seen another person, living, not from our group, so I watch, mesmerized.

She moves with catlike fluidity, creeps tiptoe inch by inch, her lithe body a shimmering silhouette against the blazing sky. She maintains a posture: head erect, spear held high in her right hand, left hand hovering out beside her to create feline balance. She's like a tightrope walker, floating across the roof towards a flock of pigeons.

Yes, pigeons have also survived, but not so much because of their instinctual advantages. Pigeons have survived only because the stupid gits can freakin' fly, and if they detect any movement, they take off in a flapping frenzy. But, like the zombies, if they don't notice you, they just keep shuffling around, cooing, looking for something to peck at.

By now, she's about an arm's length from the pigeons. She takes aim, raises her spear, and brings it down in artful silence. A gray cloud erupts around her and she disappears for a moment as the ninety-nine birds she didn't skewer flap up and away, and then she is once again in my sight, walking away with a fat feathery lump slung over her shoulder as a few discarded feathers settle around her like dirty snow.

Cat Survival Tip #2 – Shut Up

She's the most magnificent creature I've ever seen, and I want nothing more than to call out to her. But I keep my mouth shut. Cats and I know those shuffling idiots down on the remains of the street would come swarming up here in pursuit of the slightest sound. As it stands, they're currently climbing up and over each other to scale the walls of the building across the street, a former condo complex, as the love of my life disappears down the other side.

I take advantage of their distracted state to creep away myself. Like everyone else who has survived, I wear moccasins strapped to my feet like ballet slippers so I can move on silent cat feet.

I enter the roof-top stairwell and retrace my steps, rappelling down the elevator shaft like a weird, rag-covered Spidergirl, and creeping along the second-floor footbridge to the car park.

From here, I can keep an eye on the mob below as I swing my leg over the cross-bar of my ten-speed and sail away.

Cat Survival Tip #3 – Be Quick

Cats don't pussyfoot around, and neither do we. If you want to keep your skin on you and your guts inside you, you need to move faster than the braindead can shamble, and the best way to do that is by bike. It's silent (see Tip #2), you can get around most things that would block a car, and it's fast.

By the time I emerge from the car park ramp onto the street, I'm flying. As I have been successful at the medical center, finding everything on my shopping list plus a few extra goodies in an unmolested vending machine in the waiting room, I head back towards our camp, pitched on top of an ex strip mall.

But I'm an over-rated idiot. I'm so distracted thinking about her that I nearly pedal right into a nest of them.

Braindead heads pop up and look around, their sunken eyes swiveling in gray sockets and jagged yellow teeth peeking between sun-ravaged lips which part in meaningless utterances. I squeeze both hand brakes and do a sharp U-turn, nearly capsizing.

Teeth gnash and guttural moans quiver on the air behind me as I flip it into low gear and pump up speed.

I'm heading in a different direction than planned now; my mental map is ripped away and beneath my wheels the road is jagged. You thought pot holes were bad before the zombie apocalypse; I jerkily pick my way among juts of cracked asphalt.

The noise of the hungry gang draws more of them. They pop out of alleyways and from between long-ago-smashed cars.

Unbelievably, the road gets worse; it's like someone dropped a bomb here. To be fair, someone probably did. But there's another mall up ahead, the glass front smashed and the floor beyond it smooth.

I careen into it.

Cat Survival Tip #4 – Stick to the Shadows

In the shadowy darkness of the mall, I know from the smell that they're all around me, but the braindeads' vision is even worse than their hearing. The bike tires are silent on the linoleum floor, and although the mob follows me in, they lose sight of me in the dimness and end up shambling around near the entrance, muttering nonsense.

There's enough sunlight entering through the various smashed entranceways that I can just make out a glint on the floor. I pedal my way down a few corridors and out the other side, free and clear, emerging on the mall parking lot.

Not the best place to avoid zombies; it's filled with cars, hundreds of places for them to lurk. I wonder for a moment why so many cars are parked at the mall; seriously, was everyone in town shopping when the outbreak hit? Then I pass under a stack of signs: *Addition Elle, Sears, Domino's Pizza,* and I flash back to a typical day in the mall behind me, before the first bite: silent mobs shuffling around in fluorescent corridors, aware of nothing but the little screens in front of them, and I realize what I'm currently running from are not the world's first zombies.

I manage to sail on silent tires out of the desolate auto graveyard without attracting the attention of any of its denizens and I get back to camp undetected.

I'm on first shift, so it's late by the time I finally crawl into my tent and hit the sack, but I can't sleep. I keep seeing her exquisite outline, the way she stood, spear raised, like the ancient *Roman Javelin Thrower* statue. I don't know anything about her except she's cat-like. I don't know if she's single or attached, if she's even into girls, or how I would go about finding her. But I keep turning over and over, listening to the crickets, and imagining what I would say to her.

Cat Survival Tip #5 – Stick with the Colony

As a former vegan running with a pack of Texan meat-eaters, I've never fit in here. But it's ten times harder to survive on your own, so when I first met Jed, running for my life down a San Antonio alleyway with a growing herd munching at my tail, before we knew about the cat thing, and he took a liking to me and stuck me on the back of his motorbike, I figured it was better to have a pack of rednecks surrounding me than nobody at all. And we've dwindled, but we've learned and survived, and we've done it together. However, I've always felt alone in this community.

By the time the crickets silence and the birds are chirping, I've settled into a restless sleep, but the bright blue sunshine glowing through the thin vinyl of my little tent burns through my eyelids and I'm up and at 'em.

Today I'm heading farther afield with Jed in search of food. Sam and Paul are fishing; our job is to find fruits and veggies. These small towns are always surrounded by farms with gardens and orchards, and even though they've gone wild, there are still apples and carrots and potatoes and whatever else growing wild within their fences.

As we pedal through the streets, I dart my eyes around looking for a sign of her.

"Lookie here," Jed mutters as we pass some fresh carcasses. My heart springs. Was it her? Did she do this?

"Sam and Paul musta surprised a nest of 'em."

Of course he's right. I'm so preoccupied I forgot we're heading in the same direction Sam and Paul went. In a few minutes, we'll pass by them as we cross the bridge out of town.

Cat Survival Tip #6 – Stay Out of Sight

Have you ever noticed how cats like to sleep tucked away in boxes or up on top of cabinets? As I sail along, I scan the tops of buildings for evidence of her camp, but she has left nary a sign.

It's hopeless. Sam and Paul raise their free hands to us as we cross a small bridge over a creek. Around the next corner we'll be in farm country.

Cat Survival Tip #7 – Be a Ninja

Jed raises a fist in a signal to me as he slows in front of the high, white-painted posts marking the first farm. I pull up next to him and raise my spear, at the lookout as he fiddles with the latch.

Jed was a noisy ruffian when we first met, but he has become one of the most silent cats I know. He lifts this rusty old hook out of a loop covered in weeds and dust, and it doesn't make a sound.

He pushes the gate just far enough that we can get in with our bikes, inch by inch so the old unused hinges won't squeal.

I'm at the ready. I squeeze in first, holding my spear above my head, and glance around. Nothing moves.

I wave my hand to Jed. He passes my bike to me and then his. He leaves the gate ajar in case we need to make a speedy exit.

It's more of an acreage than a farm. The house sprawls at the end of a long, overgrown driveway. Beyond the weathered old building, birds chirp cheerily in a broad forest. The biggest trees are evenly spaced—this was once an orchard. We wheel towards it.

An orange cat peers down from the eaves as we pass by the house. Two others dart into the forest when we round the corner.

Behind the house, a trampoline, two faded plastic ride-on toys, and a rusted swing set, all buried in the weeds. Over to one side lies a rectangle of wild that was probably once the garden.

We'll check that on our way out. We've hit the jackpot: an apple orchard. There's even a ladder leaning against one of the trees, nearly hidden behind a tangle of growth. Jed signals to me that he's going up.

We leave our bikes and collect apples, Jed tossing them down and me catching them and putting them into my pack.

The birds suddenly fall silent. A braindead kid appears out of nowhere, shambling towards us. I catch Jed's eye and gingerly put the pack down on the ground so I can wield the spear in both hands.

They're not zombies in the traditional sense. That is, they're not entirely dead. The virus just wipes out one important part of the brain, which happens to be the part that makes you human. What you're left with makes you less than mammalian. I guess you'd call it the lizard brain.

This little reptilian shuffles towards me, a dull gleam in its dumb eyes. It starts to open its mouth to groan its excitement about having found someone to bite. I don't know why, but the braindead are very aggressive, and the virus is very transferrable.

The movies lied. So did TV and comics. It is not a simple matter to stick a sharp object through a human skull. The trick is to go for the eye socket and shove hard enough to take out what's left of the brain. I do so. The kid blinks with the one gray, swimmy eye he has left, and a guttural murmur escapes his open mouth before he slumps to the ground. I put a foot on his now entirely dead head to hold it down while I yank out my spear. Dark blood spurts over the carpet of rotting apples.

I take a step back and jab my spear into the ground a couple of times to clean it off. You don't want any of it getting on you. Never know. The way the thing first spread, and the fact that the planet went from seven billion people to three billion in just over a year, you know you don't want to get any of it on you.

I look up at Jed and signal for him to carry on.

End of the day's work, we have a pack full of apples, a pack full of carrots and potatoes, and a small dead farmer family, which we leave behind.

The cats watch us leave from their perches.

Cat Survival Tip #8 – Bury your Shit

Jed is in front, so when I see what looks like a thin line of smoke rising from a flat-roofed condo complex a block over, I can't signal him. But I know it has to be her.

I take the next corner and head back there. I'll catch up; I know where the camp is and Jed knows I'm fine on my own.

I lean my bike up against the wall next to the fire escape, a rusty ladder inside a rusty chute of steel circles. There is definitely someone up there; a rope ladder hangs from the bottom of the fire escape. Could it be I've found her? I keep my pack on and go up.

There's a camp on the roof all right, but a small one. Three tents and a small awning over a fire pit. Nobody's around. I hunker down to wait.

I'm sitting eating an apple when she arrives. They're all right; small galas, wormy for extra goodness. She comes out of the roof stairwell, not the fire escape, and she's panting.

Her breath stops when she sees me. I can't tell if that's good or bad. She starts towards me. I rise.

"I saw you yesterday. Hunting pigeons." I smile, but inside I cringe. Probably not the best way to woo her. Stalk much?

She glances at my spear, which sticks out the top of my pack, my moccasins, and the apple in my hand as I stutter, "I'm Celia."

She says nothing. Just stares at me with those brilliant obsidian eyes, no expression on her brown, cherubic face. She's at least two inches shorter than me, and I'm small.

"I just wanted to meet you." I shrug. "Do you want an apple?"

As I start to take off my pack, she goes into a crouch and raises her spear. Not good.

"Okay, you know what? I'm sorry. I'll go. I just thought you looked... interesting."

I leave my pack on, raise my hands palms out, and start to back up towards the fire escape from whence I came.

The blaze in her eyes starts to subside.

"Cole."

"Pardon?" This is good. I stop backing up.

She lowers her spear, but not all the way. "I'm Cole."

I glance at the gleaming tip. She keeps that thing in immaculate condition. It's a heavy, thick meat-cutter's knife bound to what was probably once a hockey stick with about an inch thick of leather strapping, black from the blood of all the zombies she's killed.

"Thanks for not putting that through my eye. I probably shouldn't have trespassed."

"I haven't spoken to anyone except my folks for...I don't know."

"Yeah, me, too." We stand in awkward silence. We've both forgotten how to talk to someone new. We've both forgotten all the rules. You don't hang around in a stranger's camp, waiting for them to come home. You don't pull your spear on a completely alive person you find in your camp. We ruminate on these things.

Then, she says, "Is that your bike?"

I nod, thinking she's going to commend me on such a cunning method of transport.

"There's a zombie checking it out."

At that moment there's a clatter from below the fire escape. We stare at each other, mortified. We scurry to the edge of the roof, squat, and look down over the rim.

A medium-sized braindead is standing over my fallen bike, looking rather nonplussed.

"Shit," I breathe.

In the silence of the dead world where everyone's a ninja cat, a bike falling down is like a gunshot in the Himalayas, and it has started an avalanche of shuffling braindead, blank-faced curious almost-corpses, drawn to the sound by the instincts hovering in their lizard brains, coming from between buildings, behind cars, every street in all directions.

"Shit," Cole whispers.

I look where she's looking. Down the street, two figures on bicycles pedaling towards the growing mob around our perimeter.

I look at her. Her dark eyes widen. "Are those your folks?"

She nods. The shuffling masses keep moving. The cyclists seem to notice what's going on and slow down. They come to a stop about a block from us. More zombies appear from walls, alleyways, who knows? And they're surrounded.

"Oh my God." We can only watch as the two try to fight off the many. The grunts of zombies getting their brains split through their eye sockets causes others to turn from our building towards the melee.

Silent, catlike, Cole starts down the fire escape.

"What are you..." I whisper, but she is not interested in me. She's going to save her family. It's madness; there are dozens of them now, but it's my fault, so I leave my pack on the roof and follow her.

She straddles the bottom of the fire escape where it ends, about six feet above the ground, and the braindead there look up at her. From my perch above her, I watch her spear go into a glazed eye, her small foot brace the mildly surprised head, and her shoulders flex as she pulls the spear out again. Dark blood drips off its tip and the dead zombie slumps to the ground. Five more grab for her retreating foot and the spear enters another eye. Her foot goes out again.

"No!" I breathe, but too late. Several pairs of hands latch onto her. She jabs and I shimmy down, straddle her, try to wrangle my spear into the right direction with these damn steel hoops around me, and clawing sunburnt raw hands yank at her little foot.

"No!" My surprised throat immediately aches; I'm shouting for the first time in years, but I'm done with whispering. With the amount of noise we're making, every zombie in the neighbourhood must be on its way anyway.

She wrestles her foot away and I get my spear into the eye of a tall, buzz-cut one just as his hands are wrenched free of her leg. He goes down and another one reaches up. She rams her spear into its eye, the others are clambering up on their fallen comrades and reaching for her, and suddenly the six feet of extension ladder rattles down into their grasping hands.

We both lose our footing. I manage to hold on but she is jerked, yanked, snatched into the midst of them.

I bellow my rage, my horror, all the pent up noise I've been not making for so long, and even as they tear into her, some of them look hungrily up at me.

A glance towards her folks tells me they're gone, too.

Irresolutely, I make my way back up the ladder through the rings of steel. My spear gets jammed and I yank it out, my mind burning. I have a bag of apples and a camp up there; I could live up there fine until something distracts them and they wander off, however long that takes, but why bother? What's the point?

Cat Survival Tip #9 – Don't Care

When I was a kid, my mom used to read to me from a book called *Just So Stories* by Rudyard Kipling. One quote kind of became my zombie-apocalypse new-world-order mantra: "I am the cat who walks by himself, and all places are alike to me."

Cats survive mainly because they don't give a crap. Their instincts keep them up out of harm's way; naturally stealthy, they are good at hunting and avoiding predators. They don't go falling in love and getting themselves and the objects of their affection into deadly situations. They don't care about anyone else, only themselves. Although they stay with the colony, it is only because instinct dictates it; they don't particularly care for any of those other cats they run with, and they're perfectly satisfied with their own company. They live by instinct, and it is instinct that keeps them alive.

There's no place for thinking, feeling, caring humans in this world any longer. Only the solitary, the emotionless, the cats. And who wants to be a cat?

Catspaw
A Deadly Curiosities Adventure
Gail Z. Martin

*T*hat's the last of it," I called back toward the open back door of the shop. I heaved the cut-down cardboard boxes into the dumpster. Teag Logan waited in the doorway, scanning the dark, empty alley. A cat yowled in the distance.

"Come back inside, Cassidy," he urged. "I don't know why, but I don't like the vibes I'm getting out here tonight."

Teag's intuition is fueled by strong magic, so I take his 'vibes' seriously. I'm pretty good with both intuition and magic myself, and I felt a shiver go down my back. "There's something out here," I murmured, looking down the alley toward the streetlight at the end and seeing a dark shape in the roadway I had not noticed before.

"That's what I'm trying to tell you," Teag said. "Come back where it's safe."

Wardings protected the old antique shop against dark magic. Salt and iron lay beneath the sill of every door and window to repel evil, and as an added protection, sometimes we had a nearly six-hundred year-old vampire staying in the secret room in the shop basement. Teag and I both wore protective amulets, and when it came to defending ourselves, we were no slouches. So when I lingered a moment longer, I took a calculated risk.

"We need to see what that is," I said, jerking my head toward the lump that lay near the far end of the alley. I let my athame slide down beneath my sleeve into my hand, and jangled the old dog collar on my left wrist, smiling as the ghost of a large dog appeared at my side. Teag muttered something under his breath and joined me a moment later, carrying a wooden martial arts staff and a wicked knife.

Together, we advanced on the shape, which lay still in the dim glow of the distant street light. A mangy cat paced near the body, staying just out of reach as we approached, even though Bo's ghost growled and stepped toward it. If the cat could see Bo, the ghost dog didn't intimidate him. I paid attention to what my senses were telling me, shivering at the resonance something evil left in its wake. Yet the closer we got to the thing in the road, the more certain I became that the threat itself had come and gone.

"So much blood." I hadn't realized that I spoke aloud until Teag glanced at me, eyes wide with the same horror that thrummed through my gut. A woman's body lay at our feet, clothing soaked red, wreathed in a pool of crimson. Then Bo growled, and I followed his gaze to the necklace around the dead woman's throat. For all the mess, the body appeared intact, no claw or bite marks, nothing to explain why she bled out on the cobblestones.

"I don't think this was a mugging," Teag murmured, bending down beside the corpse, careful to stay out of the blood. He brushed the back of his fingers against the cuff of the woman's jacket, one of the few places not saturated with gore. At the same time, I crouched down on the other side of the body, letting my hand hover above the necklace.

Teag's hand jerked back. "Seriously bad juju. She never knew what hit her," he muttered, having picked up that much from the brief contact. He's got Weaver magic, the ability to weave spells into cloth— or recognize magic woven into fabric. I recoiled an instant later, without ever having to touch the piece of jewelry.

"It's the necklace," I said, breathless from the dark power I sensed. "I'm certain it's what killed her—and it's too dangerous to let it out of our sight."

"Then we'd better get it off her before the cops come," Teag replied matter-of-factly. "And there's no way in hell you're touching it, so don't even try."

I'm Cassidy Kincaide, owner of Trifles and Folly, a 350 year-old antique and curio shop in historic, haunted Charleston, South Carolina. Nothing about us is what it appears. For one thing, I'm a psychometric—able to read the history and magic of objects by touching them. Teag is my assistant store manager, best friend, and sometime bodyguard, and he's got his own powerful magic. My business partner, Sorren—the vampire who keeps a safe room in the store's basement—founded Trifles and Folly back when Charleston was new, always working with a member of my family throughout the years. Sure, we buy and sell antiques. But our real job is fighting off supernatural threats and getting haunted and cursed objects off the market. When we succeed, no one notices. When we fail, the aftermath gets chalked up as a natural disaster.

Which is why we were crouched over a dead body in a back alley, preparing not just to *tamper* with evidence, but to remove a key piece from the scene of a crime—because whoever worked the magic that killed this woman was out of the league of the Charleston PD.

Teag ran back to the shop and returned a moment later with a pair of pliers, a lead box and a long strip of cloth. I recognized the fabric as a piece Teag created, with protective magic woven into the warp and woof. I kept a lookout while he wrapped the fabric around his hand so that no skin touched the pliers, then snipped through the chain that held the necklace in place, and gingerly placed the jewelry inside the lead box. The mangy cat watched every move from a distance.

"We need to get out of here," I muttered as he snapped a picture of the necklace with his phone, then flipped the lid shut. Bo's ghost wagged once, satisfied that I was in no immediate danger, and winked out. The odd alley cat rose from where it sat and padded off into the shadows. Teag and I jogged back to the store, closed and locked the back door, and exchanged a look.

"The sooner we're gone from here tonight, the better," Teag warned, placing the lead box on a shelf in my office for safekeeping, and locking the door, just in case. "The bar up the street has pay phones in the back; I'll call in a scuffle in the alley, and let the cops take it from there. Nice and untraceable."

I nodded, still feeling shaky from the sight of all that blood. "I'll call Sorren and let him know, and then I'll see if Rowan or Lucinda have heard anything or picked up any bad mojo." Rowan is a witch who's worked on a few situations with us, while Lucinda is a good friend who also happens to be a powerful Voudon mambo. If someone was working powerful dark magic in Charleston, odds were good that one or both of them sensed it.

"Okay," Teag agreed. "I'll walk you to your car. And when I get home, I'll see if I can find out anything about that necklace—and monitor the police chatter and hack their system to see what they learn about the vic. I'll call you later, let you know what they said."

"Deal."

As it turned out, Lucinda was waiting for me on the piazza of my Charleston single house, what most people call a porch. I didn't have to ask how she got past the wardings, since she's the one who put them in place. Lucinda's suit suggested she had come straight from her work at the university, and its sand and ochre colors offset the dark chocolate tone of her skin. "Child, there's trouble brewing," she greeted me.

I locked the door leading off the side of the piazza to the street, and let us into the house. Baxter, my Maltese dog, yipped and bounced in greeting until I scooped him up in my arms as we entered. "Tell me what you know," I said to Lucinda as I led us into the kitchen.

I poured glasses of sweet tea for both of us, then fed Baxter his dinner, and motioned for Lucinda to have a seat at the table. She savored the ice cold tea for a moment, and let out a long sigh.

"Someone is messing around with very bad magic," Lucinda said, giving me a sharp glance that told me she suspected I already had an inkling about that. I nodded, confirming her hunch. "Whoever's doing the magic is sloppy—which makes things even worse."

"You think he—or she—doesn't know what they're messing with?"

Lucinda shrugged. "Or maybe doesn't have the training to handle what they're attempting. Don't know. There's no mistaking that it's dark magic, so I don't think it's something someone blundered into by accident."

"Can you locate who's doing it?" I toyed with my glass of tea, reaching down to lift Baxter onto my lap, where he settled down, content to be in his rightful place.

Lucinda concentrated, then shook her head. "No. At least, nothing I've tried so far has worked. I've sensed the... ripples... of power, but it's too quick to get a lock on it. And there's something very odd about the way it feels. Not quite... human."

"What kind of 'not human'?" I asked.

Lucinda was quiet for a moment, sorting through her thoughts. "I'm sorry. That's all I can say right now. I wanted to warn you—but I get the feeling you already knew."

I told Lucinda about the woman in the alley. "I'll come by tomorrow and have a look at that necklace," she replied. "Don't you touch it. I'll look into it."

"Thank you," I said. "But we've got to hurry. Whoever's behind it—they've already killed once." I paused. "Maybe that's all there'll be. Maybe it was something personal. Still bad, still murder—but it might not be a crime spree."

She shook her head. "I don't think so. The ripples—I've felt them before, not long ago. I think there's been at least one more. We just don't know who it was." Lucinda finished her tea and stood.

"If anyone can figure that part out, it's Teag," I replied. "Let me see what I can find out from my sources, and I'll see you tomorrow at the shop."

I walked Lucinda to the door. "Cassidy—you and Teag need to watch your backs," she warned. "What's Sorren have to say about all this?"

I sighed. "He and Archibald Donnelly went to Philadelphia yesterday. I've left a voice mail, but he can't always reply when he's handling a problem." Donnelly was another ally, a powerful necromancer. He and Sorren went north to help my Philadelphia counterparts deal with something nasty and undead. "No idea when they're planning to get back."

"Then you and Teag take extra care," Lucinda said in a no-nonsense voice, the one I'm sure she used in her day job as a professor to chastise errant college students. "Someone finds out you two are looking into this, you might draw the wrong kind of attention."

"Will do," I promised as I saw her out. I locked the door and leaned against it. Baxter trotted out of the kitchen and sat down in front of me, blinking his black button eyes. "Not sure what to do, Bax," I said, running a hand back through my hair. "We've got a dead body, a cursed necklace, and a rogue witch—who might not be human. Even for us, that's a lousy way to start the week."

~

The next morning, I found a witch waiting for me as I opened the door to the shop.

"We need to talk." Rowan said. Anyone watching might have thought she was a tourist jumping the gun on a day of shopping, but I heard the serious note in her voice. I unlocked the door and gestured for her to enter first. The blast from the air conditioner made me tilt my face back in bliss, since outside was already broiling and heavy with humidity.

"Teag called you?" I locked the door behind us and headed toward the office, knowing what Rowan came to see.

"Was he supposed to?" She looked honestly surprised. I slid her a sidelong look. Tall and slender, blonde hair up in a twist and wearing a loose green summer dress, Rowan didn't look like anyone's idea of a witch—unless you knew enough to recognize the protective runes on her bracelets and the sigils carefully stitched along the hem of her dress. "I felt a pulse of dark magic last night, and came to warn you—except that the closer I got to the store, the stronger it felt."

"I might know why." I led the way into the office, and pointed at the lead box on the shelf.

Rowan's eyes narrowed, and I could have sworn she let out a soft hiss. "Oh, that is *not* good." She glanced at me. "What's in there?"

"A necklace we took off the body of a lady who bled to death in the alley with no visible wounds." I fixed her with a look. "And no, I'm not touching that box."

Rowan smirked. She knew about my magic. She said a warding against evil under her breath and pulled a cloth down from a peg on the wall, a piece of fabric the size of a bath towel that Teag wove with protective magic running through its fibers. Then she took a deep breath, centered her power, and wrapped the cloth around the lead box, lifting it down carefully. I moved ahead of her into the break room and drew a thick circle of salt on the table. Rowan placed the box in the middle of the circle and withdrew the fabric.

"Even through the lead, something is making my skin crawl," Rowan said, eyeing the box as if it might attack.

"Do you need to open it, if you can sense it from here?"

Rowan frowned. "Unfortunately, yes. The lead dampens too much for me to get a good read.

I heard a key in the front door lock, heard the chimes as the door opened, and then Teag's vice rang out. "Cassidy? I've got Lucinda with me."

"We're back here," I replied. "And Rowan's already on it."

Teag clicked the lock and a moment later, he and Lucinda came into the break room. Lucinda's gaze fell to the box immediately, and she fell back a step, as if something pushed her. "Uh, uh, uh," she murmured, shaking her head.

Teag took the warded fabric from Rowan and carefully lifted the lid of the lead box. Even though I was several feet away, I could feel the resonance of the blood-soaked necklace like dirty oil on my skin.

Lucinda clucked her tongue. "Looks like dirty deeds done dirt cheap—and dead wrong."

I caught a glance between Lucinda and Rowan. "Meaning?"

Lucinda cocked her head as if waiting for Rowan to speak first. "Whoever did the spell has power but no finesse," Rowan said. Lucinda gave a nod in agreement. "A talented amateur maybe, or a fledgling witch attempting something out of their league."

"The necklace is cursed—and there's a whiff of death magic as well," Lucinda said, frowning like a chef trying to suss out the subtle flavors of a recipe.

"If it's cursed to kill, isn't that death magic?" Teag asked.

"Necromancy," Lucinda clarified. "Remember—I told you last night something about the power wasn't human."

Teag and I exchanged a glance. "I thought Donnelly was the only necromancer in Charleston," I said.

"And that's as it should be," Rowan replied. "But there's nothing to say someone new hasn't come to town—maybe even since Sorren and Donnelly went to Philadelphia."

"Necromancy isn't beginner magic." Teag eyed the box warily, but did not move closer.

"No, it isn't—and it's dangerous power, even when it's used by a seasoned witch," Rowan agreed.

"But isn't necromancy about bringing someone back from the dead?" I asked. "How does that factor into a necklace that killed the wearer?"

Lucinda shrugged. "That's what we need to find out."

"Is there anything special about the necklace itself?" Rowan moved close enough to peer into the box, as did Lucinda.

"Unless you see modifications that I didn't, I found the same necklace online—just costume jewelry, nothing special," Teag said. When Lucinda and Rowan stepped back, Teag used the spelled cloth to carefully latch the lid and replace the box in the office.

"You said you'd felt ripples of power before last night," I said, looking to Lucinda. "Do you remember when?"

"A week ago. On Thursday."

Rowan glanced up. "I felt something then too—I just wasn't sure what. Nothing good."

"Anything else?"

Lucinda frowned, thinking. "Last Saturday, I felt a surge of something, and then it was gone. It felt… farther away than the other times." She managed a wan smile. "I remember because I was at the market and I thought I might be getting a sinus headache from rain coming in."

Teag had already pulled his laptop from his messenger bag and set it up on the table, carefully dispelling the salt circle. "Thanks. That might narrow things down."

I glanced toward the front room. "I need to open the shop. Thanks for coming by," I said, walking with Rowan and Lucinda toward the door. "Can you keep your radar tuned in and let us know if you sense anything else?"

Rowan rolled her eyes at the idea of magic being like radar, but Lucinda chuckled. "Hailing frequencies open," she deadpanned. "We'll do some digging of our own." She frowned. "Don't you and Teag go busting in on anyone without us, you hear? Necromancy's nothing to fool with, and even an amateur witch can be dangerous."

If I doubted her, the memory of a blood soaked corpse in the alley was enough to prove her point.

For a mid-week morning, the shop was busy with tourists, and then a soon-to-be bride and her mother came in to look at vintage silverware. I glimpsed Teag hunched over his laptop in the break room, but it was almost lunchtime before I had the chance to see what he had found.

"Lucinda and Rowan's 'ripples' helped a lot," Teag said, turning his laptop so I could see what he found. "The lady in the alley wasn't the only vic. Two other dead men, on the days Lucinda and Rowan felt something in the magic, both covered in blood without any visible wounds."

"Show me."

Teag's Weaver magic gave him the ability to weave disparate strands of data into information, making him one hell of a hacker.

Normal firewalls didn't even slow him down. "Charleston police found a guy in a locked parked car near the airport last Thursday. Soaked in blood, not a mark on his body." He brought up the police file on the screen and I glanced at the details.

"What's that?" I pointed at a gray blur on the dead man's pant leg. Teag enlarged the image.

"Looks like he got against something—maybe pet fur?" Teag replied, leaning closer to make out the image. "Police file said they had to send Animal Control after a cat that wouldn't leave the crime scene."

"And then Saturday, another death, same thing. This time, a guy dies in a locked bathroom at a coffee shop. Security cameras show no one went in or out except the vic. No windows in the room, no other exit—nada." We watched the security footage from multiple cameras, saw the victim go into the bathroom as no one else showed up on any of the other feeds, nothing except an alley cat pacing in front of the bathroom door.

I sighed. "That looks like the mangy cat we saw out back. Can't be a coincidence. It's got to mean something. What next?"

Teag sat back in his chair and tilted his head to loosen his shoulders, then stretched his arms, laced his fingers together, and cracked his knuckles. "Now I really start hacking, looking for anything the vics had in common—besides dying bloody and that damned cat. There's got to be a connection—but it's going to take some digging." He raised an eyebrow. "On the other hand, with three victims, I've got a better chance of narrowing down matches than I would with just two."

"I'll run the store; you dig. I'm sure you'll find the connections."

By five o'clock when I closed the store, Teag was still at his spot at the breakroom table. I ordered pizza, figuring we had a few more hours ahead of us. "I think I know the why and the where, but not who or how," Teag announced as I walked into the room.

I sat down next to him. "Do tell."

Teag turned the laptop to show me his screen. "None of them owned a cat. But all of them died wearing or holding a piece of jewelry.

And all of them went to the same jewelry repair kiosk the day before they died."

I frowned. "I get the *where* but what's the *why*?"

Teag met my gaze. "They all testified against a teenager named Ben Calvert six years ago when he went to trial for manslaughter."

"So that means Calvert's either the witch or the person who hired the witch—right?"

Teag shook his head. "Not that easy. Calvert was underage. I only got his name by hacking into the private files of a reporter who covered the trial. The media didn't release the name, and the records were sealed."

"So he changed his name and disappeared," I mused. "He could be anywhere."

"He could be—but let's start looking at that jewelry repair kiosk."

~

"So he goes by Brian Cade now," Rowan murmured from her seat in the back of the car, staring out the window at the night. "Same initials."

"Yeah," Teag replied. "The man at the kiosk said he started four months ago—a month before the murders began."

"He must have been targeting the victims all along," I mused. "And it's too much to think coincidence sent all three of them to the same kiosk right after he started working there."

Teag shook his head. "I'm betting he sent them all a special discount or coupon to lure them in. I don't think he left any of it to chance."

Teag, Lucinda, Rowan, and I parked on a dark suburban side street, watching the house at the edge of town where we'd tracked Calvert. "Can you tell anything more about his magic—or about the necromancy?" I asked. We were each fairly powerful with magic in our own ways, but none of us was a necromancer, and going up against that kind of power gave me good reason to be nervous.

"You know the plan," Teag said quietly. "Let's go."

Lucinda and I headed toward the front door, while Teag and Rowan went around back. The small house had just one floor, and what might be a loft or small attic above. Not much crawlspace and no basement. If Calvert was home, it wouldn't be hard to find him.

I laid down a salt line around the front of the house while Lucinda chalked *veves* to invoke the protection of Papa Legba and Baron Samedi, two of the most powerful Voudon Loas who held authority over life and death. Teag completed the salt line so that it went around the rest of the house, trapping the energies we released inside. We weren't taking any chances.

My phone vibrated silently in my pocket, the signal I'd been waiting for. I let the athame slip down into my hand and sent a cold blast of power toward the door, splintering the wood as it ripped from its hinges. I could hear Teag kicking in the back door, as Lucinda began to chant. With a shake of my left wrist, Bo's ghost materialized at my side, and before I could say a word, he let out a low growl and leaped through the doorway, chasing after that same mangy cat from the crime scenes.

Lucinda and I charged in the front, while Teag and Rowan barged into the back. The living room looked like the set to a horror movie, with candles burning on every flat surface and sigils drawn in blood on every wall. The carpet lay in a heap to one side and more markings covered the floor boards, along with an obsidian knife and a bowl of blood. Calvert stood in the middle of the room, looking more like a junkie than a killer. Eyes sunken, cheeks hollow, and unshaven, brown hair lank and dirty, he stared at us like he was coming off a bad trip.

"You shouldn't be here," he said in a wrecked voice. "I'll kill you like I killed them. Aren't you scared? I'm a witch."

Rowan snorted. She raised one hand and clenched her fist. Calvert dropped to his knees as if he'd been sucker punched. "I'm the witch. You're a poser with a good spell."

I kept my athame pointed at Calvert, backing Rowan up. I'd put bigger bad guys through walls with the blast of power my athame harnessed, and after seeing what Calvert did to his victims, I wouldn't lose sleep about roughing him up a little.

Teag and Lucinda each made a slow walk around the room's perimeter. "What I don't get is why he needed necromancy to kill those people with cursed objects," I said.

"He didn't." We all turned to look at Lucinda. "He needed a familiar to work the curse. Didn't you?" she added, fixing Calvert with a glare that made him tremble. Rowan held him with her power, forcing him to stay kneeling, hands at his side as if bound.

"You're so smart, you figure it out," he snarled.

"That's why that damned cat's been everywhere," I said. "He's the familiar." That's when I realized that Bo and the cat were sitting side by side like besties.

For the first time, I got a good look at the cat itself. Mangy didn't begin to cover it. I couldn't tell what color the cat's matted, dirty fur might have been originally. Chunks of fur were missing, the tail seemed abnormally short, and one ear had rotted away. The cat fixed me with a stare, desperate but too proud to beg. "He brought the cat—the familiar—back from the dead," I murmured. "Against its will."

"Where did you find the curse, boy?" Lucinda's voice held an undercurrent of power, and from the look on Calvert's face, that magic compelled him to speak the truth.

"I found an old book in a second-hand store," Calvert spat. "It wasn't hard to get everything I needed, but I've only got a little bit of magic, and that was a problem." The look on his face made it clear that we would all be next on his list if he had a choice in the matter. "Then I read that the familiar of a powerful witch can share its power with a novice. There was a guy a few towns over that everyone said was a witch with a freaky cat. I thought maybe I could buy the cat—or steal it. But when I got there, they were both dead."

Calvert licked his lips nervously. "But the old book—it had a bunch of spells on all kinds of things. And there was this ritual to bring something back from the dead. I didn't need the old guy, just the cat."

"So you used necromancy to bring the cat back to life, and used the cat to work the curses," Rowan supplied, contempt clear in her voice.

The unhinged look in Calvert's eyes said more than any confession. "They testified against me. Sent me to jail. They had it coming."

We ignored him. "So what now?" I asked. "Release the spell on the cat, and he loses his mojo?"

Rowan frowned. "A bit more than that, I'm afraid. Problem with dabbling in magic that's out of your league," she added with a withering look at Calvert. "Necromancy comes at a cost—blood, life force... souls. A trained necromancer figures out what he's going to owe before he does the spell. Our boy here didn't read the fine print, and now he has a balance due."

For the first time, Calvert's eyes glinted in fear. "What do you mean?"

"Gotta pay the power bill," Lucinda replied, an unpleasant smile touching her lips. "And it's time to pull the plug."

"Found it." We all looked to Teag as he held up a small wooden box. "Cat bones. Vertebra—bits of its tail. Am I right?"

"Go to hell," Calvert snapped.

Teag set the box on the floor and poured a stream of salt on it from a container in his pocket, then used one of the candles to kindle the old wood into flame. Rowan began to chant in a language I didn't understand, but I felt chills down my back just the same. Lucinda sang strange words in a quiet voice, while I kept my athame trained on Calvert.

I smelled pipe smoke and heard a dog bark from the front porch. I glimpsed a tall, thin man in a tuxedo and a top hat, dark glasses hiding the empty eye sockets of his skull, standing in the doorway. The mangy cat stood up with an air of threadbare dignity and walked straight toward the apparition, pausing only to fix Calvert with a baleful glare before it sauntered to the door.

Outside, two powerful Voudon Loa, Papa Legba and Baron Samedi, guardians of the underworld, waited to claim what belonged to them. The necromancer's cat went willingly.

Calvert did not.

Payback's a bitch.

Masquerade Night

Alex Shvartsman

The first time Harat saw Ada was when she was dancing with the goddess of death.

It was masquerade night, and Club Rhythm was full of monsters. An orchestra blasted the latest European tunes at their highest volume setting, filling the cavernous dance hall with music. Dance beats reverberated in Harat's temples. An engine rotated an enormous lantern of painted glass suspended from the high ceiling, which cast shards of colored light across the hall. It was the glint of light against the lapis lazuli amulet that drew his attention.

The amulet reminded him of the jewelry once worn by the women of his tribe, but the smoke and glitter of the club swallowed up the details of the trinket—much like the depths of time had long ago swallowed all memory of his tribe's existence, leaving him alone, an abandoned godling devoid of followers. It was a fate shared by most of the celestials who frequented Club Rhythm.

Once upon a time, creatures like him had ruled the world, lording it over the terrified humans. But the world had changed, the humans had multiplied, had unlocked the secrets of bronze and iron and steam. They took over, and their one-time gods, stripped of much of their power, were now confined to the shadows.

By the 1920s, they could mingle with humans freely only on rare occasions. All Hallows Eve, Purim, Mardi Gras—the holidays of masks, when gods and spirits could work the streets of New York City in their true form without anyone giving them so much as a second look. Then Jumis bought the nightclub and came up with the weekly masquerade night—costumes required—a place and time where someone like Harat wouldn't stand out despite his feline eyes and pointy ears.

Harat tapped into his Leopard aspect, using the cat vision to study the amulet from across the hall, noting the subtle differences in the design. It was not a lost artifact of his people, merely an inexpensive trinket. He felt a pang of disappointment, but then his gaze traveled upward and zeroed in on the face of the woman who wore it. She was stunning.

Her face was flushed as she danced not so much with the goddess of death, as around her. Enthralled by the celestial's power she circled ever closer, almost touching the celestial and then shrinking back, like a moth fluttering around a light bulb. The little moth would eventually get too close, and her life would be extinguished, all too soon.

Normally, Harat would not interfere. He didn't prey upon humans, but for many of the other gods the club was hunting grounds. It wasn't his business to impede the natural order of things. But this time—this one time—he was compelled to act.

Harat strode across the dance floor, pushing past the writhing bodies, human and celestial, until he was face to face with his target. Miru, the Polynesian goddess of the underworld, was tall and very thin, and her skin was of reddish hue. She could have almost passed for a severely sunburned human were it not for her shark teeth—several rows of sharp, jagged white daggers.

Harat stopped right in front of the goddess, interjecting himself into the enthralled woman's orbit. The tall celestial scowled at him and Harat threw the contents of the glass he was holding into Miru's face. Before the other celestial could react, Harat turned around and headed toward the coatroom. The confrontation was coming, and it wouldn't do for the humans to witness it. Miru roared in frustration and pursued Harat, taking on her Shark aspect as she moved. The enthralled woman stopped dancing, and was blinking rapidly, like someone who had been suddenly awakened from deep sleep.

When Miru burst into the coatroom, empty for the summer, Harat was ready for her. The Leopard aspect took over and he jumped his opponent in a blur of claws and fangs. The two primal forces clashed, Shark against Leopard, tearing into each other, cutting and slashing, and moving faster than a human eye could follow. The thumping dance beat concealed the sounds of their struggle.

When it was over, Harat limped outside. He was bleeding from several long gashes on the side of his torso just below the shoulder, but could still move under his own power. What was left of the Shark covered the floor, the walls, and some of the ceiling of the coatroom.

Harat searched the club, but the woman wearing the lapis lazuli amulet was gone.

~

"What were you thinking?" Jumis, the Latvian god of the harvest, stared Harat down. "I've got a good thing going here. I don't need you muddying up the waters."

"It won't happen again," said Harat. His bandaged ribs ached pleasantly, reminding him of the battles past.

"It better not," said Jumis. "Do you have any idea how much the repairs are going to cost me?"

Harat was envious of the other celestial. Pudgy and graying at the temples, Jumis looked human, ordinary enough to intermingle with mortals without having to pretend he was wearing costume and makeup for a masquerade ball. For that alone, Harat would trade places with this lesser god, if he only could.

"You still owe me, from when I aided you in Constantinople," said Harat.

"They call it Istanbul now, and not any more I don't," said Jumis. "You better believe this little temper tantrum of yours makes us even. Next time you feel like a fight to the death, perhaps when your sparring partner's friends decide to avenge her, you take it outside."

Harat leaned against the wall. "No one is coming to avenge her," he said. "Relics like us have no friends."

~

Harat tried to forget the incident. He had lived for too long and fought too many battles to remember the details of each kill. But, every time he closed his eyes and tried to sleep, he saw the enthralled woman's face, her eyes as blue as the amulet she wore.

He'd been with human women many times in the past. He sought some kind of connection, a balm to soothe the pain and anguish, the grief he still felt over the loss of the mortals of his tribe. None of those other women made him feel the way he did when thinking about *her*.

Harat came to the club on the next masquerade night, and the one after that, but there was no sign of the woman. She must have been scared off by the experience—some deeper part of her mind subconsciously recognizing the peril even if she had never learned first-hand how dangerous her dance with the Shark should have been.

Having existed for thousands of years, Harat knew patience. He came to the club every week and roamed the hall, a glass of absinthe in hand, watching the humans who were dressed like monsters, and the monsters pretending to be human.

His persistence paid off. He finally saw her, not on the dance floor this time, but sharing a small round table with Qarib, the Persian god of serpents and poison.

She sure knows how to pick the winners, thought Harat.

He approached the table and hovered over the diminutive form of the Persian poison god.

"Leave," he told the Snake.

The smaller celestial hissed at him, but didn't wish to fight. The word of what happened to the Shark had spread quickly among the club regulars. He scooted from the table without saying a word. Harat pulled the chair back and took the seat across from the woman. For several moments, they contemplated each other.

"That wasn't very nice of you," said the woman.

"He isn't a very nice fellow," said Harat.

She pouted. "Maybe so, but he was going to buy me a drink."

"You wouldn't enjoy drinking anything he might have offered you. Regardless, that is an easy fix. I'll buy you a drink instead. My name is Harat."

"Ada," said the woman. She continued to study him with those big, blue eyes. "And are *you* a nice fellow, Harat?"

"By the standards of this place? I should say so," said Harat.

She smiled at him. "In that case, I will have to consider letting you buy me that drink, sometime." Then she picked up her purse and walked away, without turning to look back even once.

The Leopard god wanted very much to pursue her, but centuries of experience had taught him both patience and the wisdom of knowing when not to push his luck.

～

It was many months later that he saw Ada again. She wore a flowing green dress and covered her face with a handheld Venetian half mask, but Harat knew her scent now, and could find her in a crowded club, regardless of whatever disguise a human was capable of using.

He approached just as Silenus, a satyr with a taste for human flesh, was trying out his pickup line on her. Harat inserted himself unceremoniously between the two of them at the packed bar counter.

"Hello, Ada," he said. "You've had a long time to think about that drink. Have you reached a decision?"

"You are very persistent," she said, and she nodded toward her cocktail glass. Harat motioned for the bartender to mix another. "And also very consistent. You're wearing the same costume again?"

"It suits my nature," Harat brushed at his whiskers. "I like leopards."

"I'm more of a dog person," said Ada, but she didn't refuse the drink, or another after that.

The evening wore on as they spoke about architecture and dead poets, straining their vocal chords to outshout the music. For the first time in his very long existence, Harat was beginning to fall in love.

She asked him to walk her home, and he almost refused. He cared about her, and he was afraid of what would happen if he went with her now, and she found out that the whiskers and the fur didn't come off. He never really fretted about that moment of truth with any of the other women—some denied him, some were excited by what he was—but Ada was different. So he nearly refused to go with her, but then he saw her moving unsteadily on her feet and thought back to the Shark, and the Snake, and the Satyr, and dozens of other predators that surrounded them, and he had no choice at all.

He offered his arm and the two of them left the club together. They walked the midnight streets and their two shadows, cast long in the dim light of the streetlights, merged into one.

The walk was over all too soon—it turned out that she lived only a few blocks away from the club—and she invited him to come upstairs. He looked into her big, blue eyes and, despite his concerns about losing her when she learned the truth, he followed her inside.

They came up the stairs of the townhouse and into her home, and she poured him a glass of red wine. They sat on the couch in her living room and they talked some more, until the world began to swim in front of Harat's eyes. He tried to get up but he lost his balance and tumbled onto the thick rug, the wine glass rolling out of his hand and leaving a trickle of wine that looked like blood drops in its wake.

Harat tried to shift into his Leopard aspect, but he could not. He couldn't move at all, his ageless body betraying him utterly. All he could do was to move his eyes, following Ada as she stood above him, frowning.

"Why?" he tried to ask, but all that came out were some guttural sounds.

"Poor kitty-cat," she said. "You should have known your place. You should have stayed away from me." She walked out of his field of vision, but her velvety voice continued on from elsewhere in the apartment. "You weren't my intended prey. I only hunt the really bad ones, the murderers, the monsters."

He concentrated on her voice, zeroed in on it to stay awake, stay focused, and he reached deeper and deeper within himself searching for the Leopard but finding only the abyss, its darkness inching ever closer, enveloping his mind.

"You were too persistent for your own good, kitty-cat, scaring away the game." She returned and bent over him, still wearing the flowing green dress with the blue lapis lazuli amulet gleaming against the silk. She was holding a large carving knife. "So, you forced my hand. Nothing personal, but a girl's got to eat." She shrugged and smiled at him one last time, and plunged the knife deep into his chest.

As the cold steel bit deep, his consciousness reached desperately into the furthest corners of the abyss and found the Leopard aspect. His body transformed around the blade stuck hilt-deep in his midsection. The Leopard twisted around, swatting at Ada, and his claws connected, leaving three deep gashes on the side of her neck and her shoulder.

Ada gasped in surprise and stumbled back, letting go of the knife. The great cat pounced, pinning her down on the carpet, his fangs and claws ripping into her, causing as much damage as possible before the knife wound sapped away his strength.

She pushed him off with surprising strength, throwing him toward the couch. His feline body twisted and he swatted at her one more time. She moved away with impossible speed, but the claw snagged at the string that held the amulet, and ripped it from her neck.

The blue stone set in silver flew across the room and hit the wall with a clang. As soon as it left Ada's neck, her body transformed. It changed almost instantly, the visage of a woman replaced by a thing made of teeth and tentacles, an ancient horror from long before the first humans created the first gods by worshipping the fire and the stars and the predators around them.

Harat faced the nightmarish creature and roared in pain and anger. The thing that used to be Ada roared back, and her war cry sounded like a mix of distant thunder and crumbling gravestones. The two beings, forgotten by history, came at each other.

～

Harat woke up naked, lying in a pool of blood and grime and ripped tentacles. The sun was beginning to set outside—it had been at least a day since the fight. His fingers brushed against the crusted blood and scabbing skin, where the knife wound used to be. The wound hadn't fully healed yet, but it would in another day or so. He wasn't much of a god anymore, but he could still heal much faster than mortal men. He would survive.

He got onto his feet and limped across what was left of Ada's living room. He found the bathroom and climbed into the cast iron tub, turning on the shower and letting the room-temperature water cleanse his body. He caught some water into his mouth, trying to wash out the taste of the ancient god's blood. He ran the shower until the container suspended above the tub ran out of water.

He emerged from the bathroom and stepped carefully around the worst of the mess in the living room until he reached the other side and picked up the lapis lazuli amulet. He turned to the shard of a mirror that remained on one of the walls and put the amulet on, the silver setting cold against his skin.

He watched his reflection as his cat irises expanded and rounded out, his fur disappeared, revealing smooth skin, and his ears lost their sharp feline tips. Soon he was looking at the reflection of an average young man. Even his own Leopard nose sensed only a human.

Harat rifled through the apartment's closets until he found some clothes that would fit him left over, no doubt, from one of Ada's previous victims. He got dressed and left the apartment, walking to the front door downstairs.

Although the sun was slowly setting, it was still daylight. He watched from the doorway as throngs of people walked past the townhouse, cars and horse-drawn carriages competed for road space, and street vendors called out to the passerby, advertising their wares. It was the world devoid of masks and camouflage. A new world that he hadn't been privy to, that left him and his kind behind, masquerading in the shadows. A world meant for humans.

He took a deep breath, opened the door, and stepped outside, joining them in the light.

Another Man's Cure

Joanna Michal Hoyt

*E*xcerpts *from the traveling journal of Dr. Marcus Leeds,* editor and writer of *The Journal of Cryptoethnogastronomy:*

May 11

I am through with tergiversation, and also with the attempt to explain myself to ~~Lady Bollinger~~ my backers. I depart tomorrow for the Denoresh Plateau, without my dear Gaspar. Dr. Ludwig's suggestions are far too interesting to pass over. I suppose I ought to summarize those here, as her colleagues in the Department of Cryptoethnology appear inclined to regard her last letters as a sort of practical joke. Since I cannot remember that she ever demonstrated a humanizing levity, I find this improbable; since she was not married, wanted or indebted, I can see no other reason for her to disappear in this way and imply her own death. But this is beside the point.

Dr. Ludwig's first visit to the Denoresh demonstrated, as any reasonable person might have expected, that the feared Witchfolk of the High Places were in no way supernatural and, as very few reasonable people had guessed, that the Witchfolk were not primitives either, but a quite advanced group happy to seclude themselves on a high plateau with excellent satellite-phone reception and avoid their subsistence-farming neighbors except on those occasions when they themselves required food on which to subsist.

Establishing trade would have been time-consuming and ethically complex; they found it more efficient simply to abstract foodstuffs at night, with sufficient special effects to prevent them being followed. She also reported that the Witchfolk, so-called, had their own set of possibly mythological bogeymen, to whom they simply referred as *Those People Over the Pass.*

They strongly urged her not to cross the pass, and they showed an unusually primitive reluctance to explain the danger on the other side. Her relentless questioning (a skill she had honed with great effect on her colleagues here) elicited only the information that the people and the land were both somehow accursed, and that if she absolutely insisted on going there it was imperative she carry all her own food and eat nothing beyond the Pass (possibly, she thought, an echo of the ancient warning against eating in the Land of the Dead), and also that she plug her ears before sunset every night and leave the plugs in until after dawn.

Their fear of Those People Beyond the Pass appeared to be connected to their only two demonstrably irrational customs: an absolute refusal to eat fruit of any kind or imbibe any fermented liquor, and a morbid fear of cats.

I confess I find the latter attribute repugnant. So, apparently, does Gaspar, who sat on my desk staring at the report and made no attempt to chew or it lie down upon it. Leaving Gaspar behind will be the worst part of this venture, but I dare not risk his life in High Denor, and doubtless Lady Bollinger will respect his dignity no less than that of her own feline companions. I am willing to sacrifice the pleasure of his company for a time in the interests of cryptoethnogastronomy. He, noble animal, will hardly suffer from the loss of my company.

I find that I have still not clearly explained my reasons for believing that Those People Over the Pass are legitimately part of my field of study. Besides the general statements given above, Dr. Ludwig recorded a few peculiar phrases used relative to Those People and not subsequently explained, despite all her inquiries. These included: "the two-poison balance," "the sweet-death tree", and "the living-death diet." Granting the likelihood of morbid or romantic exaggeration, it seems likely there is something there for a cryptoethnogastronomist to investigate. I said as much to Gaspar, who fixed me with his green-gold eyes and waved his tail thrice as though in measured assent.

May 24

The people of High Denor are indeed as civilized, charming, and unhelpful as Dr. Ludwig reported them to be. They remembered Dr. Ludwig's visit and her departure through the Pass. They expressed no surprise whatsoever at her failure to return, and exhibited no sense that they ought to have sent searchers after her. They did not recommend that I follow her, but they showed no inclination to hinder me. They hosted me, fed me (on a peculiar mix of drone-delivered processed foods and commandeered grains, vegetables, and meats from their more primitive lowland neighbors; (there'd be a mildly interesting study there, perhaps, if I fail to find anything significant and reportable beyond the Pass), and taught me something of their language (which they say is similar to that spoken beyond the Pass), in exchange for a large payment in bitcoin. Indeed nothing I said or did during my sojourn among them appeared to disquiet or even interest them in the slightest, until this morning.

I was making polite conversation more than anything else when I asked my hostess what creature had called outside my window during the previous night. First, half asleep, I thought I heard Gaspar crying in evident misery. Then, coming fully awake, I remembered, first that Gaspar was thousands of miles away, and second that I had never heard him make such a horrible sound.

Then, I heard the cry again. It was something like the sound a more ignoble cat might make if its tail were caught in a door, and something like some of the more disturbing noises produced by ravens, and something like something else that I could not place, yet felt that I had somehow known before, and could, if I were very unfortunate, know again. I did not, of course, mention the third component to my hostess. Nevertheless, she looked narrowly at me, said they had no place in Denor for such foul creatures, and strongly encouraged me to leave Denor before another nightfall.

In compliance with her wishes, I am departing this afternoon. She has offered to sell me quantities of freeze-dried food to take with me; when I mentioned having already packed dried fruit she shook her head and left the room.

May 26

My second day in Kopsti. I am very lucky, I suppose, that it is not my second day in another world, possibly better or possible not. Physically, I am still feeling the terrible effects of yesterday's indiscretion, though I am now well enough to sit propped up and write, but mentally I am in high glee. The food system I have discovered here is unique, possessed of sensational aspects which should draw popular attention, and capable of being fully comprehended under no other discipline but that of cryptoethnogastronomy. My Journal and my legacy are secure.

That is to say, they will be secure if I manage to avoid whatever mistake or misfortune may have led to Dr. Ludwig's demise. For it appears that she is actually dead; the young man, Lekhi, who was brought to serve as my interpreter worked with her, remembers her well, and maintains that she is buried here. He will take me to her grave when enough of the kopiat juice has been purged from my system so that I can walk.

∼

I made the acquaintance of the kopiat yesterday. After hiking through the Pass itself, I found myself on a rather overgrown trail descending a steep slope in switchbacks. The top of the Pass was bare stone. The going was slow and the sun intense. I was drinking water sparingly. At first, when that smell of peculiarly intoxicating sweetness rolled up to meet me, I feared it was a hallucination brought on by heatstroke. When I passed under the tree line, the coolness was immediately refreshing, but the scent increased tenfold. When I saw the fruit...I can remember my sensations, but I am at a loss to describe them. Suffice to say, I entirely forgot both my professional discipline and the warnings of the Denoresh. I fell to eating at once.

The fruit was considerably larger than any peach I have ever seen. Its smooth plumlike skin was crimson with a silver bloom. The flesh was green-gold, a shade that reminded me of Gaspar's eyes, and softer and more melting than anything else I have ever tasted, and the flavor beggared description.

But there was more to it than that. It seemed when I ate that fruit that the light which fell around me was richer and lovelier than anything I had ever seen, that the sound of the wind in the leaves was the most subtle and pleasing of musics, that the air itself was intoxicating. I don't remember deciding to pluck another fruit after finishing the first, but Lekhi informs me that the silver pits of four fruits were scattered at my feet, and I would have eaten more if the violent pain in my stomach and the constriction in my throat which prevented the expulsion of my stomach's contents had not caused me to lose consciousness.

When I came to myself again, I was lying on my side on a soft pallet. A basin full of foul-smelling liquid was beside the pallet, and another and fouler liquid was being spooned into my mouth by a furious-looking woman who held my head very gently while obviously berating me in a language I did not understand. A few words sounded similar to Denoresh, but I could make no sense of them. I attempted to answer in halting Denoresh, which seemed to annoy her further. Then, in desperation, I attempted English. Something complicated passed across her face. She turned away from me and shouted "Lekhi!" This, of course, conveyed nothing to me until Lekhi came.

Lekhi explained, in formal and constricted English, what had become patently obvious—the raw fruit of the kopiat is highly poisonous.

"Only raw?" I asked.

"Cooked is a slower and a more weak poison," he said, "and made to ferment it makes not death, but foolishness only. Great foolishness."

"Why do you bother to cook it or ferment it, then?" I asked after another spasm of nausea had passed.

"To eat and drink," he answered as though I had asked why he breathed.

"But if it is poison..."

He indicated the flask from which the irritable woman—Lenna—was pouring more vile fluid. "Antivenin," he said.

"You eat it and then..."

"We eat mixed, and no sickness," he said.

"Wonderfully healthy stuff, this antivenin," I said, looking unhappily at the spoonful being advanced toward my mouth. "So does everything good for you taste foul here? Is it only..." My mouth was then occupied disagreeably for some time, but apparently Lekhi had understood my question.

"Antivenin is poison, also," he said. "Taken never except with kopiat."

~

That evening, finding me weak but poison-free, he explained more to me. Apparently, they subsist largely on the products of the kopiat tree. The fruit is highly nutritious when its toxins are neutralized; the leaves are also nourishing, fibrous, and filling, and also toxic; the wood provides the material for most of their homes. And a large amount of kopiat leaf or fruit can be rendered harmless by a relatively small dose of the antitoxin.

"What plant does that come from?" I asked.

"No plant," he said. "From stiss."

In response to my further inquiries he left the room, returning with a notebook whose opening pages contained observations recorded in Dr. Ludwig's strong spiky handwriting. He riffled through these to a page mostly filled by an illustration—clearly not Dr. Ludwig's; the woman couldn't draw an envelope so it was recognizable.

My first thought was that the subject of the illustration was a cat, and I felt an acute nostalgia for Gaspar's company. A closer look revealed this thought had greatly maligned cats. The illustration's subject—the stiss, as Dr. Ludwig's caption declared it to be—was generally feline in conformation, but its matted fur was blue, its eyes a venomous magenta, and its forelegs appeared to bend in the wrong direction, giving a rather horrible suggestion of human arms. Its mouth was open to show a fine array of exceedingly sharp teeth. Dr. Ludwig's notes explained that stiss venom—or antivenin—was milked out while the stiss was asleep.

"Wouldn't it be safer if you killed it first?" I asked, and then froze, fancying that Gaspar heard me from a thousand miles away and gazed at me with profound disdain. But indeed I could not imagine this abhorrent animal was truly related to Gaspar in any way.

Lekhi's horror, however, was obvious and actual. "Never!" he said, his eyes widening in shock and then narrowing in what I took to be ferocious disapproval. "Never to be killed, kopiat or stiss. We do not make to die what we live by."

"But isn't it dangerous? And is it hard to catch them sleeping?"

"Dangerous, yes," he said. Then he proceded to explain the bite of the stiss was immediately painful and paralyzing, and thereafter fatal if it was not counteracted both with purgatives and with copious quantities of kopiat. However, the harvest could usually be accomplished without danger *of bites. Sometimes the animals were sedated with blow-darts, though their intelligence and dexterity made this difficult. "And when fed to full, they will sleep of themselves and not wake for long and long," he added.*

"What do they feed on, mostly?" I asked.

"The blood of fools," he said quite gravely. "You must stay inside at night."

That night—last night—I heard again the terrible sound which I had heard on my last night in High Denor. This morning I asked Lekhi about it. "The stiss," he said, nodding.

"That's their hunting-cry?" I said. "Do... How big are they? Do they hunt in packs?"

"So large," he said, indicating an animal about as long as my arm. "And no packing. Every stiss is always alone, except in mating time and for a small time when the young are born. And they do not hunt. They sing and they wait."

"Wait?"

"For fools to go to them."

I expressed my opinion that something beyond folly would induce anyone to approach the source of such a revolting noise.

He looked unhappy. "Stay always inside at night," he repeated. Then, he put my breakfast in front of me—a bowl of cooked kopiat, which he assured me had been treated with a drop of stiss-venom. The smell and taste were pleasant enough, but not nearly so lovely as that first taste of raw kopiat had been. That was an hour ago, and I have experienced no ill effects. I am going out now for a better look at the kopiat tree in its native habitat. I will, at Lekhi's insistence, wear a mask which dulls the scent of it so as not to succumb to the temptation of eating the raw fruit again. Lekhi appears to treat me as a dull-witted child. This is fatiguing, but I must remember he first met me under singularly unpropitious circumstances. Doubtless time will improve his opinion of me.

~

[The next several entries, apart from the very brief excerpts below, are highly technical in nature.]

May 28

Today, I saw Dr. Ludwig's grave. She is buried, according to Lekhi, at the foot of a particularly splendid kopiat tree. This does not appear to be the common burial ground. I did not inquire into the reasons for grave placement; burial customs were part of Dr. Ludwig's field of study, not mine. I did inquire into the reason for her death.

"She was a fool," Lekhi said. "She did not listen to us. She went to the stiss. We could not save her."

She is, indeed, more of a fool than I would have believed; I never suspected her of having a penchant for the loathsome.

June 1

Every night I wake to the horrible singing of the stiss. Lekhi urges me to sleep with my windows closed, but this would also exclude the delicious fragrance of the kopiat trees, and besides the air is sweltering.

Lekhi continues to treat me like a child. So, I suspect, do the other village folk...

June 3

Tonight, there is to be some a festival for the full moon. My host family is involved in some sort of final adjustments to their jugs of kopiat liquor, which I have not yet tasted. I had some difficulty in inducing Lekhi to translate for me as I asked what they were doing; he told me rather rudely to avoid the liquor altogether, and did not seem to understand that my questions were put in the spirit of scientific inquiry. He also urged me not to take part in tonight's festival, but to stay in my room and work on my notes with the windows closed.

He is young enough to be my son, and I do not intend to continue to reward his impertinence. I will not, of course, argue with him. I will merely attend the festival as an alert observer, abstract a sample of the finished kopiat liquor for analysis, and also sample some myself, the better to understand its subjective effects.

June 10

I have been a fool. I am still, I suppose, scientist enough to record what has happened to me for the benefit of future travelers, if any. I think there is some reason why I ought to care about that. At present, I find it extremely difficult to remember why I should care about anything. Lekhi says this effect is likely to last for a long time, and may be permanent. I tried to receive this news politely. I owe him my life, though I am not at all sure I am glad of this.

I went to the festival. I believe I found the music very pleasing even before I had begun to sample the liquor, although once I had begun to sample, I was hardly capable of being displeased. I remember thinking the moon hung in the sky like a kopiat fruit just out of reach, drenching us all with light as sweet as kopiat scent. At first, I found this very pleasing, too. The one thing I looked on with disfavor, was the small vial of stiss venom with which the drinkers were doctoring their cups.

My neighbor—not Lekhi, who was in another group of celebrants; I had told him I would shut myself into my room and he was free—had shown me by emphatic gestures that I must put three drops into every cup. I followed his instructions for the first three cups. Then, it occurred to me Lekhi had said the fermented kopiat did not cause illness. He had said that it caused foolishness, which I took to be a polite euphemism for plain drunkenness, but I had always had a good head for liquor. I poured a cup for myself, left the stiss venom out of it, and took a cautious sip. My neighbor by then was singing quietly and swaying and not paying much heed to my behavior.

The euphoria I had experienced upon eating the first raw kopiat fruit came over me again. I did remind myself to check for discomfort in my stomach and throat, but I experienced none. I drained the rest of the cup and poured another.

Much of the rest of that night is still hazy in my mind. I do not believe I sang or danced as the others did, merely sat and sipped while the night and the music and the moon leaped and swayed gracefully around me. For a time, the sweetness was overpowering and wonderful. Then, it was merely overpowering. Then, it was overpowering and nauseating, but I could not tear myself away from it.

I abhorred the smell and taste of the kopiat drink, but I could not stop drinking. I felt myself suffocating in a horrible sweetness, powerless against it; I saw myself as a loathsome maggot in the midst of a sweet and rotting fruit, and all I could do was burrow further in.

Then, away out in the night, under the moon, which was falling westward, I heard the stiss singing. I heard it, for the first time, truly as a song, the lament of a creature even more loathsome and more lonely than myself. I rose from the table—I was alone there, the others were dancing—and lurched into the night toward that cry. I had, so far as I can recall, no fixed intention in so doing; merely, it appeared to be the only thing outside the putrefying sweetness of the world.

I remember the rank smell of the stiss was almost strong enough to mask the kopiat scent of my breath. I remember I saw the moon reflected in its magenta eyes, purged of all sweetness. I remember I reached out to it, and I think I called it Gaspar. I remember it settling onto my shoulder, setting its face against my neck. I remember the pain was strong enough to overwhelm the nausea.

Then, I was lying in bed and vomiting again. Lekhi was tending me this time, looking as angry as Lenna had before, and scolding me as angrily. Once he saw my eyes open, he spoke to me in my own language.

"I told you," he said, scowling and shoving another spoonful of raw kopiat juice down my throat. I was not strong enough to resist him, much as I loathed the flavor. "I told you! Do none of you scientists listen?"

I couldn't answer, as he had clamped his hand over my mouth to ensure the kopiat juice went down instead of coming back up.

"How did you find me?" I asked when he had removed his hand.

"I heard the stiss to purr," he said. "It is worse even than when they sing. Worse for hearing, and worse for wondering if it is a person they have bitten, for only when they are full they purr. Most times it is a person. Most animals are not fools."

"Did you get rid of it?"

"We harvested the venom. Better not to have anyone bitten, but if people will be fools we take what we can from it."

"We?"

"The harvesters took from the stiss. I carried you home and made you to vomit."

"And you didn't get to Dr. Ludwig in time?"

"I did."

"But she died."

"After. She went to the stiss again. She chose. One stiss bite, is bad, the—" He seemed to search for an English word and fail to find it. "—the stissness stays in your blood. But two stiss bites—" He shook his head. "From two, always dead."

I heard the stiss again that night. I remembered what Lekhi had said. Precisely because of that I would have gone back to the stiss if I could have dragged myself out of bed. The kopiat poison acts swiftly and passes off as quickly when the antidote is given; the stiss venom seems to be tougher, longer-lasting stuff.

I fell asleep again, to dream that Gaspar looked down at me and purred while his eyes turned magenta.

June 10, evening

This morning it occurred to me death might be preferable to more such nights and days; that it would, at any rate, be easier than dragging myself along for no reason. I supposed Dr. Ludwig must have thought so, too, and that reminded me of the need to send back some explanation. If I vanished without a trace, I feared Lady Bollinger might send someone to look for me, and it seems that foreigners in Kopsti are fatally prone to foolishness. As I thought of that, I also realized I had no desire ever to see Lady Bollinger or even Gaspar again with my stiss-warped vision.

Under the influence of these thoughts, I completed the record above. I was writing a note informing my Denoresh hostess that she would be well remunerated for forwarding the attached parcel to Lady Bollinger's address when Lekhi came in. He read the note over my shoulder.

"You will to go back to the stiss," he said. I thought the misery on his face was not altogether due to my warped perceptions.

"No, no," I told him.

"The doctor Ludwig wrote like that before she went the second time," he said.

"And you didn't deliver her letter and notebook?"

"I told her I would not. I told her she needed to wait a moon-turn here, eat kopiat, get as well as she may be gotten, and then, take her message home by herself. I thought that would keep her alive." He looked away.

"So you suppressed her message and lured me out here..." I began disgustedly.

He sat down abruptly on the floor and put his head in his hands.

"I thought I did right. Now, I know not. Maybe it was the stissness only."

"How did Dr. Ludwig's stissness...?"

"Not stissness of her. Of me. I was bitten. I thought, also, I was healed. But maybe you are right, and I am stiss now." He was starting to shake.

"No, you aren't," I told him before I had a chance to think about it. "It isn't your fault I didn't listen to anything you told me. But how did you let yourself get bitten?"

A little bit of life crept back into his face. "Tomorrow, I will tell you," he said.

Naturally I do not intend to go back to the stiss without hearing and recording his story. And I suppose the boy will have another story to get me through the next night. Let him be a Scheherazade; at any rate don't let him think himself a stiss for my sake. I've made a bloody botch of things, but I won't do that to him.

Nemesis

Jody Lynn Nye

*H**aki leaped away from the jet of fire that shot up roaring* from the stinking pavement. Her pads felt no ordinary heat, but a searing, demonic blaze. She arched her sleek black back with indignation. If her immortal employer wanted to punish her, he had more direct ways of doing so. Haki suspected one of the imps of trying to play a trick upon her. She would deal with them when she returned to the Underworld for a nap later. No one teased Nemesis without consequences rebounding upon them. One might as well tempt one of the Fates.

Skirting the pool of molten asphalt, she stalked her current prey.

The thin man in the dark green hoodie crept softly through the alley. His pockets were stuffed with pillow cases, and he had a crowbar shoved down the right leg of his jeans. One tired yellow street light had the thankless job of trying to illuminate the whole narrow passageway, and failed miserably. Long shadows stretched out behind dumpsters and parked cars, making easy places to duck into if the lone patrol car in the area trundled down over the buckled tarmac.

He made for the jewelry store that had moved into the shop that used to be a taco stand. It had a pull-down steel gate on the front, but the new owners probably didn't know that the bars on the window facing out into the alley were loose, had been for years since the air conditioning unit on the roof had started dripping down next to the drain pipe, eating away the concrete behind the thick gray paint. All the local kids knew it. Haki trotted along behind him, invisible in the shadows, hoping he would change his mind.

Haki's eternal task set her against would-be wrongdoers, in hopes of turning them back. She didn't condemn them herself, but observed and reported. Her many selves, scattered across all of existence had saved countless souls from an eternity of pain and regret. Only those too obdurate or prideful to repent spent their afterlives suffering. Once death claimed them, it was too late to change their path. Haki's employer—she never called him master—had a particular intolerance for those who shared his own particular sin.

Souls remained as they were when taken from Earth, with all their feelings and intelligence, fears, loves, hates, hopes and idiosyncrasies intact. If they were good enough to make it to Heaven, there they stayed. The Most High never sent away a soul who showed charity and repentance, as simple as that. If they did not learn a lesson in life, they spend time in Limbo or Hell. Lucifer liked to head off potentially redeemable souls if at all possible. The paperwork to admit even one to Hell was horrendous. He'd invented bureaucracy, and in the way that Karma proved to be as much a goad to his own back as it was to others, it rebounded upon him threefold, or multiples or exponents of three.

"Don't let anyone down here who doesn't absolutely deserve to be down here!" Lucifer had admonished Haki when she had last visited the nether realm to report a prospect. The tangle into which he had disarrayed his long, beautiful hair proved how bad things were. The black feathers of his wings needed preening. Nemesis had removed herself before temptation to play with that hair or those feathers brought her close enough for a kick. She nearly felt sorry for him. When cats had too many troubles to deal with, they just walked away from them. Fallen angels who demanded their own realms didn't have that luxury. Still, he'd been the one to insist on that whole *To reign in Hell* thing.

Haki had been keeping an eye on this youth for a while. Antonio's present malign intentions had echoed through the ether loudly enough for her to hear even as far away as Singapore, where she had just persuaded a woman not to jump off a bridge. She knew he had been casing the new place, watching the two middle-aged women who owned it, learning their routine over the course of days. At closing time, they moved the chains and charms and expensive Venetian beads out of the display cases, but only seemed to take the money from the cash drawer once a week, on Friday evening. As it was Thursday, chances were it was all still there. The shop had prospered. The sum should be enough in it for one of those fancy new smartphones the young man had been craving.

Covetousness was also a sin, but as long as one didn't act upon it, Haki didn't care. Humans fantasized all the time, keeping their minds busy with self-deceptive nonsense. Intentions didn't count, regardless of what St. Bernard of Clairvaux had said. She was there to remind them in case their own conscience failed, but in the end, it had to be their own volition that kept them straight. If they failed, she turned her back on them. As long as she still had an effect on them, stayed with them, they had a chance of evading her employer. She felt sorry for them, as much as she could. They didn't see the bigger picture. After all, they were only human.

With one final look up and down the alley to see if anyone was coming, the youth slipped the crowbar free from his jeans, tucked the forked end under the edge of the steel frame and leaned into it. The bolts moaned audibly as they were forced out of the cinder blocks. Haki bounded up onto the rusting dumpster beside the door.

"Rrreeeeew!"

Antonio jumped. His crowbar fell out of his hands. Suddenly, two gigantic green orbs peered at him at eye level. He flinched away, then realized the shadow around them had a familiar shape.

"Damn! It's just a cat!"

He swiped at the shadow. The brilliant eyes didn't blink. Instead, four sharp wire whips flashed out and scored down his wrist. He clenched his fist in pain. Blood, black in the dimness, oozed from deep gouges and dripped down onto his shoes.

"What are you, a frigging tiger?" he demanded. The shadow hunched its shoulders, as if it was about to spring. That cat had to be crazy! He backed away from it, never taking his eyes off it, until he was a good ten feet away. Never mind. Never mind. No cash drawer was worth taking on a crazy animal.

Haki laughed at him as he ran away. She licked the blood from her claws. One more would-be sinner turned away from crime, for the moment.

She was Nemesis.

Haki hopped down from the crate and padded out of the alley into the busy street. People, usually in small groups, talked loudly as they walked in and out of the shops and clubs. Most of them didn't notice her. A couple that did gave her a friendly smile and perhaps a pat on her long-furred black back. One in perhaps fifty blanched at the sight of her bright green eyes, and remembered. She remembered each of them, too. She had caught them in the act, and turned them back, or perhaps failed to do so. Haki was their final pricking of conscience.

A mortal cat, a dark tabby female, wound her way out from underneath a trestle table outside a used book store and came to greet Haki with a swipe of her whiskers.

"Mistress."

"Simha called Stripey and mother-of-six, good evening. How are the young ones?"

Simha's tail lifted to vertical. To be recognized by Haki was a privilege. Haki purred low in her throat. Mortal cats, their nine lives as nine moments compared with her eternity, provided a nice change from humanity.

"They're getting big. Their teeth hurt my nipples, but they're still too little to hunt." The tabby glanced at Haki, daringly. "Do you have kittens now?"

"This body, no, but one of my ancient selves has just had two," Haki said. Though separated by eons from that avatar, she could feel the kneading of urgent little paws against her side.

"They will be… tigers?" Simha asked.

"One will be an angel. The other will be an asteroid. She will wipe out most of life on Earth."

Simha's pupils widened to overspread her golden irises with fear. "Soon?"

"Sixty-five million years ago," Haki said.

"Oh." Simha stopped to wash a paw. "That must have been quite a mating, if you gave birth to such destruction!"

Haki's throat rumbled with pure pleasure at the memory of long teeth in the back of her neck and the joining of two into one. "Oh, it was."

A thread of concern interrupted her reminiscence, tugging her to the side like a leash. Haki hissed at the interruption, but realized its source. A crisis of conscience troubled someone, threatening to overbalance that soul toward the evil side. It needed her. "I must go."

The tabby blinked. With a final swipe for farewell, she trotted back to her basket. Haki gathered herself and sprang into the air, to the astonishment of a couple of men coming out of the fruit market on the corner. No one else saw her.

Hundreds of years later and thousands of miles away, the noise and dirt of the city she had left was absent in this new reality. The walls and streets of this new city, if you could call the smooth, untrodden strips *streets*, were steel blue, with accents of silver around windows and doors. Floating vehicles like silver bubbles carried people in the same steel blue up and back. The only warm color was red rectangles etched into the blind sides of buildings: flags of a bygone era that still carried with them reminders of oppression. No comfortable chatter of cats, pigeons or rats could be heard in this place. They had been tidied out of it, along with the marginal humans who occupied the shadows elsewhere. The air smelled pure, lacking any of the ordinary scents of life. The city looked prosperous, but unhappy. Haki felt sorry for the millions of inhabitants she could sense within its walls. All the happy chaos of creativity had fled in the name of order.

Within this chill environment, a desperate soul scratched at the eggshell that imprisoned it. Mass destruction would follow its freedom. With growing concern, Haki followed its emanations. It was such a huge trace. Could she even bring this one into balance, or was it beyond her to save?

She found it at last in the center of a plaza, next to a fountain that played scented water into its precisely designed basin. A young woman with shining black hair cut short clung with both her slender arms to a lumpy device nearly as large as she was. Painted a defiant acid yellow, it stood out even at twilight. Haki recognized at once the source of potential destruction.

Around her in the square, dark blue bubbles decanted wave after wave of armed peace robots. They threw up a force shield of hot white light. Silver bubbles full of curiosity-seekers and newsgatherers hovered outside the cordon. None of them dared yet to move in close. The bomb would obliterate the entire area for kilometers in every direction, including down.

Haki sensed the young woman's fear. Social oppression and isolation had pushed Xie Chao-Xing to this final act. Haki wanted to embrace her like one of her own kittens and soothe the terror from her. First, she must prevent Chao-Xing from activating the explosion. Haki altered her shape to a plump white cat with gold paws and eyes.

She alighted on the stone bench and ambled toward the young woman, purring loudly.

Relax, child, she thought. *Easy. Let go of your intentions.*

The girl gasped. Her brown eyes filled with wonder. She must never have seen a real cat. Haki could feel the creative force within her. Chao-Xing was an artist. Her given name meant "morning star," surely a portent for what goodness she could bring to her surroundings, but society rejected her, not unlike that other *morning star* for whom Haki worked. Chao-Xing had had too much. She needed to destroy the sterility and make room for real life, even if it killed her, too.

Haki sat down just out of reach, and made the velvety texture of her fur irresistibly attractive. Chao-Xing's fingertips twitched, almost coming away from the detonator panel. Haki edged a trifle closer.

You don't want to blow yourself up, she thought, leaning toward the girl. *You want to touch me. You want to fondle me. Let go of the bomb.*

No! Another mind-voice intruded. *Set it off! Rain destruction on those who hurt you!*

The ridge of fur down Haki's back stood on end.

"Who dares challenge me?" she demanded. "This one is mine to save, if I can!"

Ululations of laughter rang across the square, terrifying the humans beyond the lighted barrier into running for their lives.

"*I* challenge you!" the voice announced.

Flames splashed up from the fountain, spreading out across the featureless square, painting it lurid red and yellow. The girl screamed as the fire devoured her. Haki felt her slip away to Heaven. At least she was spared. Her sin had gone uncommitted. Shadows poured up and out from the flames, cackling and screeching. One hovered in the center of the cascade, pointing a bony finger at her.

"Who are you?" Haki asked, peering at it through the dancing inferno. The fire melted the stone fountain and the slate-blue tiles surrounding it.

The sockets of the creature's eyes glowed with an insane red light. They were the only living feature in a ruined face with its bones exposed amid rags of skin. The skeleton beneath it crawled with maggots. The mottled, discolored flesh on which they fed hung off its incorporeal body like Spanish moss in dead trees.

"Don't you know me, Nemesis?" the hysterical voice demanded, one bony hand reaching for her. "You condemned me!"

Tail curled low around her haunches, Haki backed away, but was stopped short by an sharp obstruction. The force shield the humans had projected couldn't hurt her. She glanced back. Leering at her was a lesser imp, one of a ring of minor demons taking shape from the fire. It jabbed its pitchfork at her. How dare it! Haki hissed. The imp retreated among its fellows. They came from the hordes of Belial. She turned to stare at the figure in the ruins of the fountain. Was a major prince of the Underworld angry with her?

No, this creature wielded a prince's power, but she could tell it didn't have the power to control it utterly. Snarling hell-hounds made of black and red flame bucked and wheeled around it, threatening to escape, but held in place by sheer force of will. It harmed itself as thoroughly as it sought to harm her.

"Who are you?"

"You sent me to hell! Me, an innocent man!"

Haki thought hard, trying to place this creature. It took a moment to reclothe the bones with flesh and skin. Yes, she knew him now: a greedy merchant who sold bad food at an extortionate markup to sufferers during the plague that swept most of Europe and Asia. Never, *never* could she forget the cries of desperate souls, especially children, begging for anything to eat, only to have this man scorn them. They offered him what little they had, but he demanded gold. He might as well have demanded a purse full of stars. Many of them died at his feet, their eyes dulling as the spirits fled bodies too weak to contain them. Haki felt every loss as though it was one of her own kittens. No matter how she had stared at him, willing him to show mercy, he had nothing in his heart but greed.

"You were not innocent, Pieter Grune!" she said. "No one would have gone hungry if you had shown kindness! Those people were sick. A little comfort to suffering souls is all that justice demanded. You were fairly condemned, and not just by me."

"They were all dying already!" Grune snarled. "Because of you I have spent centuries in torment!"

"And you've learned nothing!"

He threw back his head and laughed. Scraps of flesh that had once been prosperous double chins swayed against the bones of his throat.

"I have learned this!" he said. He swept both arms upward. The restraints holding the hell-hounds fell away. Baying, they charged toward Haki.

Against her will, she was impressed. In a very short time, Grune had amassed fearsome power, exactly as he had in his mortal life. The lesser fiends gathered around him gibbered with glee as she fled the dogs, kicking her back into their path when she tried to duck between them.

She could not escape the circle of demons. Instead, Haki dodged this way and that, then clambered up and over the horned skull of a laughing cacodaemon. The hounds pursued her, knocking the demon over. They were immortal creatures like herself, but not as intelligent. When she fled between the legs of a green-skinned devil, they followed, toppling him onto others. The hounds let loose their terrifying cries, which had caused many a soul to collapse upon the ground and surrender. They shook Haki's confidence. She shrieked at the circle of devils.

"Help me! You know I am Lucifer's favorite!"

They made faces at her and laughed. A couple slapped their hairy knees as though they were watching a comedy play. She should have known they would enjoy her situation and not lift a clawed finger.

Instead, she chose the tallest and sturdiest of the demons in the ring, a horned se'irim covered with shaggy black hair. The lead hellhound was only steps behind her. She felt the flame of its breath on her back as she gathered herself. Haki leaped. The hound's sharp teeth snapped shut on the last few hairs of her tail. The se'irim scrabbled at her legs, trying to snatch her off the top of his head. She clung to him with all her claws. The dogs circled around the se'irim's feet, jumping up to try and drag her down.

"You cannot escape my vengeance," Grune's red-flame eyes glowed. "I have done more than merely serve. I have worked to earn Belial's trust! I knew one day I would find you and convince you that you were wrong to condemn me!"

"Wrong?" Haki asked, arching her back, offended. "I am *never* wrong...."

"You were!" Grune declared. He brought his fists down, and thunder echoed through the square. "I should have never been sent to Hell!"

Haki felt aghast. *Had* she been wrong? The one trait that had caused her to become Lucifer's chosen rebalancer of justice was that she always weighed the souls with the greatest of care. She weighed not only the evidence of her own eyes, but the knowledge in the minds of those around the would-be sinner. Stupidity was not a cause for eternal or even temporary damnation. Venal, petty, needless cruelty was. Vengeance could be divine. After all, hadn't Lucifer's own master called it His own? But to condemn a soul unfairly?

"I must think!" she said. "How have I misjudged what I saw?"

"My own family counted on me for their support," Grune continued. "You didn't understand! I had mouths to feed, many mouths! I gave charity where it was needed. Lots of charity! You should have sent me to Heaven, where I belong!"

Though it had been centuries, Haki recalled that to be true. His father had died, leaving him the head of the family. Their merchant company owned many ships, operated by large crews. But at the time she had been called to observe him, nearly all of those crews were dead of the plague. That might truly not have been his fault. Samael, the harvester, had taken countless lives. Grune did support their relicts, giving food and beer to hundreds. Her heart softened. He had shown responsibility. Until…

"Why did you stop feeding the employees' families?" she asked.

"I didn't!" Grune said. "They stopped coming to me for food!"

"They were starving," Haki said. "I walked among them, lying in their own filth. You never sent anyone to care for them."

"And expose my own to the plague?" Grune scoffed. "You must be joking! They were dying anyhow. I had no intention of letting myself be exposed to the evil fumes."

Haki felt her own eyes flash with fury. He had so nearly convinced her of her error. She realized that he had never changed from his moral outlook. He remained firm in his conviction that he was right and she was wrong. It had sustained him through a millennium.

"I made no mistake," she said. "You had the means and the power to do good, but you turned your back on the needy and the helpless."

"Wrong! You are wrong!" Grune screamed. "That is enough! You condemned me unfairly! For that, you must die!"

Haki's whiskers twitched in amusement.

"You had better tell your audience to let me go," she said, stretching lazily along the shoulders of the se'irim, who was too frightened of her to move. She pawed his wiry curls with one lazy pad. "I am immortal. Nothing in the power of a lesser fiend, let alone a cursed soul like you can harm me."

Grune's fury erupted in gouts and fountains of flame. He lifted his right hand to show a brilliant stream of white-hot power trailing from it, and flicked it. It cracked with the deafening force of thunder.

"My master's fire can destroy you!"

The hair along Haki's back rose in horror. Somehow, he had obtained the *tormenton*, the killing fire.

Belial's whip had only been unleashed on Earth twice before. Prophecy said that the tormenton would only be used again to flood Earth with fire in the End Times. It could bring an end to her immortal existence.

Haki's heart pounded against her ribs. She must not show fear. She had to face Grune with intelligence, not terror. Life was precious. She loved her chosen task, overseeing the foibles of humanity. She rather liked people, for all their self-centered stupidity, like kittens who had not yet learned how to void without getting it on their feet.

That truth struck her with all the force of the deadly whip. She was not frightened for herself. Death would only release her into the hands of the Most High, but her task as the one to warn the unwary would surely fall to a demon, and that she did fear. If she was not there to stand between humankind and the brink, many more would be damned, and some truly without cause. She had to fight for them as if they were her helpless kittens. Haki had to bring Grune to justice, again.

The cursed soul rode a crest of molten stone toward her, flicking the whip. The imps and fiends leaped to get out of his way. Where one was not fast enough to avoid the fire, it writhed, screaming in agony, then popped like a soap bubble. The hell-hounds abandoned the se'irim to gather around Grune. The rest of the demons crowded behind him, avid, watching. The se'irim backed away, and began to run. His legs, longer than a tree was tall, carried Haki away from them, but he couldn't outpace the pack for long.

Baying, the hounds hurtled after them, coursing through the slagged streets. The hollow between the buildings echoed with their passage. Grune flicked the tormenton, cutting burning gouges in everything that it touched. The se'irim jumped up and began to climb up the side of a building. Beneath where his feet had just passed, the bottom of the building bubbled into lava at the flick of the whip. It began to sink into the molten earth.

No matter what it cost her, she must stop Grune. Haki leaped from the se'irim's shoulders and bounded down to the street. Though she was so tiny, nevertheless her glare brought the whole oncoming horde to a halt. Grune lifted the whip, preparing to wipe her from Earth's face. Haki dodged it, though every new strike singed the edges of her fur.

From the depths of her soul, she called out to every one of her incarnations.

Our task is in jeopardy! To me! I must have all my strength to defeat this threat to our existence! Humanity needs us!

And from every corner of creation, from every age in which humans had ever walked, in whatever shape evolution found them, the cats of Nemesis came. From a primeval saber-toothed tiger, a thousand pounds and sixteen feet long of spotted muscle, to a future incarnation as a minute white fluffball bred down small enough to live in a human's ear and purr, they were all the archetypal Cat of Balance. Haki's pads burned, standing on the ruins of the street, but she glared directly at Grune.

"My judgment was just," she said. "It stands. If you had only taken your punishment, you might almost be free."

"Fools!" Grune howled. He cracked the whip over their heads, moving closer and closer. Haki felt their doom approaching. "I can destroy all of you!"

Sisters? the smilodon thought at the others.

Together or never, said the fluffball.

"Now," said Haki.

The lesser fiends that surrounded Grune could not withstand the righteous indignation of angry cats leaping at their faces to claw or bite out gobbets of flesh. One after another, Haki and her self-sisters dispatched each of them back into the hands of the princes of the Underworld with their pointed tails between their bandy legs. One after another, they fled, shrieking in pain and fear, until she faced only him. Saber-tooth sat on the ground, her tongue flicking from between her curved fangs as she washed her paws.

The pavement under Grune was beginning to buckle from the heat. Haki saw that he had changed the whip to his left hand because the fire had burned the other to a blackened stump. Nothing could stop a man so determined— nothing but her.

"I am responsible for you," she called out. "Stop now and I will speak for you. You can finish out your legitimate time in Hell and learn charity. You were admired once. Return the tormenton to Belial. I think he'll be impressed that you were able to steal it from him. Be satisfied with that!"

Grune's ruined face compressed into a grimace.

"The only satisfaction I will have is dragging you down to Hell!"

Haki yawned, showing her long tongue and all her teeth.

"So be it," she said.

With all the studied nonchalance of her kind, she ambled toward him. When she was mere lengths from him, she stopped and sat down on the ground, regardless of the burning pavement, and washed her shoulder with long, slow licks. Grune went into a frenzy, flailing Belial's fire at her again and again. Fury spoiled his aim. Haki hoped it distracted him just enough.

Now, Saber-tooth thought.

The incarnations leaped at Grune. They had to get the whip away. Saber-tooth bowled him over onto his back. Grune punched her with the coil of fire around his hand. She snarled, biting at his arm before the hell-hounds swarmed in to savage her. Haki and her smaller sisters wrestled with him, trying to get the whip. She wrapped herself around Grune's neck, shoving his head back. A slender bronze cat wearing the necklace of a pharaoh trapped Grune's forearm in her paws.

"I have it!"

But Grune twisted his wrist. The flames engulfed the Bast-cat. Her wails of dire, soul-killing pain faded. Horrified, Haki felt her true-death. Her sorrow would have to wait. The balance was about to be redressed. She felt the ground shift beneath her. One moment. Two moments…

Belial's fire had destroyed so much of the earth under them that the very fabric of reality was weakened. With a mere gesture of will, she, Grune, and all the rest of her incarnations plummeted downward, into the Pit.

They tumbled through the spheres of Hell, passing through bitter cold, parched pale desert, stinking poisonous seas, darkness, burning, drowning, choking, past wailing, tormented souls until they landed with a splat in a pool of lava. Lucifer appeared in a puff of sulfurous smoke, more beautiful than ever in his fury, and put one perfectly-shaped foot on the cursed soul's neck. He snatched the tormenton from Grune's fist, heedless that his fingers came with it.

"Belial!" Lucifer bellowed.

The stocky red devil snapped into existence and dropped to his hairy knees. Lucifer hurled the brand at him.

"I had come to trust this creature over these centuries! And now the paperwork has to be done all over again!"

"I am sorry, Master," Belial said.

"He was very convincing," Haki said, lounging back in the bubbling lava in studied nonchalance, though every part of her body ached from the battle. Her silver-tabby self, who had come from a spaceship nine millennia hence, licked the top of her head. "I was almost fooled. But then, I am not a human or an angel."

Lucifer glared.

"Get back to work! If there's no rest for the weary, there's none for us, either!"

Haki rose slowly and stretched, arching her back in a leisurely manner to show that his scolding did not concern her. She walked out of Hell, followed by all her surviving incarnations.

She took no satisfaction in the suffering of the twice-damned soul behind her, but she was no longer concerned with his fate. She hadn't committed his sins. She had only pointed them out.

Haki's time belonged to kittens who could *learn*.

The Neighbors' Cat
Gregory L. Norris

The green one—an old New Englander with peeling white trim and black storm shutters—was that place in every neighborhood neighbors talked about. During my three-plus years living next door to Mike and Linda Talmadge, their notorious flop house had been the epicenter of several police raids—I'm talking guns drawn type—and, once last autumn, by the bigger arms of law enforcement. One of their tenants, it turned out thanks to a tip from another disgruntled flopper, was cooking meth in an upstairs bedroom.

Life in my quiet, sane little house with its postage stamp-size yard, perfect for lazy lawn mowings without the added threat of stroking out beneath the noonday sun, had been a nightmare since they bought the place as a foreclosure at bottom dollar, and then turned it into an endless revolving door of low-lives and desperates.

Even their cat was a menace.

A scrawny, orange tabby with a big head and obvious rib bones, I woke that sunny Sunday morning to find him plastered on the outside screen of my sun porch door, holding on by his nails. The nervy little terror had already plucked several jagged holes in the mesh, creating future entry points for mosquitoes and mayflies. So much for calm nights at sunset spent on my favorite part of the house. Their cat had ruined that for me, too.

I swore, my rosary a blasphemous counterpoint to the dreamy carillon playing from Saint Luke's on Church Street.

"What's your problem?" the cat asked, his voice male, from the tenor to baritone range.

"My problem?" I huffed, and then swore again, "Is that you people are a monsoon of crazy. You have no respect for your neighbors and the neighborhood. You're loud, nasty, filthy—you don't take care of the place. Hell, even your bedbugs are cleaner and have better manners."

Then, I realized I was talking to their cat.

I narrowed my gaze on the cat's eyes, which were all pupil.

"Did you say something?" I asked aloud, feeling foolish. Foolish? After some of the ludicrousy committed on the other side of my single-car driveway, what did I have to worry about? Even if I'd finally cracked after so many years of living alone, at least I'd kept the crazy confined to my side of the property line.

"Yeah," the cat said, his little mouth moving between pants. "I said, let me in—they're bananas over there!"

He tipped his chin, indicating my neighbors' house, where my neighbors' cat lived.

"Okay, I'm going to lie down now," I said. St. Luke's carillon tinkled and tintinnabulated over the neighborhood, the notes drawing out, dragging downward, as I turned. Some unaffected register in my dazed thoughts heard the sharp *plink plink* as cat nails detached from what had been until that morning perfect door screen, and reattached, tearing fresh holes in the mesh.

"Mister, you gotta help me," the voice continued. "I don't got a lot of options."

"How about Lithium, Thorazine, or catnip," I said on my way into the house.

I had vague understanding of the fan on the dresser turning, its motor struggling, groaning, as it spun air for what I remembered was its ninth summer—not bad for an appliance purchased on the cheap from a big box store that sourced all of its inventory from China. My heart wasn't faring as well. I collapsed onto the bed. The bed was catty-corner between the room's windows. At some untimed point in the cottony-cloud fugue that followed, I heard the cat jump into the window box outside, showing the same lack of care for my royal purple petunias as he had the sun porch door screen.

"*Look*," he said.

I rolled over. An orange beast had flattened the flowers. "No, *you* look."

"Don't you sense it, man? The wrongness emanating from that house of horrors?"

I did, and nodded.

"You seem like a jake guy. Not at all like that twisted idiot and his she-devil common-law boozehound of a wife. Help me, that's all I'm asking."

"I'm not a cat person," I said, my head mashed onto the top pillow.

"You're in luck, because right now I'm as much people as I am cat."

"I'm not really a people person, either."

That removed some of the little monster's moxie. He pretended to sniff around one of the surviving flower trumpets, nipping at the purple velvet petals. "So, you're not a cat person, and you're not a people person. But aren't you at least curious?"

"About?"

"About what's really going on over there, one house away from your fine, happy home. Let me in, mister—I'm dying out here!"

I shook my head. The growing bald patch rubbed unpleasantly against the pillowcase. "No—you've likely got fleas."

"Fleas?" the cat parroted. "Mister, if you don't put a stop to it, *to what they're up to*, fleas'll be the least of your worries!"

∾

I opened a can of tuna and put it in a bowl, juice and all, along with a glug of two-percent in another. The cat wolfed them down, his purrs juicy and rabid. Soon, both bowls were clean.

"Next?" he asked, and licked his lips.

"What do you mean?"

He eyed the bowls.

"That's albacore—the good stuff. *Expensive.*"

"Cry me a river," the cat said. "You try living on bugs and frogs and the occasional field mouse like me, because the rats you were unlucky enough to wind up with don't have an ounce of common decency."

Sighing, I pulled another can of tuna out of the cabinet and cranked it open by hand. The cat's striped tail snapped in anticipation. I lowered the bowl. He helped himself, this time leaving a few flakes for later enjoyment. When finished, he groomed his face with a paw.

"Now?" I asked.

"And now, we nap."

"Nap?"

"Still a cat, buddy. But when we wake up…boy, do I have a story for you!"

∾

We snuggled together on the bed, one lonely man growing older beyond simple seconds and days, and a scrawny tabby with a moth-eaten orange coat. In lieu of words, the cat purred beside me, the cadence soothing, strangely reassuring. As the afternoon drifted forward at an unhurried pace, I forgot that I didn't like cats. Half asleep, I scritched his head. The cat leaned into my touch. At one point, he stretched out contentedly, offering his stuffed belly for me to stroke.

"You got a name?" I asked.

"Gunther," the cat said.

"Really?"

He snorted a sarcastic laugh through his nose, half of it sneezed. "No, but seriously, you people...needing to name everything. Cat. House. Flower. *Ancient evil...*"

My eyes inched wider open. "Come again?"

The cat stood, stretched his spine, and kicked out his legs, one at a time. "That was the most comfortable catnap I've enjoyed since—"

"*Gunther,*" I admonished.

He glared at me through one eye, the other cloaked behind its third lid. "You sure you're ready for this before we've enjoyed another fine, fine meal?"

"I'm not hungry."

"Not even for a morsel, a scrap?"

"Elaborate on what you said about 'ancient evil.'"

The cat's other eye unstuck. It was all pupil again. "Your neighbors are low-lives, it's true. Among the lowest of the low. You could say that disgusting house of theirs is where pets go to die. I tried to get out, but when they leave a door open, and there's rain in the forecast...God, I hate rain!"

"Screw the rain. What kind of ancient evil?"

"You know all those people coming and going, renting floor space in that house?"

I rolled my eyes. "I'm aware."

"One of them came, went—though not in the manner you'd think. *Expired* right there in the middle of that dark tabernacle they refer to as a living room. Oh yeah, while you're in here having your chamomile tea and scones, dreaming your dreamy little dreams, Lord and Lady Talmadge are murdering him because of this book he has, a book of dark magic older than the U-S-of-A. Then, they're out back digging a shallow grave by the light of the moon, and dumping the corpse of that dead slob in it."

I listened, forgetting to breathe until the last bottled sip of air began to boil in my lungs. Forgot blinking, too—I imagined my eyes were all pupil as well, like the cat's. "They buried his body in their backyard?"

Gunther fixed me with a look. "Oh, it gets better, friend. And it gets worse. Much worse. You see, while they were forgetting to feed me and I was out foraging for Kobe rat and salamander tartare, I seen it."

"It?"

"The body. Only it wasn't dead no more. Dug its way out of the dirt and dragged itself back in there."

"Maybe he wasn't really dead," I said. "Just stunned."

Gunther scratched at his jowls with a hind foot. Fleas—I knew it!

"Oh, he was dead, chum. Still is. You see, everyone's favorite neighbors, Ole Mikey and that pillar of virtue Linda, they opened that book and brought the stiff back from the dead using one of the spells inside. Consider necromancy just another of their nastier habits, like smoking crack and getting hammered by nine in the morning. They're not very good at this stuff, mind you. And you know that old chestnut, the one about a little knowledge being dangerous? Blah, blah, blah, in the wrong hands, with idiots? That's them. That's what you're up against. A couple of loony dirt bags, who are likely, even as we speak, tampering with dark forces best left alone."

∼

I closed the bathroom door and sat. Gunther scratched at the outside. When that failed to grant him entrance, he passed several clawed front toes under the frame, making grabs at air.

"Come on, let me in," he begged.

"Why? Why do cats always want to follow you into the john?"

"That's just how we roll, kemosabe. Would you prefer to have this conversation in this seedy fashion, or can we do it face to face?"

Sighing, I flushed, dragged up my pants, and opened the door. Gunther streaked in. When I exited, he followed.

"So, do you believe me?"

"About the evil goings-on next door?"

"Yeah, yeah," the cat said.

I poured a cold one—tap water. I might have opted for something stronger, but I wasn't like my neighbors, to whom it was always beer o'clock. "I do," I said. "That we're having this little chat at all proves just how frigged life has become as a result of living next door to them."

He told me about the spell that had given him the power of human speech, which had left one of the undesirables in the green house, a man named Kenneth, yowling like a cat in heat.

"Another of their botched experiments. I think I was supposed to be sacrificed."

I caught the note of sadness in Gunther's voice and felt sorry for him. Reaching down, I stroked the cat's spine. Gunther chirped and arched his back into my palm.

"I really hate those people," I said.

Gunther purred.

"Now, about this dead man?"

"The sun's almost down," the cat said. "Come on, I'll show you."

~

Creeping around other people's houses and peering in through windows was more *their* style. I was raised by strict parents who taught me to respect rules and boundaries. It didn't matter that it was Mike and Linda, or that I was seeking proof of the danger those two dirt bags were putting themselves and others in through their tampering with sinister cosmic powers. It felt wrong—and worthy of near-future Hail Marys.

"Over there, that one," Gunther whispered.

He brushed against my leg and indicated a window over which a football throw had been haphazardly tossed. Light oozed through the length of fringe dangling just above the sill. Aware that my heart was doing its best to jump out of my ribcage, I peered in. A bird shrieked a piercing note from one of the nearby trees. I jumped. Gunther smacked his chops.

Exhaling through my nostrils, I looked again. The wedge of visible window revealed a scene that should have appeared normal in any other house, under most circumstances. Only a talking cat was urging me to break the law, and the longer I stared, the more wrong that glimpse became.

A recliner, beige. A man seated in that recliner, his eyes aimed ahead at the television. The TV was on low—and tuned to one of those worthless reality shows populated by spoiled rich families and manufactured drama.

The walls of the room had been mostly stripped down to the studs, with chunks of drywall hanging at angles from the paper skin. As I stared, afraid to blink, a thought crossed my mind—that the scores dug across the surviving pieces looked like nail marks. Like—

He tried to claw his way out of that room, I thought, turning my focus down, to the man's hands, folded upon his lap. Right as my consciousness took note of the sickly color of the man's arms—jaundiced yellow on top, purplish-blue on the undersides—I saw that his fingertips were damp and crimson, and missing several nails. The man's clothes were filthy with dried dirt.

"That brain-dead show's the only thing that'll keep him calm," Gunther whispered.

"Huh?" I asked, shooting a glance down at my partner in crime.

"That mindless garbage on the idiot box—the living dead eat it up, apparently."

I returned to the window to see two rheumy, angry eyes now staring through the gap, aimed directly at me. A foul, cadaverous smell invaded my lungs as I sucked down a breath, readying to scream, only my body forgot how. I turned. Another figure stood between the neighbor's house and my driveway, which seemed a mile away in the darkness. Farther. Light-years.

"What the hell are you doing?" a woman's voice demanded.

Linda. Her long, dark hair and pinched face materialized fully, pulling free of the shadows. Instead of a scream, I produced a maniac's laugh.

"Funny thing," I said. I then offered what seemed the cleverest of explanations, improvised right on the spot. "I'm returning your cat."

Then pain exploded across the back of my skull, and the darkness turned red around me. Through the exquisite glare, as the strength departed my legs and I dropped to the weedy, untended lawn, I saw Mike had snuck up behind me, a length of lumber held in his grip like a Louisville Slugger.

~

I surfaced from the sea of blood and shadows, aware of the welt rising on the back of my head, and of the dank smell lingering in my nostrils. Not my close brush with a dead man this time, I realized I'd woken face down on a patch of dirt cellar floor. Theirs, I assumed. Resisting the urge to moan, even though the scream that had blossomed in my guts outside was now a ball of thunder ready to claw its way up my throat, I surveyed my surroundings. Their cellar, oh yeah—a length of rickety countertop made from an old door set across two saw horses was littered with empty longnecks and drug-making equipment. At least, I deduced as much, given that there was an open flame and noxious chemical fumes rising from what looked like your average, ordinary kitchen crock-pot.

"You made it crooked," Linda carped.

"Where?" Mike asked.

"That angle—it's supposed to be straight."

"Does it matter?"

She tisked. I tipped my eye up to see them in the process of digging a crude pentagram into the dirt floor around me. Linda sipped from a fresh bottle and directed traffic. Mike clutched at an ancient tome—the book of spells they'd already murdered once over—and stabbed at dirt with a garden trowel. Both wore black ceremonial raiments. I blinked, and realized their attire were terrycloth bathrobes, belted at waists.

I attempted to move, only to discover my arms were bound.

"He's awake," said Mike.

"So?" Linda countered. She knocked back the last of her beer and belched.

"Classy," I said while also doing my best to ignore the miserable pulse radiating outward from what I assumed to be quite the swollen egg on my skull. "But then again, you two always are a couple of beauts."

"Shut up, *meat*," Linda said.

"Yeah, ask anyone in the neighborhood," I continued, not heeding her initial warning. "We all love you guys. Can't thank you enough for moving in and driving up property values with your fancy renovation work—and voodoo."

"Hey, this isn't *voodoo*," Mike corrected. "And we're sorry!"

"You look it."

"We're sorry, but what do you expect us to do? If you had an unwanted ghoul camped out in your living room, you'd do whatever it takes, too, to get rid of him. Even make a blood sacrifice to the *King of the Underground Tide* in order to evict him, dammit!"

I absorbed the idiot's words. "King of the Underground Tide?"

Mike straightened and opened the tome. A few flips, and he aimed the horrific image of an amphibian face from an old woodblock illustration down at me. "The spell is very specific—if it's not done with the blood of the innocent, instead of taking the dead away to the underground realm with him, the King's rage could spill over across the surface world. You understand, right neighbor?"

I peered above the hideous picture to the equally repugnant face inside the bathrobe's cowl, as clueless of his guilt as the danger they flirted with. And then, I shouted one of those words my parents had forbidden me to utter during my youth to the threat of a mouth washed out with soap.

"That's straight enough, boo," Linda said, and tossed her empty beer bottle. She then faced me. "Sorry to say it, but your house is about to go on the market, meat."

Outside the pentagram, Mike began to recite from the book: "*Ungh! Ungh! Inzwichen und under das Bluet…*"

I struggled against my bindings. "You sound like you're hacking up a hairball, you moron!"

"I said, shut up!" Linda spat.

She risked a kick past the spokes of the five-sided star and nailed me in the kidney. Now, two places on my body stung.

Mike sighed. "We have to start over—you contaminated the crux."

"Fine, but before you resume, gag him so we don't have to listen to his yapping."

Mike searched among the makeshift counter's drug laboratory. I was about to scream for help—not that anyone would hear me—when a scratch sounded on the other side of what I assumed was the cellar door. Furtive at first, it quickly grew more insistent.

"It's that damn cat," Mike said.

Linda answered, "The *cat*-cat, or, you know…*Kenneth*?"

"How do I know?"

The scratching became a banging.

"I'll kill whichever one of them it is," said Mike. He tromped up the cellar stairs and banged open the door. "What, dammit?"

A ribbon of orange color darted between his legs and down the stairs.

"Stupid cat," Mike said.

"Forget about him," said Linda. "Let's do this. My TV show comes on at nine."

Mike plodded back down the stairs, the book again opened. He coughed, clearing his throat. "Keep that mangy little puke out of the crux."

Linda spat at the cat. Gunther, meandering past the pentagram, tensed. Ears back and eyes wide, he moved sideways away from the pentagram, me, and his two dirt bag owners.

"What? You got nothing to say tonight?" Mike said to the cat. "'Cause you sure were chatty earlier."

Gunther receded. Mike and Linda turned to face me. From the cut of my eye, I saw the cat spring onto the counter and nose around whatever illegal substances were cooking there.

"*Ungh! Ungh!*" Mike bellowed.

Gunther nudged. Something tumbled across the table, catching fire before spilling to the ground. Sparks erupted. Little fiery pinwheels crackled, one catching Linda's cheek as she turned toward the building conflagration.

"Son of a—!" she exclaimed, cut off in mid-speech by another projectile cutting close to her face.

"That mangy cat!" Mike added.

He scrambled after Gunther, who raced through his clutching hand. As their attention turned to the fire, Gunther's weight landed on my back.

"I'll get you out of these, friend," Gunther said.

Nails and teeth dug at my bound wrists. Nails and teeth also jabbed through my flesh.

"I think I'm good," I said, and maneuvered to my knees, coaxing the cat off my spine.

On my feet, the world spun. Ignoring the dizziness, I hastened to the staircase, taking the steps unsteadily.

"The meat's escaping!" Linda howled.

I was at the top of the stairs when the explosion at my back propelled me through the cellar door.

∼

The floor was on fire. Part of the ceiling, too.

"Wake up! Wake up!" Gunther yowled.

I reached for my face. My wrists were free. Either the shockwave had twisted the bindings loose or Gunther had done more to release me than I'd thought. Of course, it was also possible that Mike, the idiot, had done a lousy job at tying my wrists.

I got up, dazed and bleeding, sputtering on the growing smoke, unsure of where I was or which direction to take.

"This way," the cat said.

I followed him down a dark and hazy hallway, only to stop when he did.

"Well, look at that," said Gunther.

I looked up to see a shadowy figure blocking our escape. It was the dead man.

"*Neighbors*," I said.

From somewhere else in the smoke-choked landscape, a human voice began to meow—*Kenneth,* I thought. The dead man raised his bloodied hands at me and lunged. Aiming my head low, I rushed the animated corpse and drove my noggin into its gut. Dead weight collapsed. Gunther and I pounded over the cadaver, and to the house's rear door.

I pulled chain, flipped deadbolt, and unlocked lock. Then, Gunther and I were running into fresh air, away from the green house and toward home.

At my driveway, I turned back. The flames engulfed the ground floor and were spreading quickly to the upper level. The same window covered in football throw blew out. As fire and oily smoke billowed through the gap, for a terrible second the explosion took on a familiar image, that of an amphibious face, there one instant, gone the next.

∾

They pulled four sets of charred human remains from the wreckage. The house burned completely in what was assumed the result of a meth lab fire. A tragedy, my neighbors agreed. And a relief.

∾

"So," said Gunther, waiting beside the empty food bowl.

"So?" I parroted.

"Can we make this official? You and me? Because I think you've earned the right to have yourself a great forever cat, pal."

Smiling for what felt the first time in years, I pulled a can of albacore tuna from the cabinet. "I agree. We make a great team."

Grimmun
Oliver Smith

It was an unseasonably mild Wednesday when the Grimmun came marching in again.

The Grimmun came marching in. He jumped off the forty-eight bus surrounded by a fug of evil with his long grey coat flapping in the back draft. He stirred up a cloud of dust and malice with his big hobnail-hammered boots and marched down fuming like a stove pipe past the gnarled crouch of the Raven Tree.

An old crow watched with thousand year old beads from a gnarled hole in the Raven Tree's crouch. A bad old crow in a grey hood with moth-chewed wings and a worm-holed beak, a black-souled crow that shadowed and scavenged on the little green hill called Seven Kings Sleeping.

Grimmun tumbled down the hill and somersaulted over Mr. Lucitus's machine in an awful hurry. Sweet-Caraway Hisop saw him park the Grimlaw Stone in the corn-stalk stubbled Longfield. He stood back to look at his work, gave a grim nod and descended into the valley of Whipple's Po like a bad-luck mucked-up winter fog.

Under the broad brim of his wrinkled whale-skin hat a shadow mask lay over his eyes.

Or where his eyes should be.

All Caraway could see was the gristled grim old mouth. Grimmun came marching in after a thousand years or so of absence. His lip pealed at the edge from the cold bite of the north-frost. He dog-snarled it up over his canines, showed a mouth full of gold teeth.

Biters, nippers and grinders.

He came striding down that rough, ice-glittered gutter-path in the low November sun. At a terrible hasty pace down the old stream-track.

Grimmun came down among the remains. The devastation. Dada Hisop's timber harvest. As Grimmun came down he paid no heed to the small creatures beneath his feet. They popped splat splat splat under his iron-shod feet.

They burst, ruptured, exploded.

He looked around at the fallen tree trunks, purposefully wiping the invertebrate yolk from his feet in the late afternoon glow.

He looked unhappy.

Caraway didn't care. She had cakes from Mrs. Waldice. She sat on her log outside of the Bungalow eating her cake and Ratter, the cat, ignored her. Ratter was more interested in the hooded crow that had flown down from the Raven Tree and strutted up and down the roof cackling and mocking him.

Grimmun said, "The grove, the trees, my sacred trees."

He put a big wind-up book before Caraway and said, "Tell me child, tell me in the name of the Grimlaw what marauders ravaged the land."

"The Tacks-man came to see Dada. If Dada don't pay him, the Tacks-man will knock tacks into his face and nails in his knees. Then if he still don't pay his due, the Tacks-man will hammer a tin spike into his tummy. Dada has gone sell the timber for the Tacks-man's tribute."

Grimmun nodded and tapped on the windup book, "Book of the Grimlaw; Law Grimgods gave to men. Grimlaw is as you must, you must offer hospitality and I must accept."

He opened the book and pointed to a line-word clockworked into the pages. "Stranger, that's me, you must offer the Stranger your hospitality." He tapped the page. "I must accept. Well, ain't you going to offer?"

"Yes. Please, Mr. Grimmun, accept my offer of hospitality."

"I do," he said, and his mouth turned even downer.

"…in the name of the Grimlaw."

His face quivered in the shadow and the grim mouth said, "I shall heal this."

He didn't look like the sort to heal anything. Not with the Grimblades glittering under his coat.

The Grimmun unlatched a word-spring and set it pulsating so it keened and sang in the paper page so loud that Ratter legged it into the boiler shed to hide, then decided the boiler shed wasn't safe enough, and legged it off towards the cliffs and terraces of the Oolites.

In the lee of the limestone cliff, a cloud formed a small thunderstorm that rained right over from the Seven Kings Sleeping down to the clearance. The storm spread to the hollow Raven Tree where the lightening sang in the crooked branches. The stony old crow flew back to his home and his throat heaved with the thunder song.

Weed upon weed grew from the stone and soil: little green shoots coiled aside the rocks. Sturdy saplings curled out, thickened, and became sun-lead spirals following the precession of years. Twisting green branches ran through unremembered decades in minutes. They unfurled fresh green leaves. Where the trees had been felled there grew a new stand of pure prime springtime oak woods.

Grimmun picked a flea off the crow's feathers and said, "Now, they'll be a price to pay, the magic don't come for free. I never got it for free and I don't do it for free. Under the Grimlaw you will be under an obligation. I demand a gift in return. Why, for nine full nights…"

"My Dada ain't going to be chuffed with that," Caraway said.

"What do you mean? What do you mean?" His mouth turned down into two hard creases.

He looked grimmer, upset even. Under the grey beard heathering his granite chin, his peeled lips quivered like limpid snail flesh.

"Well, he was getting a nice price for them. Cash down, my Dada would have paid off the tithes. Kept the Tacks-man away. Dada really ain't going to be happy with tacks being hammered in his face."

"What gift could make amends?"

"Don't think nothing will. He'll be gutted."

~

On the second day, Caraway saw Lucke setting a mole-trap in the short field and told him she'd seen Grimmun.

"So he's back is he?"

"Guess so."

"What we need is the mortal enemy unsubjected to the Grimlaw."

"I thought everyone had to obey the law."

"There are laws and laws. Now Grimmun, he's the Old Law; the Grimlaw, the law of obligations of gods and kings and victims, each pint of blood measured against gold and gold priced by the slaughter of the souls that held the gold. Before the Grimlaw there was the Wildlaw, the law of tooth and claw. That's the Wulfer's law. We need the Wulfer, the dog of the Wildlaw, as deep and wicked as Dead Man's Cran. He has jaws of frost and winterwind. He'll stare Grimmun down with his ice blue eyes of freezing screaming squealing pain. His coat is glacier ice, his teeth sharp as icicles. One look of him will pour the fear of death into Grimmun's cup. Fill him up so he overfloweth with the terrors. We'll just whistle him up and send misery-guts packing."

Caraway didn't like the sound of Wulfer.

"Are you sure the medicine ain't worse than the ill?" she asked, "Are you sure the cure ain't badder?"

"Well of course there's always recourse to the Greylaw made by men learned in dusty books and precedents and woven from hairs that are split into quarters, hundredths and thousandths; and costed by each splitting, then charged and invoiced in guineas per hour. Have you got any money for the Greylaw? Neither have I. I don't see much choice."

"How do you get him then?"

"I don't know—I'll look in Ezzy's book."

~

On the third day, Caraway was disturbed by shouting coming over the valley. She could see tall Tom Vander stood toe to toe with the Grimmun below the Grimstone. There were all the folk of Whipple's Po watching; looking grim. Even Mr. Lucke, among them, arm in arm with Miss Ezz. Tom Vander shook his head.

Grimmun was nodding at him.

"You owe me, you took the gift and so you owes me."

"We didn't take any gift," said Mrs. Waldice. "And we don't want any."

"She's right," said Tom Vander. "No one's took a gift, now get."

"Not likely, sonny," said Grimmun. "It took me too long to get back to be leaving so soon. You tell 'em, son, all your tribe. I must have sacrifices. It's the Grimlaw. I must have blood sacrifice; an eye for a tooth and the truth for an eye, bring a strong man for Grimmun's tribute. Get captives; bring a ploughman, a priest, a warrior, a strong one from over the hill. How about a king? A Christian one that'll take a long...

...time...

...dying."

Mr. Lucitus stepped out. "Supposing there were strong young people in the valley, supposing there were any Christians left and we were willing to sacrifice them to someone. Why would we sacrifice them to you?"

The Grimmun grimmed his mouth up tight and started winding the big rusty key in the back of the book.

"For nine full nights I swung in the windy tree, wounded by the spear..."

The gears and escapement clicked and ticked.

"...consecrated to myself..."

A mainspring creaked and wheezed.

"...on the tree whose roots have no name..."

The book rattled an evil old rhythm and a stain-all ran down his face and dripping down over the dusty trench coat.

"...that's why."

The book sang and the words raced round and round like a runaway rat. His fingers carved great bloody drops in the darkness and night fell all around him.

Mr. Lucitus said, "Now, I know I'm a bit slow, but that don't sound like a reason. Call me dim, but it don't sound like anything."

"Well," said Grimmun, "you need a teaching Mr. Lucitus. Look into my eye."

We all looked, but there were no eyes.

Just the darkness. We were all alone with the book in the clockwork-grinding darkness. It promised us things. Not nice things though. Terrible things. It creaked and rumbled in its gears. "You're mine," it said. "You will give me slittings and hookings and hangings and skinnings. You owe me, for nine full nights I hung on the windy tree..."

"You've only been here two nights, Mr. Grimmun," Caraway said.

Caraway saw the flash of gold biters, nippers, and grinders grimace—the darkness evaporated.

"So far," he said, and headed off into the woods. "So far," he shouted back over his shoulder.

"If he wants a sacrifice, why don't we give him the Tacks-man? Two with one stone," Caraway said.

Tom seemed to like the idea of giving up the Tacks-man to Grimmun, but then answered, "Sacrificing the ones you don't like, is all very well, but that ain't no real sacrifice. Grimmun'll know he's done you a favor, and then, you'll owe him more. We've got a week, and if we haven't got him out by then…"

~

Caraway saw Lucke looking at the old mould mound of Seven Kings Sleeping. She saw Lucke digging down.

She made her way over and asked, "What you digging for Mr. Lucke?"

"For the Wulfer," he pointed at the barrow. "Bones," said Lucke, "the smell of the old bones'll get him back."

It was only a small hole: Caraway could see a few worms and some pale roots coiled among rocks.

"Can you crawl inside?" he said. "See if you can get a bone out?"

There was room for a little 'un. Caraway landed in the dust and darkness; she could feel the soil all dry and sandy between her fingers. It was cozy and warm away from the winter down in the tump. She groped her way into a passageway. Caraway gave Ratter a soft kick to move him on faster. She must have walked a mile in the dark. It was getting hot, and a blue glow showed up ahead so she could make out some coils and curves carved into the rocks around her.

She came out in a big stone room where men with long dark hair slept around a big stone table. They were wrapped in grey cobwebbed coats snoring and dreaming. There were stars shining off their foreheads and there was food set in front of them. An old man sat among the food wearing a long grey wig coiled about his body; wearing nothing but his wig-tails. He was weaving cobwebs—finely spun and twisted and knotted from the thinnest fibres. They stuck to every surface binding and entwining and coating the kings.

"Are you looking for me? Did Mistress Whipple send you?" he asked.

"Mr. Lucke sent me down for a bone."

"Bone? I could let you have one for a fee, I suppose."

Mr. Whipple picked up a lump of yellow cheese and took a big bite. He broke off a crumb and offered it to a spider than scurried out from his wig.

"Tasty m'lud?"

The spider just bounced up and down on its eight legs, grabbed the piece of cheese and scurried back.

"Are you coming back with me, Mr. Whipple? I'm sure I'll need help getting out," said Caraway.

"I stay here to keep the Kings in check, to bind them under the webs of the Greylaw to keep the Dreamlaw at bay."

"What's the Dreamlaw, Mr. Whipple?"

"Shh, it's a secret, you'll wake them," he answered.

One of the seven around the table muttered, "I am an eagle swooping low over endless grassland."

A second said, "I fly a white owl in the eternal darkness."

A third said, "I am a swan on a lake of stars."

The others were a magpie in a tower, a skylark falling in the void, a sacred ibis, and a gull over the green sea.

Master Whipple said, "Just hold this thread for me."

The cobweb was composed of thin grey text of surprising density and stickyness. Caraway started to read: "under the precedent of the judgement of Justice Polisher in the case of Scraggins vs. Copral, in the second role of judgement Justice Polisher amended the legal basis of reason and weighting in the uberdivision of the third demesne of the hypothicated nomenclature of the tenacity thus..."

She felt her eyelids sag, sapped of life, they rolled limp and flaccid over her eyes.

She dreamed that she flew a moth in the night.

There was a howl. Ratter was at Master Whipple. Caraway's eyelids unstuck themselves and she found herself bound in the grey webs he wove from the split hairs. She tore the adhesive bindings from her arms and legged it back, calling for Lucke.

There was a terrible screaming behind her.

Caraway could see the green eyes of Ratter following. She could see a pinlight of day up ahead. As she scrambled up, the earth ran down and the daylight at the top shimmered in the dust. She caught a stick, but it was smoother than a stick and heavier than a stick. She shouted for Lucke and held the stick tight. A rope came down, and she held on as he hauled her up.

"Well done," he said. "A bone."

Lucke said, "You take that bone to the Elderwoods and see if you can tempt Wulfer back."

~

On the Fourth Day, Caraway wandered: calling and whistling for the Wulfer. She was doing it quiet in case he actually came. Caraway looked in the Elderwoods where the trees were frozen to the pith. Caraway looked on the grey clouded heights. Caraway called beneath dark-bellied snow clouds. She called on that high stone table and sniffed the frosty air for the spoor of the Wulfer.

There was no hint of him.

Ratter hid behind a shrivelled clump of mushrooms. His green eyes shone as he laid himself pancake-flat on the ground. There was something in the undergrowth.

A bright tailed Mudpecker broke cover, but too late for Ratter. He launched himself and flew silent though the air.

The long claws tore and small sharp teeth razored through the birdflesh like Grimblades through a sacrifice. He sucked it down whole.

On the way home, Caraway saw Mr. Lucitus and Tom Vander. They were there looking in a book.

"Just how many victims does it say he has to have?" asked Mr. Lucitus.

"All of them," said Tom Vander, "all of them."

~

On the fifth day, to her relief. Caraway still had no luck finding the Wulfer.

The smell of apple strudel drew her out as it came up through valley. She let her nose lead her. and she passed the old scarecrow which stood on the Spatt. It wasn't a good scarecrow. An unscared crow sat on its hat. It poked its worm eaten beak from beneath a wing and called at her.

Ratter eyed the crow with a mean green eye and yowled up at it.

The crow flew up showering with pine needles. It came to rest on a dead bare spruce branch and cackled at Ratter.

When they got home, Ratter climbed onto the boiler shed roof and practiced jumping down. Caraway ate her strudel.

∾

On the sixth day, Ratter had graduated to jumping from the windows of Mr. Lucitus's tower.

Caraway saw Ezzy on the old mound pouring milk onto the turf. "Why you spilling milk. Miss Ezz?" she said.

"There's seven kings waiting for fresh milk. Seven kings sleeping beneath the little green hill all waiting for me."

Caraway felt a bit guilty knowing they were a bone less than seven.

∾

On the seventh day, Caraway climbed up the cliffs, and Ratter followed. In the deep woods, there were skeleton escapements dancing and grinding teeth of bright brass and shivering their bones of laceworked metal. She didn't like them, so she went home. Caraway came back down the stone-face when Ratter fell past her. Ratter dropped silent and slow-motioned from the rocks, his legs coiled like spring-traps around a rock-pigeon in flight and the two of them fell in a cascade of feathers.

Ratter picked himself up and licked the gizzards and gore from his lips and slipped off among the shiny leaves of an ornamental laurel.

∾

Wednesday next, the Raven Tree was grey against the snow that had fallen in the night, and the old crow sat in its branches shivering and quivering.

Ratter caught a rat in the yard and dragged it off towards the boiler shed for breakfast.

On Seven Kings Sleeping, Caraway saw Ezzy with her jug. She poured milk onto the ground again. She looked up a bit sharp over the gold rimmed glasses.

Caraway's bag gave a shake.

"Someone wants a word with you."

"Who?"

"He says you have his upper leg."

The ground began to quiver and eight white shoots started to wriggle up through the snow. The shoots became fingers that tore back the frozen turf. A rather yellow skull looked out from the grass covered in abundant snails of the genus Cepaea having a good ooze, and a sharaliggo slipped from a socket. A white owl settled out of the air and perched on the skull. A cross looking owl eyeing Caraway with a look of evil yellow fire.

"Oh."

"What you doing with my leg?"

"We needed it to get the Wulfer back."

"Not keen on dogs. Dogs gnaw on bone. Destructive. Give it back."

"We need it to get rid of the Grimmun."

"Why d'you want rid? What's he done?"

"He wants a sacrifice."

"Nothing wrong with a nice sacrifice, nice drink of sacrifice from the cows keeps your teeth strong."

"Full of calcium," said another king popping his yellow skull out, showing a full set of white teeth, a swan alighting beside him.

"I don't think he has teeth, not his own grown ones."

"Better give him some milk."

"He don't want milk, he wants people," Caraway said.

"Ain't no way to behave, we never sacrificed people."

"Not much."

"Not unless they did us wrong," said the King with the owl, which pointedly eyed Caraway and scratched at the frosty ground with a scimitar talon.

She tossed the leg-bone back. A thin arm dressed in grave rags reached out to catch it in its finger-bones and sank back into the ground.

The birds snorted, hissed and piped according to their species and rose up into the white air. All hope of the Wulfer's return gone with them. It was a relief.

Caraway ran through the fierce frost that gripped the valley. She nearly ran into the Grimmun walking down the Burdhaze road, a tall old scarecrow in a big battered old hat, his turnip face hidden in the shadow. He brought out a big timepiece from his pocket and tapped it.

"Grim-clock says times getting on Grim-crow: we'll feed you soon."

He paid Caraway no mind but the dark bird floated and swooped and rasped in a dry voice and tried to spear her with its worm gnawed beak. Caraway took shelter in the metal cabin of Mr. Lucitus's machine.

~

On the Thursday with the ninth full night bearing in, we all assembled in the new grown grove. He'd hung the branches with sharp steel hooks, and the Grimstone towered high in the field making a black shadow in the wintery sky.

He stood there sharpening the Grimblades.

"Where's the victims?" he said, looking grim.

He looked down at Caraway with his shadow face. There could have been empty skull sockets concealed in that umbral shadow. There could have been nothing at all hidden in the deep shade.

His mouth bittered up as if he had a bite of a crab-apple.

"I have swung in the windy tree, and under the Grimlaw you will owe me the victims, tomorrow. My soul has suffered; those grim cold nights alone in the windy tree. How could you leave me swinging there all alone? You are cruel and bad and you all owe me. You all owe me so much. Everything."

The old crow on his hat swayed and cawed in approval.

Six-foot-eight-in-his-socks, Tom Vander stepped forwards. He held a machine saw in his hand.

He looked up straight into the Grimmun's eye-area. "I defy you Grimmun, I defy you with the honest steel of a good honest chainsaw."

"You'll owe me if you lose," said the Grimmun.

"Your magic cannot triumph over an honest man."

"You're not a virgin are you?" said the Grimmun.

"I am indeed pure of heart, body, and mind," said Tom Vander. "And you cannot triumph over an honest man who is pure of heart, body and mind armed with the honest steel of a good honest chainsaw."

"'Course I can, I was just curious," said Grimmun, popping a snail and throwing it to the bad old crow. "What shall it be Tom Vander? The hooking? The hanging? The slitting? The skinning?" said a grim mouthful of shiny metal teeth.

Mrs. Waldice said, "I think you should run now, Tom."

"Wait," said Ezzy stepping forward. Ezzy had a wind-up book of her own, and she turned the little gold key.

"Do you dream at all, Mr. Grimmun?"

The Grimmun's mouth grimmed up as if he was sucking a bitter-berry.

"For nine full nights…" he began.

The book tinkled and trilled, and Ezz sang: its pages fluttered like moth wings and shadowy figures danced round and round the grove in clockwork steps. They shimmered like a mirage. Dream people marching in circles. Each drew a shimmering Dreamblade of gold and spread Dreamdust over everything. They flew in dreaming silence sort of very slow, but also very swift across the grove, spreading great rings of violet Dreamfire.

Grimmun placed his own book carefully on the ground.

The Book of the Grimlaw opened wide its pages so Caraway could see the precision meshed gears and pinions whirring together in the calligraphy.

There was a sucking noise. A wind ruffled Caraway's hair, then a gust untidied it, then a blast blew them all off their feet. The Dreambook was sucked out of Ezzy's fingers and down into the dark jaws of the Grimlaw. Its cover snapped shut and it whirred a while then ejected a pile of shredded paper.

The crow sat in a branch and cackled. It raised its moth-chewed wings and its black beads sparkled.

The Grimmun reached down and retrieved the Book of the Grimlaw.

"What shall it be Ezzy? What shall it be, victim number two? The hooking? The hanging? The slitting? The skinning?" said a grim mouthful of biters, nippers, and grinders. The crow settled back on the hat and cackled down at Ezzy. It opened wide its beak and poured out a torrent of laughter. It teetered on the brim of the hat and hooted. It fell flat on its back helpless with wicked glee.

It was the chance Ratter had waited for. He dropped silently from the top of the tree. He landed hard on the crow with his back snaking and his tail chasing around the battered old hat; his eyes shone with green hunger. The crow in the grey hood struggled to right itself, tried to squawk, but Ratter was too quick and black feathers fell as he caught its throat with his full set: with biters, nippers, and slicers. The crow in the grey hood's song was silenced by the rat-trap grip of the teeth. It fluttered and fought and the two of them tumbled off the Grimmun's head onto the Book of the Grimlaw knocking it out of the Grimmun's hands.

"Oh dear, the poor crow," said Miss Ezz, who was soft-hearted in these matters. "But I suppose its nature's way," she added, being of a pragmatic turn of mind.

Grimmun's face had seized up.

Ratter sucked and licked bits of dead crow from the Book of the Grimlaw which did not sound well. It rattled, there was an awful grinding and the snap and squeal of collapsing clockwork, the tearing of paper, the sighs and shrieks and curses of dying words.

Grimmun backed away from Sweet-Caraway Hisop. His mouth turning down so deep she thought his jaw was going to snap. "You broke it...

...You...

... broke...

...the Grimlaw."

Lucke nodded and brought a muddy boot hard down on the Grimmun's book. Caraway felt a pain in her head, but not the noise as hidden gears wound down, stopping the thin winter sun in its tracks.

The Grimmun ascended the valley like a bad-luck mucked-up winter fog. Holding down the broad brim of his wrinkled whale skin hat so the shadow mask remained over his eyes.

Or where his eyes should be.

Grimmun tumbled up the hill and somersaulted backwards over Mr. Lucitus's machine in an awful hurry. Caraway saw him pull out the Grimlaw Stone like a rotten tooth and carry it across the corn-stalk stubbled Longfield, and then he marched up past the gnarled crouch of the Raven Tree fuming like a stove pipe. A pair of green cat eyes watched from deep in the hole in the Raven's crouch.

Grimmun jumped backwards onto the forty-eight bus and left the valley of Whipple's Po for good.

They hoped.

About the Contributors

When she was in third grade, her teacher told her to "write what you know," so from that point onward **K. I. Borrowman** set out to experience as much as possible. She has lived on five of the planet's seven continents, earned two bachelor's degrees, and hand-reared a human child. She has owned twenty-one different vehicles and lived in thirty-four different homes. She has climbed many mountains, dived many seas, and carried many back packs. Borrowman is currently living in Dubai with her husband, who wants to believe in aliens, and two Qatari cats. She hopes to know more, and continue to write it.

Jeremy M. Gottwig wakes at 4:30am each morning to write speculative fiction. As a result, he is addicted to caffeine. He currently works for the University of Maryland libraries and lives in Baltimore, MD with his wife and young son. Find him online at StrangeShuttle.com or at twitter.com/jgottwig.

Elektra Hammond emulates her multi-sided idol Buckaroo Banzai by going in several directions at once. She's been involved in the copyediting and proofreading end of publishing since the 1990s for presses small and large and nowadays concocts anthologies, writes the occasional short story, and is a freelance editor and movie reviewer.

She lives in Delaware with her husband, Mike, and the cat herd of BlueBlaze/Benegesserit catteries. When not freelancing or appearing at science fiction conventions she travels the world judging cat shows.

Find Elektra on Facebook (Elektra Hammond), Twitter (elektraUM), LiveJournal (elektra_h), g+ (Elektra Hammond), and building her website at http://www.untilmidnight.com.

Joanna Michal Hoyt lives with her family (and without any cats) on a farm in upstate NY where she spends her days tending gardens, goats and guests and her evenings reading and writing peculiar stories.

Her writing has appeared in publications including *Crossed Genres, Daily Science Fiction, and Mysterion: Rediscovering the Mysteries of the Christian Faith*. She has had some opportunities to observe the quaint behavior of expert researchers at firsthand, though she has yet to encounter a real live cryptoethnogastronomist.

A. L. Kaplan's love of books started at an early age and sparked a creative imagination. Born on a cold winter morning in scenic northern New Jersey, A. L. spent many hours developing her ideas before translating them into words.

Her stories have been included in several anthologies, including *Young Adventurers: Heroes, Explorers and Swashbucklers, Suppose: Drabbles, Flash Fiction, and Short Stories*, as well as Indies Unlimited's *2014 & 2015 Flash Fiction*. You can find her poems in *Dragonfly Arts Magazine's* 2014, 2015, and 2016 editions, and the BALTICON 49 and 50 BSFAN. She is the President of the Maryland Writers' Association's Howard County Chapter and holds an MFA in sculpture from the Maryland Institute College of Art.

When not writing or indulging in her fascination with wolves, A. L. is the props manager for a local theatre. This proud mother of two lives in Maryland with her husband and dog. Read A. L.'s short works and poems at alkaplan.wordpress.com. Twitter: @alkaplanauthor Facebook: https://www.facebook.com/AuthorA.L.Kaplan/.

Christine Lucas lives in Greece with her husband and a horde of spoiled animals. A retired Air Force officer and mostly self-taught in English, has had her work appear in several print and online magazines, including the *Other Half of the Sky* anthology, *Daily Science Fiction*, and *Space and Time Magazine*. She is currently working on her first novel, and in her free time she reads slush for ASIM. Visit her at: http://werecat99.wordpress.com/

Gail Z. Martin is the author of *Vendetta: A Deadly Curiosities Novel* in her urban fantasy series set in Charleston, SC; *Shadow and Flame* the fourth and final book in the Ascendant Kingdoms Saga; *The Shadowed Path*, and *Iron and Blood* a new Steampunk series, co-authored with Larry N. Martin. A brand new epic fantasy series will launch in 2017 from Solaris Books.

She is also author of *Ice Forged, Reign of Ash and War of Shadows* in The Ascendant Kingdoms Saga, The Chronicles of The Necromancer series (*The Summoner, The Blood King, Dark Haven, Dark Lady's Chosen*); The Fallen Kings Cycle (*The Sworn, The Dread*) and the urban fantasy novel *Deadly Curiosities*. Gail writes three ebook series: *The Jonmarc Vahanian Adventures, The Deadly Curiosities Adventures and The Blaine McFadden Adventures. The Storm and Fury Adventures,* steampunk stories set in the Iron & Blood world, are co-authored with Larry N. Martin.

Her work has appeared in over 30 US/UK anthologies. Find her at www.AscendantKingdoms.com, on Twitter @GailZMartin, on Facebook.com/WinterKingdoms, at DisquietingVisions.com blog and GhostInTheMachinePodcast.com, on Goodreads https://www. goodreads.com/GailZMartin and free excerpts on Wattpad http:// wattpad.com/GailZMartin.

Gregory L. Norris is a full-time professional writer, with work appearing in numerous short story anthologies, national magazines, novels, the occasional TV episode, and, so far, one produced feature film (Brutal Colors, which debuted on Amazon Prime January 2016). A former feature writer and columnist at Sci Fi, the official magazine of the Sci Fi Channel (before all those ridiculous Ys invaded), he once worked as a screenwriter on two episodes of Paramount's modern classic, Star Trek: Voyager. Two of his paranormal novels (written under his rom-de-plume, Jo Atkinson) were published by Home Shopping Network as part of their "Escape With Romance" line—the first time HSN has offered novels to their global customer base. Norris judged the 2012 Lambda Awards in the SF/F/H category. Three times now, his short stories have notched Honorable Mentions by Ellen Datlow. He won

Honorable Mention in the 2016 Roswell Awards in Short SF for his short story 'Mandered'. Norris lives and writes in the outer limits of New Hampshire with his husband, their small pride of rescue cats, and his emerald-eyed muse. Follow his literary adventures on Facebook, or at www.gregorylnorris.blogspot.com.

Jody Lynn Nye lists her main career activity as 'spoiling cats'. When not engaged upon this worthy occupation, she writes fantasy and science fiction books and short stories.

Since 1987 she has published over 45 books and more than 150 short stories, including epic fantasies, contemporary humorous fantasy, humorous military science fiction, and edited three anthologies. She collaborated with Anne McCaffrey on a number of books, including the New York Times bestseller, *Crisis on Doona*. She also wrote eight books with Robert Asprin, and continues both of Asprin's Myth-Adventures series and Dragons series. Her newest series is the Lord Thomas Kinago adventures, the most recent of which is *Rhythm of the Imperium*, a humorous military SF novel.

Her other recent books are *Myth-Fits, Wishing on a Star,* an e-collection of cat stories, *Cats Triumphant; Dragons Run* (fourth in the Dragons series) and *Launch Pad,* an anthology of science fiction stories co-edited with Mike Brotherton. She is also happy to announce the reissue of her Mythology series and Taylor's Ark series from WordFire Publishing. Jody runs the two-day intensive writers' workshop at DragonCon, and she and her husband, Bill Fawcett are the book reviewers for Galaxy's Edge Magazine.

R. S. Pyne is a freelance writer/research Micropalaeontologist/ Mental Health First Aider based in rural West Wales, near the University town of Aberystwyth. Ravens regularly visit the back garden and the only traffic problems are caused by sheep. Working in the historical fiction, horror, Science Fiction, and fantasy genres, she is currently enrolled in a screenwriting module as part of a certificate in Creative Writing (the equivalent of the first year of an undergraduate degree).

Previous fiction credits have included *Bête Noire, Aurora Wolf, Albedo One, Bards and Sages Quarterly, Christmas is Dead - a Zombie Anthology, Eschatology, Fifth Di, Neo-Opsis Science Fiction Magazine, Hungur, Lacuna*, and many others, but she also writes sonnets and evil haiku. Someone has to do it.

She shares an eighteenth century mine captain's cottage with a hyperactive rescue sprollie (springer spaniel x Welsh collie) and a black tortoiseshell cat which appeared on the doorstep one rainy day in August 2015 and decided to move in. "A Canticle for Grimalkin" features a black tortoiseshell cat with attitude ('tortitude') and, although the real life inspiration for the story has never caught a fairy at the bottom of the garden—it is not from lack of trying!

Alex Shvartsman is a writer, translator and game designer from Brooklyn, NY. Over 80 of his short stories have appeared in Nature, Galaxy's Edge, InterGalactic Medicine Show, and many other magazines and anthologies. He won the 2014 WSFA Small Press Award for Short Fiction and was a finalist for the 2015 Canopus Award for Excellence in Interstellar Fiction. He is the editor of the Unidentified Funny Objects annual anthology series of humorous SF/F. His collection, *Explaining Cthulhu to Grandma and Other Stories* and his steampunk humor novella *H. G. Wells, Secret Agent* were both published in 2015. His website is www.alexshvartsman.com.

A. L. Sirois is also a developmental editor, graphic artist and a performing musician. He has had fiction published in *Isaac Asimov's Science Fiction Magazine, Fantastic, Amazing Stories, and Thema,* and online at *Electric Spec, Every Day Fiction and Flash Fiction Online,* among other publications. His story "In the Conservatory" was nominated for the Pushcart Prize. He's published several novels and a short story collection. Other works include a children's book,

Dinosaur Dress Up. His graphic novel, *The Endless Incident*, based on a video game, was published in February, 2016.

A. L. has contributed comic art for DC, Marvel, and Charlton, and has scripted for Warren Publications. He wrote and drew "Bugs in the System" for witzend #12, the famous comics fanzine started by Wally Wood. His illustrations have appeared in many publications and on book covers.

He lives in rural Bucks County, Pennsylvania with his wife and occasional collaborator, author Grace Marcus. Together they are writing a Young Adult novel set in ancient Egypt. A. L. has been a drummer for five decades, and currently plays in a jazz quartet. In his spare time he is teaching himself how to play piano.

Oliver Smith is a visual artist and writer from Cheltenham, UK. He was born in 1966 and recently returned to university twenty-five years after graduating in Fine Art to study Creative Writing as a post-graduate research student.

His writing practice developed from an interest in various surrealist techniques and his stories and poetry generally involve the weird, fantastic, and speculative: a mermaid in the bath, pickled brains plotting in the pantry, and a green man who has lost his head and isn't going to take it lying down. All this and more are included along with many of his previously anthologised stories and twenty poems in *Basilisk Soup and Other Fantasies* available as a Kindle download from Amazon.

Oliver's writing has been described as "literary splatter-horror, and wild-conceited ironic fantasy to die for." (D. F. Lewis), "richly textured and shaded through a dark and subtle palette", "hauntingly poetic", "beautifully written with a superb poetic turn of phrase" and "not my cup of tea." (Amazon reviews)

His short fiction has appeared in anthologies from Inkermen Press, Ex Occidente Press, Dark Hall Press, History and Mystery LLC, and Horseplay Press.

His poetry regularly appears in S. T. Joshi's *Spectral Realms* journal from Hippocampus Press, and has been published in the *Horrorzine* and on *NewMystics.com,* and is scheduled to appear in *Illumen, Eye to the Telescope,* and *Fossil Lake.*

Oliver lives with his wife, Claire, and they both share their home with Ishtar, a very spoiled two-year old Tonkinese female.

Steven R. Southard has been described by some as one cool cat, and as the cat's meow, but when he hears it, that sort of talk rubs his fur the wrong way. Busier than a one-eyed cat watching two mouse holes, he's had short stories published in over ten anthologies, including *Hides the Dark Tower, Dead Bait, and Avast, Ye Airships!* He's the author of the fourteen-story series, *What Man Hath Wrought.* An engineer and former submariner, Steve has pounced into the genres of steampunk, clockpunk, science fiction, fantasy, and horror, and managed to land on his feet each time. He has marked the following territories: a blog and website at www.stevenrsouthard.com, www.facebook.com/steven.southard.16, and www.twitter.com/StevenRSouthard, where you can find him grinning like a Cheshire...well, you know.

Doug C. Souza Doug C. Souza began his story "Tenth Life" when the first line, "I found Mr. Gary confessing to the cat one evening," popped into his head. It was a random image that seemed to have the makings of a fun story. He had no idea where the characters would end up, but one thing was certain: the cat would be a gray tabby. A couple years earlier, Doug C. Souza had to say goodbye for the final time to the greatest cat that ever walked the face of the Earth. He's glad his pal Remy found a home in one of his stories.

Recently, he won first place in the Writers of the Future Contest, and has a story featured in "The Young Explorer's Adventure Guide" due out later this year. His story "Mountain Screamers," a novelette about cougars, appeared in *Asimov's Science Fiction Magazine.*

Doug C. Souza hopes you enjoy "Tenth Life," a story where a cat gets into (and out of) trouble the way only a cat can.

You can follow Doug C. Souza at dougcsouza.com.

Sir Arthur Conan Doyle is a Scottish writer and physician, known chiefly as the author of the Sherlock Holmes mysteries, though he wrote non-fiction, poetry, novels and over 200 short stories.

About the Editors

Kelly A. Harmon used to write truthful, honest stories about authors and thespians, senators and statesmen, movie stars and murderers. Now she writes lies, which is infinitely more satisfying, but lacks the convenience of doorstep delivery.

She is an award-winning journalist and author, and a member of Science Fiction & Fantasy Writers of America. A Baltimore native, she writes the *Charm City Darkness* series, which includes the novels *Stoned in Charm City, A Favor for a Fiend,* and *A Blue Collar Proposition.* Her science fiction and fantasy stories can be found in many anthologies, including *Triangulation: Dark Glass; Hellebore and Rue; Deep Cuts: Mayhem, Menace and Misery; and Swords & Steam.*

Ms. Harmon is a former newspaper reporter and editor, and now edits for Pole to Pole Publishing, a small Baltimore publisher. She is co-editor of *Hides the Dark Tower* and *In a Cat's Eye* along with Vonnie Winslow Crist. For more information, visit her blog at http://kellyaharmon.com, or, find her on Facebook and Twitter: http://facebook.com/Kelly-A-Harmon1, https://twitter.com/kellyaharmon.

Vonnie Winslow Crist, MS Professional Writing, has had a life-long interest in reading, writing, art, science fiction, fairy-tales, folklore, and legends. A cloverhand who has found so many four-leafed clovers that she keeps them in jars, she strives to celebrate the power of myth in her writing and art.

A Pushcart nominee, she is a member of Science Fiction & Fantasy Writers of America, Society of Children's Book Writers & Illustrators, and Pen Women. Her award-winning books include *The Enchanted Dagger, Murder on Marawa Prime, Owl Light, The Greener Forest, Leprechaun Cake & Other Tales, River of Stars and Essential Fables.* Her speculative stories can be found in *Chilling Ghost Short Stories, Cast of Wonders, Faerie Magazine, Dia de los Muertos, Les*

Cabinets des Polytheistes, The Great Tome of Fantastic and Wondrous Places and elsewhere.

Editor of The Gunpowder Review, Ms. Crist co-edited Pole to Pole Publishing's *Hides the Dark Tower* and *In a Cat's Eye* with Kelly A. Harmon. For more information, visit http://vonniewinslowcrist.com, http://vonniewinslowcrist.wordpress.com, http://facebook.com/WriterVonnieWinslowCrist, or http://twitter.com/VonnieWCrist.